This is a work of fiction. Names, characters, businesses, places, events and incidents are either the products of the author's imagination or used in a fictitious manner. Any resemblance to actual persons, living or dead, or actual events is purely coincidental.

Catalyst

Cameron Phoenix

Catalyst

Vanguard Press

VANGUARD PAPERBACK

© Copyright 2023
Cameron Phoenix

A CIP catalogue record for this title is
available from the British Library.

ISBN 978 1 80016 365 2

Vanguard Press is an imprint of
Pegasus Elliot MacKenzie Publishers Ltd.
www.pegasuspublishers.com

First Published in 2023

Vanguard Press
Sheraton House Castle Park
Cambridge England

Printed & Bound in Great Britain

PROLOGUE

Michael Harding sat staring out of the window from his carefully selected seat in a North London coffee shop. His second cup of coffee had turned ice cold, completely untouched and bought for no other reason than to add to the facade of him being there to casually drink a coffee.

Harding had an exhausted, dishevelled appearance. His untamed grey and brown beard coated his sunken cheeks. The greasy, shoulder-length blond hair on his head was covered by a touristy 'I heart London' cap. His skin was a pale white, contrasted by the deep pits of black surrounding his eyes. Having not washed for a few days, if the appearance didn't put you off him, the smell would. The only saving grace was a relatively new, well-fitted blue North Face coat complementing his dark denim supermarket jeans that edged him one step closer to 'tired dad' from his otherwise 'derelict' appearance.

For moments between darting madly about the place, his eyes would meet one of the other customers'. A group of three suits from a local law firm, two builders on their tea break, a young family of French tourists. Their conversations all mundane and for all intents and purposes, normal and uninteresting. Harding would kill for 'normal'. He felt sick with envy of the 'uninteresting'. In his increasingly anxious state, it almost brought him to tears imagining how much of a relief it would be if he too were just in this coffee shop to pass the time over a hot beverage, eating a muffin with a shockingly high calorie count. This had *seemed* like a good place for a meeting; it had *seemed* like it might have been a way out of his situation, but the inescapable reality of this meeting was that it was made out of complete and utter desperation and was morbidly ill-judged.

Harding was not one to make a mistake like this under normal circumstances. From a very young age, he had exhibited great intelligence and within a very short time of knowing him, it was clear to most that he was a gifted individual. As is often the case, his intelligence was accompanied by a sort of social awkwardness. A lack of

7

understanding for other people and their feelings coupled with his unusual interests had left him somewhat alienated throughout his life. In school, he excelled in maths and the sciences and was a self-taught electrical engineer by the age of fourteen. When most other children were reading *Goosebumps* or playing Knock-Down Ginger, Harding was at home taking apart a household electrical item, building a new gadget or delving deep into the inner workings of the most dangerous type of device that he came into contact with during the course of his life. A Computer.

It's a cliché, but the seconds in that coffee shop really did feel like hours. Michael's brain raced at an intolerable speed. As quick as a thought entered his mind, the next rushed in and took over. He had been waiting just over forty-five minutes for the unidentified man he was supposed to be meeting to arrive. With the ever-increasing concern that his heart might actually explode if it continued to beat this fast, Harding began to come to the conclusion that he should perhaps reconsider this rendezvous and simply get up and leave.

This meeting was his idea, *he* had insisted on a public place, but the perceived 'comfort' of having other members of the public around was heavily outweighed by the anxiety-inducing mixture of conversation going on around him. It was a distraction and it just seemed to be getting louder and louder.

Just then the burner pay-as-you-go phone that Harding had in his left jeans pocket started to ring. It might have offered a break from the intense anticipation of his upcoming meeting had it not been for the fact that he *only* owned this phone for the purpose of arranging it. This could only be one person and its ringing denied Harding of the subconscious hope he had developed over the past ten minutes that his mystery guest might have been a no-show.

The connected call served as a final verification to the surveillance team on New Bridge Street. An unassuming blue Mercedes van parked down a nearby side road made the call to a black BMW X5 two roads away. The latter was filled with a team of four armed SO19 Metropolitan Police officers. Having received the orders to proceed, they pulled their black balaclavas down over their heads and readied their Heckler & Koch semi-automatic rifles as the van engine shuddered into life.

Harding's instinctive reaction to the phone ringing had been to push his chair back and stand up from the small table he'd been sitting at. The abruptness with which he did this and the sudden noise it made caused the groups of people at the two closest tables to turn and look at him, momentarily pausing their conversations mid-sentence.

He slowly slid the bashed and beaten-up silver Nokia out of his pocket, his hand shaking uncontrollably. As he lifted the phone up he reluctantly turned the screen to face him, allowing him to see the number calling.

He hesitated, standing frozen in the centre of the coffee shop in a state of limbo, the reality of what might be happening hitting like a freight train. Suddenly it's utter panic. This was not the golden ticket he had hoped for, or the helping hand his desperation had allowed him to believe was real.

Has someone recognised me? What was I thinking coming here? What the fuck was I thinking?

Hyperventilating, Harding put his head down and marched forward at a determined pace, pushing past an elderly couple who were walking in through the coffee shop door. They let out a yelp. All conversation in the shop immediately stopped as everyone turned around to see what was happening.

Harding briefly turned to exchange a panicked and desperate look with some of the shocked customers. As he stumbled out of the coffee shop doorway and into the street, he turned back round to face a surreal scene unfold in front of him, as if in slow motion.

An eerie silence seemed to fall over that London street as the black BMW X5 came thundering towards Harding from his right-hand side at an alarming speed. Having shot through the red light at the intersection next to the shop, it skidded to a loud, dramatic, screeching halt about five metres from where he was standing.

Time appeared to move slower and slower as the adrenaline surged through Harding's body. The BMW continued to slide in his direction as blueish smoke from the seemingly motionless tyres rose into the air. He froze there in total shock, staring wide-eyed at the driver and passenger of the car through their balaclavas. As the milliseconds passed, the car slowed down and the doors on either side of the vehicle began to fly open.

At that moment, Harding's instincts kicked back in and without checking for traffic in either direction, he turned to his left and ran blindly into the road. Amidst all the madness he could still pick out the thud of the first officer's boots as they landed on the ground behind him.

"Armed police! Armed police! Get on the fucking ground now!"

Harding dared not look back, his focus now entirely on an alleyway down the side of a shop on the opposite side of the street. He made it halfway across the road in seconds in a mad, primal sprint.

Officer Max Carter took a deep breath. At this point, he was out of the car with the sights of his firearm trained directly on Harding. He was walking at speed both towards Harding and away from the van, out into the road. Two cars and a bus approached from either direction and slowed dramatically as the drivers observed what was happening in front of them.

"Stop, or we will fucking shoot!"

The chorus of aggressive warnings coupled with the clicking sounds from the guns made it feel as though there was a physical wave of heat approaching Harding from behind. The crippling fear that a shot might ring out at any moment overcame him. He stumbled forward and nearly lost his balance before slowing to halt about half a metre from the pavement on the other side of the road.

"Armed police. Get on the fucking ground!"

Officer Carter approached from the rear left side of the four-strong formation of officers. He calmly raised his sights, now aiming directly into the upper centre of Harding's back. He knew what his orders were. He knew what it would mean if he pulled the trigger. And what it would mean if he didn't.

Harding turned to face the officers, slowly and cautiously raising his hands in the air. He was trembling with fear and all of the colour had left his skin.

"Don't shoot please… I… I give u—"

"Don't fucking move! Keep your hands up!"

Harding was now confronted with the menacing sight of the four officers approaching, all with their guns trained on him. All of them seemed to be edging forward slowly to make the arrest, except one.

Max Carter stood to Harding's front right, slightly further back than the other officers. He kept his gun trained and began slowly strafing to the side to widen the angle between him and the other officers.

Harding noticed his differing movements from the other three. In a split second, he watched the officer move his thumb down and flick off the safety catch on his firearm, readying his finger on the trigger.

"*For fuck's sake!* I'm unarmed… I don't have anyth—"

Carter stared down his sights. He took one last breath and fired two shots into Michael Harding's chest.

The gunshots echoed violently through the London streets like a hammer hitting a nail that ignited a bomb. Michael Harding's lifeless body instantly crumpled to the ground in a heap.

***

One man who understood Michael Harding, perhaps better than anyone else, was his close and in fact only *real* friend, Timothy 'Alpha' Rolfe.

The pair had met at university while they were studying computer science almost ten years ago to the day. It was during this period of their lives that their passion for computing, and more specifically, hacking, moved from an inquisitive pastime to a way of life. At first it was friendly competition. Who could break into this system, take down this network, crash this corporation's servers, gain access to this celebrity's social media account, all under the alias of their online alter egos, 'DOSPhreak' for Harding and 'Alpha166' for Rolfe. Over the years, they had gained some notoriety across the dark web and its various hacker forums. By the age of twenty-two, with both men working dead-end jobs to keep the money coming in, they had formed their own fully-fledged hacking clan named 'blackNet'.

Although it only *really* had two active, consistent members in Michael and Tim, like Anonymous and similar groups, the blackNet quickly gained a cult following in the online community. The pair's discovery and exposure of corruption, fraud, illegal activities, and on occasion, international conspiracy had spurred them to move from one exploit to the next, often 'dumping' the uncovered data online for the world to see.

They strictly considered themselves to be 'white hat' hackers — that is, they performed their exploits for the good of mankind. They had *never* taken down a system out of spite, written a virus to infect random people's computers or exposed 'celebrity nudes' to gain attention. In their minds, the dirt that they dug up belonged in the public domain and they were doing a service to the world by putting it there. With their knowledge and abilities, they could expose information that would otherwise need an investigation from a legal body to obtain. Warrants, writs, court judgements, legal permission, they could bypass all of it in a way that legitimate organisations could not.

Their ethos was nothing new in the world of hacking; many groups had come and gone since the 1980s that had taken a similar position. Their uniqueness came in the form of the sophistication of their methods and how far it meant they could go without detection.

The group's pièce de résistance was a combination of a unique way of connecting to the internet through 'backpacking' on public satellite communications and a series of machine learning algorithms that, subject to a few other variables, theoretically allowed them to break virtually any mathematically-based security system on the planet. These were one-of-a-kind techniques that the pair had developed themselves and they enabled them to operate in a manner that was essentially untraceable. Because of this, regardless of their intent, blackNet had made it on to the radar of many of the world's intelligence agencies as one of the most dangerous internet-based groups in the world.

The blackNet side of their lives was obviously a closely kept secret and the men were confident in their ability to remain in hiding, turning up to their nine-to-five jobs every day and assuming the habits of a normal lifestyle. They were both extremely smart and rarely took anything for granted in their exploits, their carefulness evident in the fact that in ten years of operation, they hadn't even come close to being caught or even leaving enough of a digital footprint to be traced effectively. Inevitably of course, with the level of criminality they were involving themselves in, they lost sleep some nights worrying that tomorrow might be the day they finally get caught.

Although they were conscious never to underestimate the security systems they targeted, there was one force that they did underestimate: the desperation of the people they were targeting to keep what they were exposing under wraps and the lengths that some of these people would go to, to do so.

Amongst their impressively long list of exploits, blackNet had exposed the illicit sexual affairs of senior police figures, revealed illegal offshore accounts held by politicians, brought to light the details of illegal arms deals and implicated huge media outfits in all manner of nefarious and immoral activities. Naturally, this had gained them the attention of multiple organisations and individuals across the world. Some of these parties were willing to hire private detectives, spread counter-rumours, denounce the revealed information as false. Some would contact the police or even government agencies to try to enlist their help in tracing the culprits. But there were other groups that were not interested in pursuing a legal means of shutting the group down — along the way blackNet had amassed some powerful and in some cases, dangerous enemies.

The mainstream media and elements in the government and police had stepped up their public criticism of the blackNet in recent years. It was easy to understand this targeting, after all, most people would agree that an organisation with this kind of capability could not be allowed to continue to grow unchecked and unregulated. Most people, that is, outside of the million-plus blackNet fans and supporters across the world. The group's symbol had taken on a hard-left notoriety akin to Che Guevara. Market stalls from Camden to Las Ramblas sold out every week of T-shirts bearing their logo, a black-and-white depiction of the globe with a spherical dark net covering it. Copycat groups appeared all around the world; every teenager with even a slight interest in computer hacking idolised them. It was a love affair, however, that was to be relatively short-lived.

The claims in the media fell mostly on deaf ears initially: how much the latest exploit had cost the taxpayer in damages; the national security risk posed by the latest leak and the potential link between groups like these and other dark-web activities, such as arms sales and illegal pornographic content. People had heard the scaremongering all before and amongst their most staunch fans, this only fuelled blackNet's popularity.

As the group's online cult status grew and their name and abilities became known around the world, the number of concerned potential targets increased. GCHQ and the FBI had files specifically dedicated to the blackNet and although the two agencies had no evidence to suggest the group was intent on doing any serious damage, they were deeply alarmed by their lack of ability to effectively detect or control its activities.

The reality was that, although it was the clear consensus that the group was a concern, the blackNet had a very clear MO. The *real* potential targets were those in some kind of position of power with something to hide. As the hackers were beginning to find out, however, there are a lot of powerful people and organisations in this world with an awful lot to hide.

***

On the morning of October 12th, 2015, the world awoke to the news that there had been a terrorist bombing in London.

HP Stanthorpe, a long-standing financial institution with a tall building that stood in the heart of Canary Wharf, had been targeted. A package around the size of three shoeboxes had been delivered to the reception, addressed to a 'John Doe'. Having been taken to the postage room as normal and then delivered to the relevant office manager up on the sixth floor, at 09:05 GMT on a regular Thursday morning, the package exploded without warning.

The timing meant that there were people in the hallway arriving for work, as well as staff sitting metres away from the post room. London was no stranger to the threat of terror, but the likes of this kind of attack had rarely been seen of late. Six people were killed by the blast and a further fifteen injured.

The attack, according to a claim of responsibility that was verified by police, was the action of members of the 'blackNet internet-based activist group'.

This narrative was given some additional credibility by the fact that the organisation had been a target of blackNet in the past. The group had openly posted the results of an exploit just over a year ago, detailing examples of the bank's policy of paying bonuses into offshore accounts and their culture of ignorance towards tax avoidance.

The resulting series of internal investigations in the organisation had led to the expulsion of two employees, found to have been members of online communities that sympathised with the blackNet. This act was itself exposed, causing its own controversy and a polarisation in public opinion. The subsequent bombing was quickly framed as a sort of retaliation for the employee dismissals a year earlier and was painted as another battle in the 'war' between the two parties.

The narrative, though, was a fallacy. The followers and supporters of blackNet knew this, as would anyone who knew Michael Harding or Tim Rolfe personally in any capacity. The long-building media story of an out-of-control anarchist group and their recent support from outspoken hard-left activists, however, made this version of events seem all the more plausible and real.

The HP Stanthorpe bombing was the first of two incidents that quickly moved blackNet's image in the public psyche from a 'playful menace' to that of a dangerous terrorist group. A huge explosion at a large oil storage facility in Hertfordshire six months later was also pinned on the group, supposedly having tampered with the computer systems at the site as a 'punishment intended for the evil oil corporations that store their black gold' there. Four workmen and two local residents were killed in the blasts and resulting fires, and over a quarter of the site was irreversibly damaged.

The attacks had two major impacts. They turned public opinion further away from the group, but also meant that Internet Service Providers and more importantly, the UK police and government, were now galvanised into spending serious time and money on finding and shutting down the blackNet. It was a deviously clever acquisition of resources and one that had Harding and Rolfe shaken to their core.

Becoming aware of their invisible enemies and the tactics that they were prepared to use against them, both men were understandably deeply disturbed and paranoid. For this reason, very soon after the incidents, the pair almost completely ceased all blackNet-related activity. The one and only project that either of them had any interest in was finding out who had framed them for these atrocities. The willingness of whoever was involved to let innocent people die in order to create this scenario was a particularly worrying element that remained at the forefront of their minds.

All the while, a part of both of them wanted to just run away from it all and try to live a normal life. Alas, of course, it was too late for that. In light of the attacks and all of the other negativity being attributed to the group, several anonymous witnesses had come forward to the authorities and named Tim Rolfe and Michael Harding as the founding members. Being former friends of the two men and fellow hackers, these witnesses had a pretty convincing story to tell and soon after, the men had no choice but to live a life on the run.

The information that Harding and Rolfe had exposed themselves to over the years; the enemies that they had made and the noise they had caused in the online community meant that they would now be hunted, in all likelihood, for the rest of their lives.

CHAPTER ONE

Jayden Amare Fox lived alone in a two-bedroom 1960s-style flat on the third floor of the Aylesbury estate in East London. He had spent the past ten years working as a mechanic for a local car garage just off the estate. Like many of us, he'd had ambitions and dreams that were 'not yet' fulfilled and saw his current line of work as a temporary measure, a stepping stone to get to where he *really* wanted to go.

Although he kept himself to himself and led a somewhat humble existence, Jay was a handsome, relatively confident thirty-year-old man. He was five foot ten, relatively stocky and had striking brown eyes and a chiselled jaw. His ever-so-slightly receding hairline streamed across the top of his head with this hair tied into a tight ponytail at the back.

Jay hadn't always felt blessed in the looks department though. He had been skinny and pale in his youth and, coupled with the fact that he was a foreigner, he'd suffered some degree of bullying throughout most of his childhood and adolescence. Growing up through school with a strange accent and Ghanaian adopted mother didn't help matters. Kids are cruel.

Jay had always felt a certain lack of identity. He didn't know much at all about his real parents. He never questioned Sonya as his mother, but the elephant in the room that was their strikingly different skin tone soon came up in conversation when Jay reached a certain age. She had always been vague with him about who his biological family were, primarily because she genuinely didn't know herself. She took Jay in at the age of five, an event that he could only just about recall.

Jay was put up for adoption by a family that had come over to the UK from Chechnya to flee the political situation there at the time. Within a year of being in the country, they had found the stresses of trying to work two jobs each and look after a four-year-old too much and decided to do what they felt was best for all parties. They themselves had taken Jay in as foster parents in 1992 when he was just two years old, not foreseeing the instability that would lead to them fleeing the country so soon after.

The details before that were very sketchy. The foster parents that had brought Jay to the country had told the authorities that his birthday was on 7th January 1990 and that he was born in a small hospital on the outskirts of Grozny. The pregnancy was apparently unplanned and his poor, single mother had made the heart-breaking decision to give him away at birth.

One attribute that had intrigued everyone along the way was an unexplained set of markings at the top of Jay's back. Just on the inside of his left shoulder blade, there was a two-inch black outline of a Fox's head tattooed into his skin that had been there since he was a baby.

Sonya and Jay had gathered all of this information and nothing more. He had never heard his real mother's name and had never attempted to trace either his biological or previous foster parents.

Sonya had been a good mother to Jay and as far as he was concerned, she was his only family. Although his previous carers had already named him, one of the first things Sonya had given Jay was a *new* name. Jayden had been the name of a baby boy that she had miscarried a number of years earlier and the surname 'Fox' seemed appropriate, in honour of those mysterious markings on his back. *'Amare'* meaning 'good-looking' or 'handsome' in many African dialects was chosen as his middle name.

From day one, Sonya cared for Jay whilst working as an NHS nurse in several local hospitals. She moved in to the third-floor flat on the Aylesbury estate two years after adopting Jay and the two had lived there ever since. That is, until September of 2009, when after a long battle with breast cancer, Sonya Abimbola sadly passed away at fifty-three years of age.

Jay continued to live in the apartment alone following his loss. As time went by without Sonya around, in the back of his mind he became more and more curious about where he had *really* come from. Old questions that he had let go of for some time began to bubble to the surface as he wondered what other family he might have out there.

As Jay had grown up, he had developed an interest in the martial arts. As well as giving him a way to defend himself, it had provided him with a sense of self-confidence and was a sanctuary away from the 'outsider' feeling he was used to in other areas of his life. At the age of seventeen he became a black belt in Tae Kwon Do, having quickly risen up through the belt grading system. During his teen years, other teenagers at the youth centre had nicknamed him 'Jean Claude' since he bore a slight physical resemblance to the nineties film icon.

Jay could also fix cars from a young age. His single foster parent Sonya had a long-term boyfriend who was a mechanic and he'd somewhat taken Jay under his wing in this regard. Jay worked with him, and then in several other garages in the area from the age of sixteen. Although he enjoyed aspects of working as a mechanic and it had kept his food on the table, it definitely wasn't his dream. His long-term goal was to start his own gym and martial arts academy locally, somewhere where he could teach a unique combination of his favoured techniques from the various disciplines he had practised over the years. He wanted to share what martial arts had done for him with other kids who might have felt the same way he did as a boy. Just weeks before his twentieth birthday, these dreams — along with multiple bones in his body — were brutally shattered.

On the evening of the 18th of May 2010, Jay was riding his Honda CDR 150 motorbike home after finishing a shift at a mechanic's yard in Croydon. A friend of his boss was short staffed and had called in a favour. Jay was partial to the variety of working from a different location for the day, not to mention the extra money, so he had volunteered when it was offered.

At quarter past nine that night, as Jay slowed in the approach to a T-junction near the entrance to the Aylesbury estate, a white van came careering round the corner on the wrong side of the road. The van was doing in excess of 50 mph and was closely followed by a pursuing police car. Jay had little time to react but having heavily applied his breaks, he tried to swerve to avoid a collision with the van coming in from his left. It had all happened far too fast for him to do anything about it.

The heavy braking had meant that in the seconds before the impact, the rear of the bike had raised slightly into the air as both locked wheels skidded across the road, carrying the bike and Jay forward in a plume of tyre smoke. The front of the bike and Jay's body smashed into the bonnet of the van, his limbs flailing around limp like a mannequin as the bike slipped under the wheels. The impact of his body on the van was enough to crumple the body work and smash the windscreen. They travelled together for a further few feet before the van finally came to an abrupt stop, flinging Jay's body forward for one more violent impact with the ground. Jay's cracked and dented helmet was also thrown off in the process. The driver and both passengers had enough time to jump out of the van and flee in various directions before the pursuing police could get near them.

Jay regained consciousness some hours later, laid out on a bed in Whitechapel Hospital. He had fractured his skull, jaw, collarbone, left arm and six of his ribs. Several bones in his right arm and leg, having been sandwiched between the bike and the van at the combined 60 mph speed of the two vehicles, were almost completely shattered. Moreover, his left wrist had smashed into the handlebars of the bike and suffered severe, irreversible damage. Doctors later concluded that his head injury caused by the hard impact with the ground may also have led to mild brain damage, as well as permanent damage to the upper section of his spine.

Jay spent weeks in the hospital in and out of induced comas and operations and although the doctors had achieved the amazing in keeping him alive, they were forced to acknowledge that his injuries would more than likely be life-changing to some degree. His recovery was unlikely to be complete.

Despite the prognosis, however, after the initial recovery in the hospital and the several months of rehabilitation that followed, Jay managed to at least attempt to return to a relatively normal way of life. He had to learn how to walk, pick things up, speak at a certain pace and build strength up in his body, all from scratch. The shattered bones and muscles in his legs, chest and arms meant he now walked with a sort of awkward hobble. Walking fast remained a struggle. Running was out of the question and would probably remain that way indefinitely.

The weakness in his hands meant his job as a mechanic was far more of a challenge, but his boss Pete had kept him on in the garage working reduced hours. His football, basketball and of course, his keen interest in martial arts were all brought to an abrupt and tragic halt. The brittleness of Jay's body coupled with the complications from his head injury meant that these activities were now out of the question for him, which understandably had devastated him.

Fast forward to the present day. Having lived through an initial period of isolation, Jay had come to terms with his injuries and managed to find other areas of interest to keep himself occupied. Where sports and martial arts had been a pastime in his old life, he had recently found new hobbies in reading and computing. Between these and focusing on his work, Jay had managed to achieve a relative degree of happiness and stability. Perhaps the most stabilising factor of all, was that six months before his thirtieth birthday, Jay had met, and very soon after fallen in love with a girl.

Julia Campbell, a twenty-five-year-old nurse from Hackney: five foot four, bright strawberry-blonde hair and a pretty round face that most of the time, wore a wide beaming smile. Her infectious bubbly personality and louder-than-life laugh meant she was a girl you wouldn't quickly forget. The daughter of one of Jay's boss' business associates, she would often drop by the garage to pick up or drop something off, dressed in her blue NHS nurse uniform paired with a gleaming pair of white trainers.

Like Jay, Julia had humble beginnings, born and raised on the Bridewell estate just a few miles down the road. She had followed in her mother's footsteps in becoming a nurse at the local Queen Elizabeth Hospital and loved her job. After watching her walk in and out of the garage hundreds of times over the years, Jay finally plucked up the courage one Wednesday afternoon to ask her out for a drink. She agreed, and the pair clicked almost immediately.

Julia's bright and energetic conversation was just the injection of colour and positivity Jay had needed in his life. He had a sarcastic, dry sense of humour that had for too long been suppressed underneath the grey-bitter tone of his everyday life. Julia felt the connection in their personalities instantly as well. By the third date, all of the initial awkwardness that comes with meeting someone new had gone. The pair had become completely relaxed in each other's company. They'd spend hours on their 'dates' doing impressions of the people they knew and laughing their heads off like a couple of kids.

After just over a month of their as yet unlabelled 'relationship', Jay had saved up some money to book an expensive restaurant in the West End of London. Aside from just wanting to treat her to a decent night out, he had decided that this would be the night that he would ask her to become his girlfriend. Although he thought of this kind of thing as cheesy and a tad pointless, he knew that Julia would appreciate the gesture. He also knew that in a few weeks, they could both look back and take the piss out of him for being so soppy as well. Neither of them could have known that this evening of positivity and the celebration of starting a relationship together would be part of a series of events that would lead, unavoidably, to disaster.

It was 11.35 p.m. on a dark, chilly March evening in East London. Jay and Julia were walking hand in hand through the estate after what had, so far, been a predictably pleasant night. As they turned the corner into the ground-floor corridor, they saw a group of men huddled around drinking and smoking, only metres in front of the set of stairs that led up to Jay's flat. This wasn't a particularly uncommon sight; in fact, it was something that both of them were used to. This group seemed particularly sinister, though, and they had appeared to immediately take an interest in the couple's presence. As Jay and Julia approached the group, one of the men turned round and opened his mouth into a sleazy smirk, revealing a set of badly stained, yellowy black teeth. The kind of teeth that you feel like you can smell and taste just by looking at them.

With his heavily glazed, bloodshot eyes focused on Julia he quipped in a snaky, gravelly voice, "Well, well, well, ain't you a sight for sore eyes luv?"

Both Jay and Julia could smell the foul tobacco, booze and puke-smelling mixture emanating from the man's breath. Julia leant in towards Jay and gripped his hand tighter as the couple picked up their pace to get past the group faster. A chorus of muffled sniggering faded away in the background as the pair made their way up the three flights of stairs, along the dimly lit outdoor corridor and into Jay's flat.

Julia walked straight along the narrow hallway and into the kitchen at the back of the flat. She took a freshly washed glass from the drying rack next to the sink and began running the kitchen tap to pour herself a tall glass of water. There was a few minutes' awkward silence as Jay hung his coat up in the hall and leant against the doorway of the kitchen, watching Julia.

"I'm sorry about them."

Julia turned to look back at Jay with a mixture of appreciation and regret.

"Don't be silly; it's not your fault! Besides, I'm not fazed by what some loser says on the street."

She looked down at the glass of water in her hand and then back up at Jay, holding the glass out in front of her.

"I'm just a bit thirsty."

Jay looked up from the floor and through a forced smile replied, "OK, good… Thank you."

Julia walked over and put her hand on Jay's shoulder. There was an unspoken understanding about Jay's injuries and how vulnerable they made him feel in situations like the one they'd just experienced. The two briefly hugged before Julia turned back round to face the sink, knocking the 'boil' button down on the kettle.

"Tea?"

Jay sniggered and walked up behind Julia, kissing her on the neck and reaching round to pat her stomach.

"Yes please."

As is routine, Jay walked out of the kitchen and turned left into the living area. There was an open square 'hatch' between the kitchen and the living room, so the pair could still see each other. He slumped back into his usual position on the sofa with a sigh before reaching for the remote. Their thirty-two-inch plasma television hummed into life and the picture faded in, just in time to catch the day's news round-up.

"Just after twelve p.m. today, armed police officers shot and killed a suspected international terrorist outside a coffee shop in North London. Thirty-one-year-old Michael Harding was purportedly a founding member of the infamous blackNet hacking organisation. Having received a tip-off as to his whereabouts, armed officers confronted Harding before fatally shooting him. The blackNet is suspected of committing various acts of international terrorism over the past ten years. Prior to the shooting, police had stated that they

considered any member of the organisation to be 'likely armed' and extremely dangerous. It's unknown at this point whether Harding was armed during the confrontation or whether indeed he was in possession of an explosive device as some have suggested. The investigation has been handed over to the IPOC in line with standard procedure."

Jay shook his head at the television with a disgusted look on his face.

"Terrorist my arse."

Just then, a series of loud and urgent knocks at the door caught the couple off guard. Jay and Julia exchanged a surprised look through the kitchen/living room hatch but did nothing for a few seconds.

Once more, loud knocking thudded down the hallway followed by a muffled voice from behind the door.

"Open up, Jay, I need that fing you've got."

The expression on Jay's face morphed from surprise to a calm disappointment.

As he got up and walked towards the door, Julia snapped in a whispered voice, "Who is that Jay?"

Jay looked back at her apologetically and reluctantly opened the door.

In the outdoor corridor getting soaked in the rain was twenty-four-year-old Colin Norris. Tipped off from one of the youths Jay had seen just minutes ago, he had on a 'full tracksuit' attire with an old pair of blue-and-white Nike trainers to complete the outfit. His bald head was covered by a worn and faded cap and he stood with his hands in the pockets on either side of his fleece, furiously chewing gum. A strangely welcoming cheesy smile stretched to either side of his face upon the opening of the door.

"Well... you gonna invite me in then or what?"

Jay again looked back at Julia. Before he could turn back to face Colin at the door, he was pushing past him and into the flat.

"Come on mate, it's fucking soaking out there."

Jay reluctantly closed the front door behind him as Colin breathed into his grubby hands, rubbing them together to try to warm up. Each time he did, Jay could smell the foul, boozy odour of Colin's breath.

Julia had started to cautiously follow behind Jay as he had walked down the hall to open the door, but upon seeing this unknown, unsavoury man enter the apartment, she naturally retreated into the kitchen. She could sense Jay didn't particularly want this man in the house, but that he didn't seem *worried* about it either. She thought it best to let the two of them talk and then quiz Jay about it afterwards to her heart's content. She took a plate from the top of the pile ready for washing and began running the hot water from the kitchen tap. The conversation continued behind her out in the hallway.

"So Jim says he left sumfink here last night — you got it or w—"

"Shhhh…"

Jay interrupted Colin, holding his hand up to his face before nervously looking back towards the kitchen. He looked back at Colin with a frustrated, angry frown. Colin cracked a smile and leant forward to peer over Jay's shoulder towards the end of the hall. He leant back and locked eyes with Jay once more with a smug smirk on his face.

"Ohhh you got company have ya? You soft bastard! I better not stay long then eh?"

He let out a cackling laugh, showing off his own incredibly poorly maintained set of teeth in the process.

Jay turned to the left and opened the small storage cupboard in the middle of the hallway. He crouched down and reached right into the back of the cupboard to rummage around the pile of coats and boxes. After a few seconds he emerged holding a green shoebox, sealed shut with several layers of thick, dark brown adhesive tape. He stood for a second looking down at the box, leant to one side to peer nervously towards the kitchen again before reluctantly handing the box over to Colin.

Julia was now nearing the bottom of the pile of plates. She was pretending to be busy, but while she couldn't see much in the reflection of the window above the kitchen sink, she was concentrating as hard as she could to listen to what was happening in the hallway with a nervous intrigue.

Colin pulled a small penknife from his jeans, flicked out the blade and quickly sliced away a strip of the tape covering the lip of the green shoebox. He stretched open the corner of the box just enough to see the pile of £20 notes packed inside before promptly shutting the box and nodding at Jay.

"Looks all good mate, well done. Seems you're not a completely useless cripple after all."

Colin displayed another menacing smile. Jay nodded once and wasted no time walking over to pull down the handle and swing open the front door. He moved to one side in order to let his uninvited guest walk out.

Colin took one final look over his shoulder towards the far end of the hall, walked over to Jay until he was eye level with him, nodded and then walked out of the flat. Jay quickly shut the door behind him. He leant his head against the door and sighed. As he turned to walk back down the hallway of the flat, he saw Julia was now standing at the entrance to the kitchen facing him. She had her arms crossed with a dishcloth folded over them, and a very angry look on her face.

"So … are you gonna tell me what that was about then?"

She turned her head to one side and raised her eyebrows with a sort of 'well?' expression.

Jay awkwardly shuffled over to her in a way that made it immediately obvious that he was about to lie.

"Oh he's just some guy from the estate I know. Ended up coming here for a few beers the other night. He left his coat here… he told me he'd swing by tonight and get it… I just forgot"

There was an awkward silence as Jay inched closer to Julia. She took a step back into the kitchen away from him.

"It didn't seem like he was a friend of yours Jay."

She waited for some kind of response, but he just looked down at the floor with a blank expression. She tried again to prompt an explanation.

"It didn't really seem as though you wanted him here… you looked… uncomfortable…"

Having had a few more seconds to adjust to the situation and react to the pressure of Julia's questions, Jay finally looked up at her, attempting to adopt a more sincere expression on his face.

"Well I didn't, you know… me and you are having a nice night together and I don't want someone interrupting and ruining it for us… I don't want *anyone* interrupting."

He walked over and reached out to put his hand on Julia's shoulder. She turned her head and parried his arm away, huffing as she did it.

"I'm not stupid Jay. Something was very weird about what just happened there. Why do you let him talk to you like that? What on earth did you give him? What is he coming here for?"

Jay laughed nervously in a vain attempt to try to make what Julia was suggesting seem ridiculous. He wasn't used to lying to Julia like this. It wasn't in his nature to lie, especially not to someone he loved as much as he did her.

***

In the months following Jay's accident in 2010, he had understandably become very depressed. It had happened less than a year after the extremely painful loss of his mother Sonya, something he was already struggling to deal with as a twenty-year-old man with no other family.

Following his discharge from the hospital, he had spent weeks alone, unable to move and in constant pain. For a time, he managed the sleepless nights and constant feeling of fatigue with the medication and advice that the doctors had given him. Before long, though, it was becoming too much for him to bear physically and mentally and he began looking elsewhere for relief.

Alcohol was the first port of call in this search. On those dark nights alone in the apartment, it meant a brief release from the compounding misery, numbing the physical pain in the process. Having seen Jay hobbling through the estate every day on crutches, a few of the local gang members had approached him and introduced him to the second of his borderline addictions: ketamine.

Jay working only part time had meant that the money coming in was very limited. Combined with his increased spending on drink and the £20-a-bag sleeping aid he had fallen victim to buying on 'subscription', his finances had quickly become stretched. Not managing to keep on top of things and having reached a point of desperation, at twenty-three years of age, Jay accepted the offer of a short-term loan of £5,000 from Jeremy 'Jez' Weaver, a well-known loan shark on the estate. From that point on, he was tied in.

Two years down the line, having ended up in hospital after collapsing at work, Jay had taken control and immediately stopped both the medication and the drink. His brush with ill-health had given him a new perspective on life and he had realised that drinking himself into oblivion was not going to fix anything, no matter how sorry he felt for himself. At the same time, some aspects of his injuries had improved; he had become slightly more mobile and had better use of his hands for working. He put in double shifts to get his finances back on track, including paying back his ill-gotten £5,000 loan, plus interest. This, however, was not the full extent of the debt.

Anyone familiar with loan sharks will tell you that the interest rates on such loans are often extortionate and can be adjusted as the lender sees fit. Jez Weaver, as well as being known as a loan shark, was one of the most feared 'hard men' of the estate. He had demanded an additional £2,000 repayment on Jay's loan, with an extra £500 for every week he didn't receive the full amount. Having initially tried to argue with this, Jay had quickly realised that no matter how hard he tried to reason with Weaver, there wasn't going to be an easy way out of this debt. He had since seen and heard about the countless shootings, stabbings and slashings that had taken place on the estate relating to other 'unpaid loans' and realised that he couldn't take any chances. After multiple frosty exchanges and several years of partial payments, a negotiation had eventually culminated in a reluctant agreement between them.

Weaver and his associates could ask Jay to keep money and/or other 'packages' at his apartment from time to time. This was especially valuable to the men since most of their homes were well known to the police and rival gangs. Having another 'drop-off' point was useful and it also meant that the gang could pass certain things between each other without having to meet. At first, they had used this service sparingly since it was only required under certain circumstances. More recently, however, with some increased tension between the group and rival gangs and more attention from the police, the men had begun taking liberties with the storage option. Naturally, Jay was extremely uncomfortable with the arrangement but at the same time, he knew that there was little else he could do to avoid paying back this ever-growing debt he had been burdened with.

Jay did have a plan though. Almost immediately after taking on this arrangement, he had started planning a way to leave the estate for good. He didn't know exactly where he would go or when, only that one day without any warning, he would take the stash of money that he was slowly building in a safe box at work and just leave. A plan that had been both accelerated and complicated when Julia had come into his life.

CHAPTER TWO

Tuesday, 17th March.

Panting heavily after running almost a mile through residential streets and gardens, Daniel Boulton had successfully evaded an intense police pursuit. It had started almost twenty minutes earlier in the middle of a busy East London high street.

After spotting Boulton in the passenger seat of a car known to be linked with drug dealing in the area, a sharp-eyed policeman had U-turned at the roundabout at the end of the street, switched on his lights and sirens and attempted to pull the vehicle over. The car didn't have road tax registered against it, but that was only a convenient excuse for the attempted stop.

As well as the car itself, the two occupants were known to the police and the officer in the car had a suspicion, just from looking at the pair, that they were in the middle of something dodgy. His suspicion was justified. The men had just left a house three miles down the road after picking up fifty wraps of cocaine to sell on their estate. Having noticed the undercover police car before it had even turned round to pursue them, the driver had accelerated rapidly and driven into oncoming traffic to put some distance between themselves and the police.

As they reached the corner of Roman Road, Boulton signalled for the driver to let him out. After diving out of the car and sprinting down a long alleyway in between a row of shops, he continued to run through various adjacent streets, hopping the fences of two gardens and finally reaching the southwest entrance of the Aylesbury estate.

Walking at a more controlled pace and constantly looking over his shoulder for any sign of a pursuit, Boulton climbed the three flights of stairs and walked calmly up to the front door of flat 46, the home of Jayden 'the cripple' Fox. He spent around three minutes knocking the door and peering through the letterbox before coming to the conclusion that no one was home.

Breaking protocol, Boulton decided to open the door using a bent pipe through the letterbox to pull the inside handle down, an operation he was more than used to performing from the years he had spent burgling properties in the area as an adolescent. Jay would have normally bolted his front door being relatively security conscious, but he and Julia had been up late the previous night and he'd left in something of a rush for work that morning.

After letting himself in the flat and closing the door behind him, Daniel opened the cupboard in the hallway and stuffed the wraps of cocaine and £6,000 cash he had on his person into a bag at the back of the cupboard. He then quickly closed the cupboard door and left the flat, pulling his hood down over his head as he emerged. Having got back to his mother's flat on the edge of the estate and for the fifth time this month explained to her why the police had been calling, he received a phone call from Luke Weaver.

Luke was the younger, more volatile brother of the loan shark, Jez. The Weaver brothers were notorious on the estate and in the surrounding area. They had a reputation for violence and intimidation and were even nicknamed 'The Krays of Aylesbury' by some of the fearful residents.

Jez had preferred to stick to the more 'traditional' and 'cleaner' crimes of money laundering, loan-sharking and extortion that he had grown up watching his elders on the estate take part in. He wasn't a big fan of the drug trade and didn't like to make a big show out of the lifestyle they were living. He preferred to keep things low-key and relatively controlled. His brother Luke, however, did not share these ideals. His approach was far louder and he revelled in the reputation that the brothers had gained in the local area. If anybody messed with them or any of their associates, he wanted to make examples of them and make sure that others took note. His business ventures were almost exclusively in the area of A-Class drug trafficking on and around the estate, having always seen it as too much of an easy money maker to ignore.

Boulton informed Weaver that he and his associate had picked up the 'gear' and temporarily stored it in 'the cripple's' flat after picking up a tail. He had failed to mention the crucial fact that the items had been left in the apartment without Jay's knowledge, an omission that would cost everyone involved a great deal.

Thursday rolled around and for Jay, the week had been long enough already. A busy and frustrating few days at work meant he was looking forward to spending a relaxing evening with Julia even more than usual.

The couple were now spending most of their free time with each other and were practically living together. For several reasons, they both much preferred her flat to his and they were staying there around five nights a week. Tonight, however, they had decided to stay at Jay's since he had to work late and it would be too much of a pain for him to get over to her place when he finished.

Julia arrived at the door of the garage that Jay worked at wearing the familiar nurse uniform and white trainers combination. Jay never got tired of seeing those big beautiful blue eyes and the beaming smile on her face every time she turned up.

"There's a gorgeous bird at the door, Jay. Listen I'm as shocked as you mate, but I think she might be here for you"

A typical attempt at piss-taking from Jay's boss Pete.

"I'd better call it day then eh?" Jay replied.

Pete smiled and nodded his head towards the front door of the garage, giving Jay the go-ahead to leave for the day.

Jay and Julia walked hand in hand back to the flat to have the customary debrief from work in the kitchen as Julia prepared the evening's dinner.

As usual, the two took their cups of tea into the living room and slumped onto the sofa with an exhausted exhale. Jay sat with his eyes half closed, still covered in black stains from his day in the garage, playing with Julia's hair with one hand as he took occasional, slow sips from his cup. Similarly fatigued, Julia was lying across Jay's chest as they took in the evening's dose of television.

Unbeknownst to them, this would be one of the last content moments the pair would spend together. Just as the relaxation began to set in, once again, the aggressive knocking on the front door disturbed them.

"For f…"

Jay felt like he wasn't getting a moment's rest and grunted at the thought of having to get up and open the door.

Julia reluctantly moved to the side to let Jay get up. This time, far from being fearful of the visitor at the door, her feelings were more of frustration and inconvenience. The unscheduled visit had caused an argument last time and the two knew instantly that this was probably going to cause another one.

There was another series of more pronounced knocks as Jay approached the door.

"OK, OK… I'm coming…"

"It's me, hurry up!"

The painfully familiar voice of Colin Norris. Jay rolled his eyes as he reached out to unlock the door.

Standing in the corridor was a far less jovial-looking Norris. He wore the usual tracksuit getup and was chewing his gum, but this time at a more manic pace. His usual cheeky smile was replaced with a look of angry concern.

"The filth haven't been ere ave they?"

Norris pushed the door open and attempted to slide past Jay into the flat, getting about half of his body through the semi-open doorway. Reacting instinctively, Jay tried to close the door further and created a bar with his right arm, attempting to stop Colin entering. Feeling this resistance, Colin paused for a moment to look up at Jay, as if to say, 'You're not actually stopping me… are you?'

The pair awkwardly exchanged eye contact for a few moments before Colin broke the silence.

"Move!"

He shoulder barged the door hard, squeezing through the gap and knocking Jay off balance. The two men now stood facing each other in the hallway of the flat with the front door wide open.

"You're out of order Colin — I'll call the fucking police!" Jay shouted.

Jay straightened himself up, both men panting slightly from the brief but intense physical altercation at the door.

Colin gritted his teeth and puffed out his chest, taking a step closer to Jay.

"You'll do what? You're fucking lucky the Weavers ain't here to hear you say that mate. Just give me the fucking bag and I'll be out of here."

Jay's expression instantly morphed from anger to frustrated confusion as he scrunched up his face.

"What bag?!"

Colin's patience was very thin and it would not last long. He was getting the increasing feeling that Jay was attempting to mess him around and this was the wrong day to be doing that.

"Look mate — I ain't got time to be playing these fucking games with you all right? I'm getting grief to get this shit back over to the boss and I—"

"There's nothing here! No one has been here since the last time I saw you!"

Jay cut Colin off mid-sentence and threw his arms out to either side in defiance as he spoke.

Colin looked back at him with a confused scepticism before panning over to the hallway cupboard. He looked back at Jay and then nodded his head over to the right.

"Open the cupboard."

Jay laughed nervously.

"What?"

"You heard. Open the fucking cupboard — it better be in there. If it's gone you're fucked."

With no action from Jay, Colin walked over to the right-hand side of the hallway and began to force the cupboard door open. Shocked and confused, Jay reacted by grabbing Colin on the shoulder, pulling him backwards with a sharp tug.

The two men jostled over the cupboard door for a few seconds before Colin leant back, swung, and punched Jay hard in the side of the head. He fell to the ground.

By this time, Julia had heard the loud thumping noises and heated verbal exchanges between the men and made her way to the living room doorway. She arrived at the entrance to the hallway with a rolling pin in hand, just in time to see Jay lose consciousness on the floor. She quickly became hysterical and started screaming.

"Jay... Jay! Are you all right? Oh my God! What have you done, you psycho?"

Hearing Julia approach from behind, Colin emerged from inside the cupboard. He had thrown the various shoes, coats and bags into a heaped mess that spilled out into the hallway but was yet to find what he was looking for.

"Where is that fucking bag? What the fuck are you two playing at?"

Julia was terrified and at the same time infuriated by this man's presence. She stared down at the surreal and horrifying sight of her boyfriend laid out on the floor in front of her. Her heart was pounding at an uncontrollable rate. Fight or flight had taken over.

"We don't know what you want! Just leave us alone now, get out...get out!" she screamed.

She walked backwards into the living room, holding the rolling pin out in front of her, and reached behind her to the coffee table where her mobile phone was plugged in charging. She was shivering with fear, barely able to hold the rolling pin steady.

Colin was just about to lean back into the cupboard when he saw what Julia was reaching for.

"Don't you!"

Julia screamed as Colin leapt over Jay's motionless body towards her. She swung the rolling pin at Colin's head, but he put his arm up in time to block it. As she continued to shriek, Colin grabbed hold of her by the arms and shook her violently, shouting in her face, *"Why are you fucking me about so much you little cunt?"*

Julia kneed Colin hard in the groin. He winced for a second, loosening his grip on her. She turned around to face the living room and leant over to make one more frantic attempt to reach out and grab her phone.

Just as the tip of her fingers made contact with the phone, Colin leapt forward and violently pushed Julia with full force. She was thrown over the solid wood coffee table in front of the sofa and landed on her side on the living room floor. She immediately curled up into a sort of foetal position, slightly winded from being thrown onto the laminated flooring. Shivering in fear, she fully expected to feel the weight of a hard kick or punch to come crashing in from behind. She wondered if he might even kill her.

As Julia lay whimpering on the ground, Colin leant over and picked up her phone, removing it from the charger. He lifted it up into the air above his head and aggressively threw it down to the floor. As it smashed into pieces, Julia let out another terrified, whimpering shriek. With her eyes now closed, she wasn't even sure what had made the noise.

Colin took a couple of deep, panting breaths as he turned around and walked back into the hallway of the flat, dusting himself off in the process. He stepped over Jay and once again leant in to the storage cupboard to resume looking for the package.

As Colin rummaged through the cupboard, Jay started to come round. From where he was lying, he could partially see the bottom half of Julia's body curled up on the living room floor through the doorway. He groaned and blinked his eyes a few times as they came back into focus, frowning in disbelief at what he was seeing. The side of his head was pounding from the already swelling lump, courtesy of Colin's fist.

Jay slowly shuffled round and started to crawl towards Julia, awkwardly dragging his body across the floor with one elbow at a time. Within a couple of seconds, the feeling of limpness in his body began to fade as he fully regained consciousness. He stumbled up to his feet and adjusted his balance as he approached the entrance to the living room. Julia let out another shivering whimper that let Jay know she was at least still breathing and conscious.

Just then, as he heard movement in the hall behind him, he remembered that Colin was still in the apartment.

Jay was suddenly overcome with anger. He gritted his teeth and tensed his whole body, forming a tight first with each hand as he stared down at Julia on the living room floor.

Without a rational thought entering his head, he turned into the entrance to the kitchen, reached up and slid out the old, dusty baseball bat that he kept on top of the high storage units.

Jay took hold of the bat firmly with both hands, swinging it behind his head to a ready position, and marched out into the hallway. He was panting and growling with anger. His mouth was wide open with a thick, stringy line of saliva swinging down like a rabid dog.

At that same moment, Colin emerged from the hallway cupboard with a bag stuffed in the inside of his coat. Catching him completely off guard, Jay began wildly swinging the bat at him with all the force he could muster.

The first few overhead swings of the bat didn't do much. Colin had just enough time to assume a crouched position with his arms over his head, effectively shielding him from any significant damage.

After the fourth swing, Colin managed to reach out and grab the end of the bat and the pair began struggling for control of it. Both men had both hands firmly gripped on the bat, staring wildly at each other from either end.

"What the fuck is wrong with you? You fucking nutter!" Colin cried.

Jay simply roared in response, his eyes fixed on Colin with nothing else going through his mind except his desire to hurt him.

After a brief tussle, Colin, being the stronger of the two men, managed to prise the bat from Jay's hands. He grunted as he threw the baseball bat off to his right side. Jay lunged forward with both hands in an attempt to grab Colin by the neck.

Colin swung his whole body weight round from the left into another 'hook' punch that crashed into the side of Jay's head before he could get close. Colin moved off to the left as the momentum of Jay's advance carried him forward into a leant-over position, dazed from another blow to the head.

Colin quickly followed up with a powerful right uppercut straight into Jay's ribcage. The wind was taken out of him as he gasped for air and dropped down on to all fours on the hallway floor.

Norris immediately turned and switched his attention to getting out of the flat. He had what he needed now and had already spent far too long on these extracurricular activities in Jay's flat.

"They are going to fucking have you for this!"

Colin barked the parting threat as he marched down the dark hallway towards the front door.

He pulled down the door handle and swung open the door.

Colin glanced back into the flat just in time to see the thick end of the baseball bat swinging down from a height at him. He instinctively raised his arms once more to try to block it, but this time he was too late. The bat crashed down hard on the top of his head.

The sound of the violent cracking impact was followed quickly by a grunt and yelp of pain.

A second bat swing hit Colin across the top of his back as he stumbled out of the flat and into the more brightly lit communal hallway of the block. From a hunched position, he turned to look back into the flat with his hands above his head to protect himself.

Still enraged, Jay took two more swings of the bat, the latter side-swing crashing into Colin's unprotected chest, instantly breaking two of his ribs.

"Arrggghhh... fu—"

As Colin's left arm moved instinctively down to his broken ribs, an enraged, emotional and exhausted Jay swung the bat over his head and then down, thumping it against the back of Colin's head.

Void of any energy, Jay dropped the bat and stood limp with both arms down by his sides. He took deep, panting breaths as he looked down at Colin, who was now retreating in a hunched stagger down the outdoor estate walkway.

After a few seconds, the red mist began to clear. Still out of breath and panting, Jay turned to head back into the flat and check on Julia. The two met in the hallway. She had slowly been edging her way down the corridor to try to see where Jay was and what was going on.

Julia threw her arms wildly around Jay and gripped as tightly as she could. As she did, she let out a wail of emotion and began sobbing loudly and uncontrollably as tears streamed down her face.

Jay simply stood with a blank, solemn expression on his face. His arms were around Julia, but loosely. He was in a completely emotionless daze. His left eye was swollen and blood was slowly pouring from one of his ears. Several of his teeth were loose. His head felt like it was continually inflating and there was a loud buzzing in his ears.

The two stood there for at least a minute in this position, Julia occasionally loosening her grip on Jay to lean back and kiss his face a few times before grabbing on again firmly.

Colin Norris stumbled down the corridor of the flats, swaying from left to right as he lurched from one drunken stride to the next. He was left heavily concussed after the sharp blows to the head, his mouth pouring with blood.

Holding his arm out and using the wall to stabilise himself, he managed to make it to the top of the stairwell and began hobbling down step by step. As he lifted his leg forward to attempt the third step down, Colin felt an overwhelming faintness come over him. His skin had turned completely white and his lips a dark blue as he fainted from the shock of his injuries.

Colin's limp body crashed against the cold concrete steps as he tumbled over himself repeatedly before finally coming to rest at the bottom of the stairwell. A dead silence filled the hallway as he lay sprawled out, bloody from his injuries. He floated in and out of consciousness for several minutes, his eyes rolling around in his head before eventually losing consciousness completely.

Fifty wraps of cocaine and a large pile of cash lay scattered all around him, spread out during his fall down the stairs. Lodged under his right arm, there was an unloaded Glock 17 pistol wrapped tightly in a black bin liner.

CHAPTER THREE

Thursday, 19th March, 9:37 p.m.

Tommy 'Trigger' Boulton was finishing his second post-dinner brandy at his gated, detached five-bedroom house in the Essex suburbs. His partner Suzie was filling what he saw as the traditional wife roll, dolled up in the over-the-top marble and LED-light-ridden kitchen, clearing up the plates and glasses. She was only three years younger than Tommy at forty-seven, but after years of Botox, a facelift and a nose job, you'd be forgiven for thinking she was in her twenties. At least from a distance.

Tommy was a six-foot-five bulldog of a man. He had razor sharp 'jarhead' jet-black hair and bulging, pronounced muscles in his chest, back and arms. His face was mean-looking with a wide, flattened boxer's nose and a permanent scowl. His wide, thick neck was draped in a heavy 18-carat gold chain contrasting nicely with his fake-tanned, dark brown skin. He mostly wore tight black or white T-shirts to show off these 'assets', even at his age. He was the stereotypical ex-bouncer-cum-football hooligan.

Tommy was quiet at home; the intensity and stress of his working life meant these times were a much-needed sanctuary from the madness. That madness was a brutal and unforgiving but successful life of crime.

Tommy had grown up on the Aylesbury estate and by his early twenties had become deeply involved in the world of organised crime. He'd moved from extortion, to armed robbery to firearms and drugs trafficking operations that reached across much of South East England. Being one of the more calculated, clever and of course ruthless of his peers, Tommy had found ways to legitimise his ill-gotten gains in the form of several 'front' businesses. One of said businesses existed in the world of boxing promotion and management — Boulton Boxing.

As time went on and Tommy became more and more revered, his access to extensive amounts of money, along with his reputation and affiliation with hardcore criminals, made him behave as though he was untouchable. On the several occasions he'd had run-ins with the law, he had managed to avoid serving any serious prison time through either the appointment of high-power lawyers or the intimidation and bribery of susceptible police officers and witnesses. For all intents and purposes, he was an established and seriously feared criminal and most people in the local area knew his name.

Being the driver in a police chase that ended in a van/motorbike collision on the edge of the Aylesbury estate ten years ago had been the final 'close call' for Tommy and it was the point where his common sense and discipline began to outweigh his greed. It was the moment where he took the decision to no longer do any of his own 'dirty work' himself, since he had far too much to lose. Although he and his co-conspirators had got away from the crash scene before the police could catch them, the incident had left a twenty-year-old local man in a critical condition. When the van was searched, police discovered a record haul of semi-automatic rifles, handguns and even grenades.

Despite the motorcyclist having seen and recognised the notorious Tommy in the van that day, he knew better than to say anything to the police about it. Although he never told a soul, he had remembered whose face he'd seen. He remembered the unapologetic grin on that same face on the occasions he had seen him since. He remembered, and in the months he had spent recovering from his injuries, he had nurtured a deep, unrelenting hatred for him.

Although Tommy had initially planned to keep his family well distanced from his business interests, he had reversed that decision some years ago and introduced his son Daniel to the criminal underworld.

Daniel was never really all that good at anything else. He wasn't a looker either. He had a tall, skinny, gangly appearance and a mouth full of long, wonky teeth. His shoulder-length curly blonde hair always looked dirty. From a young age he had exhibited a tendency for violence and was known for having an extremely short temper. At some point, Tommy had come to the conclusion that his son was always going to fall into a life of crime and if that were true, it might as well be under his guidance.

Tommy had taken on the role of a mentor to his son Daniel and some of his childhood friends, including Luke and Jeremy Weaver. Over the years he had given them access to weapons, offered them places to stay and acted as a consultant in their various criminal activities, often in exchange for something, of course.

In more recent times the boys had filled numerous roles in Tommy's 'legitimate' business affairs, including collecting money from those who owed, working as security on fight nights for his promoted boxers and, occasionally, ensuring that his associates had the women and drugs they needed when they were out socialising in one of East London's more seedy clubs.

On more than one occasion, Tommy had been forced to get his own hands a little dirty in order to dig his son and his friends out of whatever trouble they'd found themselves in. Tonight was one such occasion.

Tommy had answered the phone to a frantic Daniel, who had explained that about one hour earlier, his childhood friend and 'business associate' Colin had been found unconscious by a middle-aged woman at the bottom of the stairs on the Aylesbury estate.

When the paramedics and police arrived, they found money, enough drugs to warrant a 'possession with intent to distribute' charge and an illegally converted semi-automatic Glock pistol.

Daniel explained that the gun was one that had been on the street for a while and that there was a good chance it could have some forensic history that might point back to them. That was only a side concern though. Colin was a lifelong business associate and family friend and given what he had been discovered with, he was more than likely going to receive a serious jail term. Both father and son knew that this was also going to bring a whole wave of police attention to the wider group, many of whom still worked for Tommy from time to time.

Naturally, Tommy was furious to be receiving this news in the comfort of his own home on what would otherwise have been a quiet Thursday evening. All the work he had done to make calculated moves and keep himself at arm's length, all the things he had taught the boys over the years. How the fuck could they have allowed this to happen? Who had left Colin in this state?

Amidst the torrent of information that was flowing through the phone at a pace that made it hard to understand, a name emerged from the noise. Jayden Amare Fox.

CHAPTER FOUR

Jay sat on Julia's bed, holding a plastic bag full of half-melted ice to the side of his head. The lump on his left eye had now swollen up to the size of a golf ball. The seriousness of what had taken place earlier on the estate was beginning to hit home and his stomach churned with a worried sickness. He sat in virtual silence as Julia darted around her room, gathering together some clothes for a few nights' stay away.

The couple had decided that they would both call into work sick tomorrow and spend some time at her auntie's house in the Hertfordshire countryside, since she was away at her holiday home in Cyprus. Julia had put together an overnight bag for Jay back at his flat after partially recovering from the shock of the confrontation with Colin. Since the pair had left the estate through another stairwell at the east side of Jay's block, they were unaware of the full gravity of the situation they had left behind.

After a few minutes of silence between them, Jay briefly snapped out of his worried preoccupation.

"I'm really sorry, Julia."

The constant sound of drawer shutting paused as Julia turned to look at Jay. She could see the sincerity in his eyes and although she resented that they had been dragged into this mess, she genuinely felt sorry for him. After all, in the moments of Colin's attack at the flat, she had felt in very real danger and in fear for both of their lives. If she'd had a weapon on her at the time, she thought, there's a high likelihood that *she* would have used it. She didn't blame Jay for his actions under the circumstances.

Of course, there was still the unanswered question around what exactly Jay had got himself involved in that warranted Colin's visits. Julia thought it best to leave it until they had arrived at their weekend retreat before confronting him on that subject again though. For now, she was just grateful that they were both safe.

Julia walked over to the bed and began stroking Jay's arm, leaning in to kiss him on the lips.

"I know you were just trying to protect us," she said. "You have to leave that place Jay; those people are fucking evil. They'll never leave you alone. Whatever it is with them, it's obviously not just gonna go away is it?"

Jay nodded his head slowly in agreement as Julia spoke.

"... with what's happened... they're dangerous people and it's only a matter of time before..."

She paused and looked down to the floor with a concerned expression as she thought about how to end that sentence. In the moment of silence, Jay looked up at her and the two exchanged an expression of solemn understanding.

After a few more seconds of silence, Julia continued packing her bag. The pair had decided that a change of scenery at her aunt's house was the best way for them to both forget about what had just happened and decide what, if anything, they would do next.

Jay had left a message on his boss Pete's phone letting him know that he would be gone for 'at least a week'. The thought had already entered his mind that he might actually never go back. They could spend a few weeks, even months at Julia's auntie's place and he could get a local job and then find somewhere more permanent to live. Pete would be upset and there might be complications with Julia's work but so what? People had worked around bigger complications. Maybe he would never have to see the goons from the estate again. It was worth making whatever sacrifice was necessary to allow that to happen.

***

Thursday 19th March 11:30 p.m. — Hackney South Train Station.

Jay and Julia sat huddled together on a metal bench on the northbound platform. It was a dark, chilly evening and at this time on a Thursday night, the station was barren.

The day's events had been traumatising, but they were now trying their best to move forward. Emotionally exhausted, the couple were looking forward to a nice cosy bed in the country tonight, away from all the madness. Julia was back to laughing and joking and for brief moments, it felt as though nothing was wrong again. Jay had thought to himself a couple of times, maybe this isn't such a bad thing after all. Maybe this kind of horrific event is *exactly* the kind of push they needed to make a big change in their lives and find happiness in the process.

The near-empty 11.32 train slowly crept in to platform one. This was a slower, 'all stops' service that wouldn't get Jay and Julia to Hertfordshire as fast as the later .50 train, so it was one that they were going to let go.

Three carriages down from where the couple were sitting, Dave Shilling stood at the carriage doors waiting to get off.

Dave was a six-foot tall, skinny and slightly goofy-looking young man. At twenty years old, he was considered the 'baby' within his group of older, tougher friends. He had big baby-blue eyes and a young-looking face to match. That being said, he had one of the worst receding hairlines of the gang, with large spaces either side of a small island of black hair in the middle of his head.

Having had a few drinks that evening, Dave was talking loudly and jovially on his phone to his childhood friend, Luke Weaver.

As Shilling stepped off the train, he glanced to the right and recognised Jay sitting on the bench with Julia. Julia was on the side closest to Dave and the two briefly made eye contact as he flashed a sleazy smile her way. Unimpressed, she immediately turned her head away to face forward. Jay had not seen this interaction take place. He sat hunched over with his hands clasped together, once again lost in thought about their current situation.

Dave turned to the left and began walking along the platform towards the exit stairs.

"Yeah, mate I told him he's taking the piss — I told him if he keeps being so lippy, I'll have to shag his bird again."

The pair laughed incessantly together down the phone. Their conversation continued as Dave walked up the platform stairs leading to the small Hackney South concourse.

About one minute into the phone call, Dave left the station entrance and turned right out on to the main road. This led directly onto a road bridge that crossed over the railway lines, with a pavement on either side.

"The cripple's bird is all right ain't she? Ow's he done that then?"

Dave sniggered to himself as he said this.

There was a moment of silence on the phone; the jovial tone of the conversation was killed stone dead.

Dave continued, slightly confused by the lack of response.

"Fucking fit, no?"

Luke Weaver replied in a solemn, serious tone, "You spoke to Colin today?"

Dave, confused by this seemingly out of context question, stopped in his tracks and screwed up his face.

"Colin...? Nah I haven't... why?"

Another silence. Luke's voice took on an increasingly angered and assertive air.

"You sure about that mate? Ain't seen him today? Ain't spoke to him?"

Dave's confusion quickly turned to nervousness. He could tell that Luke was seriously concerned about something and he knew all too well how volatile the Weavers could be.

"Luke mate I ain't seen him... is everyfing OK?"

"Why did you mention the cripple's bird?" Luke asked.

Dave nervously chuckled as he replied to the question.

"First time I've seen her that's all — just fought he was punching above his w—"

"*Where?* When did you see her then?"

Luke cut Dave off at the end of his sentence.

Dave turned round to look back into the entrance of the station.

"Erm... I've just seen both of em sitting at the platform."

There was another brief silence.

Dave nervously walked over to the wall of the road bridge. He stretched his neck up to peer over the top of the thick brick wall. From there, he could just about see the legs of Jay and Julia, who were still sitting on the bench at the far end of platform one.

Luke replied, slightly taken aback by what Dave had just told him.

"Right now? They're at the station right now, yeah?"

Dave replied once more, nervously.

"Yeah mate... I'm looking at em now... what's all this ab—"

47

At that moment, the call was abruptly cut off. Dave took the phone away from his ear and held it in front of him to look at the screen. He stared at it in confusion and then once again over to the platform. Instead of carrying on with his walk home, he decided to stay where he was, leaning against the side of the bridge in anticipation of finding out what the end of that call was all about.

Jay and Julia sat at the deserted platform for ten more minutes before the relative tranquillity they were experiencing was suddenly brought to an end. This time, however, it wasn't because of a loud passing train.

Jay had subconsciously noticed the distant sound of footsteps pounding down the station stairwell but thought little of it. As they came nearer, however, the addition of deep, angry sounding exchanges between the approaching group had caught his attention. He gently moved Julia's head off his shoulders and leant forward on the bench to look past her, right down the platform.

In front of the glaring yellow lights, he could see the silhouettes of three men walking in his direction. They walked with an urgency and a thuggish lean, swinging their shoulders from left to right. With each step the image of the men became clearer. The man in the centre pulled his hood up over his head. A second later, the two six-foot-something men on either side reached up and pulled balaclavas down to cover their faces. As they neared another set of platform lights, Jay could see that the smaller man standing in the middle had a bandanna covering the bottom half of his face. All three men were wearing slightly different varieties of black hooded sweater and worn-looking denim jeans. A sick feeling instantly set deep into the pit of Jay's stomach.

Jay turned to look at Julia. She was caught up in looking at her phone, holding it with both hands out in front of her. She had her wireless headphones in, smiling whilst looking at an amusing video that had been sent to her. Ignorance is bliss.

Jay quickly turned his focus back towards the far end of the platform and the approaching gang. They were now a couple of steps closer and about twenty metres away from the bench that Jay and Julia were sitting on. The even more disturbing sight of what each of the men held in their hands came into view.

The glint from the blade of a machete caught Jay's eyes as it reflected the yellow light beaming down from above. It was stuffed in the jeans of the man on the left, with the handle and a couple of centimetres of the blade visible above the belt. Jay's eyes darted frantically between the group as he tried to scan the men for other weapons. The man in the centre had his hands in the pockets of his hoodie. To the right of him, the tallest of the three men had a cosh semi-hidden inside his left sleeve. He cuffed the tip of it in his hand.

Jay whipped his head round to look in the exact opposite direction. To the couple's immediate left there were two more benches spaced a few metres apart, followed by a large advertising billboard. After that, about thirty metres in the distance, the platform sloped down to meet the railway. There was no safe way out of the station that wasn't in the direction of the approaching group of thugs.

As the group moved closer to the platform bench, the man in the middle distanced himself forward to lead the pack. Jay instinctively stood up and walked over to the right, past Julia and the end of the bench. Julia looked up from her phone and removed the right headphone from her ear, surprised to see Jay suddenly get up. As she looked up at him with a confused expression, the sight of the three approaching men caught her eye for the first time. Her jaw slowly dropped and the colour immediately began to fade from her face. A feeling of complete dread washed over her.

Jay extended his hand out behind him, giving Julia the unmistakeable command to stay where she was as he took a few steps in the direction of the group.

Jay wasn't the confrontational type; in fact, he had stood up for himself on only a handful of occasions in his life. It was his instincts that drove him to stand in front of Julia. No matter how terrified he felt at the prospect of what was approaching, he knew that these men were here because of him.

Julia looked over at Jay and then back to the approaching group, her teeth now chattering with fear.

As the two larger men at the rear slowed and stopped a few metres away, Luke Weaver continued walking. He advanced directly over to Jay, raised both arms up and pushed him backward, hard.

The other two thugs — Steven Norris (brother of Colin) and his close friend Jamie Knight — stood menacingly behind him holding their weapons. They turned their heads around every few seconds to see if anyone was coming or if there was anyone around on the neighbouring platforms. No one.

Jay managed to right himself. He now stood about a metre in front and to the right of Julia. She screamed for the men to leave them alone, frozen in a sort of foetal position on the bench with her arms firmly clutching her knees.

Luke edged forward to stand with his balaclava-clad face almost touching Jay's.

"You've fucking done it now cripple ain't ya."

Luke reached up and grabbed hold of Jay's face, squeezing hard on his cheeks.

Out of pure instinct and to break the painful hold, Jay dropped his right shoulder to swing a punch at Luke. The punch had a weak connection as Luke had dipped his head down and leant to the side to avoid it.

Luke responded by immediately grabbing hold of Jay's sweater with both hands and throwing him against the clear fibreglass shelter panel that stood adjacent to the bench. At the same moment, the two other thugs bounced over from behind Luke and leant in to hold Jay even more firmly against the panel, one on each arm.

Luke wasted no time. He took a step back, cracked his knuckles and began swinging blow after blow of violent punches into Jay's body.

Jay tried to resist and wriggle free as the first few punches landed against his stomach and ribs.

Julia couldn't just watch the torturous sight of her boyfriend being so helplessly pummelled. In a panic, she leapt off the bench and grabbed hold of Steven Norris on the nearer side of Jay, who was holding him against the panel by his left arm. She dug her nails deeply into his right arm and pulled backwards as hard as she could, screaming and crying uncontrollably as she did.

Norris let out an angry grunt of pain, and letting go of Jay temporarily, swung round and punched Julia directly in the nose. He leant in with the full force of his body. Julia's nose exploded with blood as her head and neck violently jolted back. She dropped to the ground with a cold, hard thump. She was immediately rendered unconscious.

Caught off guard by Julia's sudden intervention off to his right, Luke briefly paused his beating of Jay to allow his associate to deal with her.

Jay looked up from his hunched position just in time to see Julia's head bounce off the concrete platform floor. He screamed out in anger and swung his full weight round to punch Jamie Knight with his now free left hand. The hard, accurate punch connected with his temple and Knight fell back, lifting both of his hands up to protect his head.

Jay slid his back up the fibreglass and rose to his feet, now free from restraint. At the exact same time Luke Weaver, still standing directly in front of Jay, lunged forward to throw another flurry of fists in his direction.

Jay raised his clenched fists up beside his head.

The two exchanged a series of blows but Jay, screaming with rage and running on pure adrenaline, began to get the upper hand. Luke's head began to drop and his hands came up to defend his head as Jay continued his assault.

Jay was wildly swinging punches from the left and right, saliva flying out of his mouth as he landed multiple blows on Luke's arms and ribs. Several of them broke the guard to connect with the small, exposed areas on Luke's face.

Suddenly, a loud whipping crack echoed along the platform as Knight struck Jay across the back with his cosh.

Jay was met with an immediate rush of pain but still in his adrenaline-fuelled rage, turned to his right to face Knight. Knight stood with the cosh raised above and behind his head, jerking his shoulder forward, threatening another strike.

Meanwhile, Steven Norris wiped the blood from the open wound on his arm. He looked down at Julia in disgust and drew the long machete from his jeans. He turned round to face the ongoing fight just in time to witness Jay swing four more punches, taking two more hits from Knight's cosh to the arm and chest in the process.

Luke Weaver angrily wiped the blood from his own mouth and steadied himself. He looked to the right and nodded at Norris, who, without uttering a word, reached forward and handed Luke the machete.

Luke calmly walked towards Knight and Jay, pulled his right arm back and violently thrust the machete blade into Jay's ribcage.

A moment of silence and stillness came over the platform. Luke grabbed the handle of the knife and firmly pulled it back out. It was followed by a stream of blood that splattered out onto the concrete floor.

Jay stumbled back, falling to once again rest on the clear, fibreglass panel behind him. He clutched the wound on the left side of his torso firmly with both hands. For a second, he slowly edged his left hand away to watch the blood pouring from the gaping hole. The sight of this drew his hand back over to cover it, almost magnetically.

There was another moment of silence as all three thugs stood around Jay.

The electric adrenaline that had pumped through Jay's veins only moments ago was replaced by morbid fear and shock. Jay felt the energy immediately begin to drain from his body and a wave of weakness rush over him, his legs shuddering underneath him, struggling to hold him up.

Jay looked up at the re-assembled group of thugs standing menacingly around him like a pack of snarling wolves. He was pale and wild-eyed with an expression that seemed to say, 'have mercy'. The blood was now streaming out through the gaps between Jay's fingers. He could tell, even in the milliseconds following the impact, that this was bad.

During a two-second pause the thugs looked at each other, back at Julia lying unconscious behind them on the platform and then once again at Jay. Luke handed the machete back to Norris, who stuffed it down in his jeans. The group began attacking Jay wildly once more.

He was kicked, stomped, and battered violently as he curled up in a crouched position against the shelter wall with his hands up. The vicious melee only lasted about thirty seconds, but it was enough to do some more, serious damage.

Jay's jaw was broken, several teeth had flown out of his mouth and the bones in his hands and fingers had cracked as he'd tried to use them to defend himself. He began to gurgle with all of the blood accumulating in his throat.

An overwhelming fear and sadness ran through Jay's body as he realised that he was no longer just being injured or maimed: these men were killing him.

And Julia. What state was she in? He could only just about see the bottom of her legs behind the three burly attackers in front of him, even then it was only for a moment at a time.

Just then an automated announcement came over the platform loudspeaker stating that the .50 train would be arriving in two minutes. The thugs paused their beating as Luke Weaver threw his hands up to either side, signalling the group to stop.

Jay was now sitting slumped to one side, slipping in and out of consciousness. There was a large, torso-shaped bloodstain smeared down the transparent fibreglass panel, now cracked and shattered in several places from the force of the frenzied attack.

Luke noticed out of the corner of his eye that just behind and to the right of the group, Julia was now conscious. She had rolled herself on to one side, got on to one knee and almost raised herself up onto her feet. Her strawberry blonde hair was draped wildly across the front of her face, stained with blood near the tips. Her head swayed from side to side as she staggered with a concussed balance.

Luke looked at Norris and nodded in the direction of Julia.

"Sit her down."

Norris immediately walked over to Julia, grabbed her by the shoulders and threw her to the floor towards the edge of the platform. This time she was conscious enough to put both her arms out in front of her to break her fall. She let out a groggy moan as she once again hit the floor. Holding herself up by her elbows, she attempted to turn her head back around to face the men, desperate to see if she could see Jay.

Luke Weaver walked over in Julia's direction, reached under his belt at the back of his jeans and pulled out a black revolver pistol.

Without any hesitation, he stopped, extended his right arm to point the pistol down at Julia in a diagonal trajectory and fired two shots into the top of her back.

The loud cracks of gunfire echoed and reverberated along the platform.

Knight and Norris jumped back in shock; instinctively turning away and holding their hands up to their ears.

A deafening, shock-filled silence washed over the place — everyone experiencing a loud but fading ringing in their ears.

"Luke for f... who told you to bring a fucking gun?!"

The panicked and shocked voice of Steven Norris came from behind him.

Luke immediately swung the gun round to point it in the direction of the criticism.

"No one fucking tells me to do anything," he said flatly.

Luke walked toward Jay, once again extending his right arm out to one side, aiming the gun down at him. By this time Jay had all but lost consciousness.

Luke pulled the trigger twice more, firing two bullets directly into Jay's chest.

Another two extremely loud booming shots echoed off the structures on the platform and into the nearby station car park.

Still shocked, the other members of Luke's crew stood silently, in awe of the level of casual, murderous violence on display in front of them.

Jay's pulse was already fading; he'd lost more than two pints of blood and taken a savage beating. Those two shots were going to be more than he could possibly survive.

His pulse slowed and slowed.

Jay took one last deep, gargled breath and opened his eyes. For a second his vision was almost clear. It was the first time he had clearly seen Julia's lifeless body lying metres away in front of him on the platform.

His heart beat two more times. And then stopped.

With only just over a minute before a train pulled into the platform they were standing on, the three men began stuffing their weapons back into their hoodies and jeans and walking quickly up the platform to the station exit.

Luke laughed menacingly as he pulled his hood up over his head once more, walking at the front of the group.

"Fucking showed them cunts, didn't we?"

***

Jayden Fox's eyes shot open. They were now a deep, blood red.

His neck snapped up to face forward as he took a primal, gasping breath. All of the muscles in his body instantly tensed and began swelling in size. His heart was now beating so fast and with such force it felt like it would burst out of his chest. It was as though fifty thousand volts of electricity were running through his body. He began shuddering violently, his jaw clenched so hard that he could feel his teeth cracking in his mouth.

Fox immediately looked over towards Julia. Although he could see what was in front of him, his vision was altered. There was a sort of indigo tinge that covered everything. The lights on the station platform appeared to shine brighter, creating a powerful haze around them.

As his eyes processed the objects around him, he was overwhelmed by the chatter in his mind. The minute details of every object, the distance between things, the feeling of the wind touching his skin and the amplified sounds coming from all around him. His brain was in overdrive, relaying more information than he could possibly handle.

Thinking he'd heard a noise coming from behind him, Luke briefly turned his head. He stopped, turning round to do a double take. The thugs on either side of him continued walking for a few steps until they noticed Luke had stopped walking and then also turned around.

Amongst the deafening sounds in Fox's mind, he could hear the wind whistling in the air, the cars driving on the road just over half a mile away and the distant sound of the train approaching. He could also hear the heavy breathing of the three thugs further along the platform. And the lack of breathing from the body that lay directly in front of him. In his heart he wanted to check her, to race to save her. But in his mind he knew, beyond a doubt, that she was dead.

Fox threw his arms out to either side of him, slamming them into the concrete platform floor with such force that it threw him up into a standing position. A cloud of dust from the smashed concrete floated off him. He immediately turned to his right to face the three men once more.

Luke Weaver was now marching down the platform towards Fox, growling with frustration. He once again reached down into the back of his jeans and pulled the black revolver out to hold in in his right hand. His two comrades reluctantly followed a few metres behind him, exchanging a concerned look.

As Luke closed to around five metres from Fox, he stopped suddenly and pulled the trigger twice more. This time two metallic 'chink' sounds were all that followed. The gun was out of ammo.

Holding the pistol out in front of him, Luke turned it on its side and looked down at it in disgust.

Just then Fox leapt forward, closing the gap between the two men at an impossible rate. At the same time, he took hold of the revolver with his left hand and drove his right elbow hard into Luke's chest. Three of Luke's ribs cracked loudly. The force of the impact was so great that it lifted Luke off his feet, both arms trailing out in front of him. His eyes and mouth were open wide in shock as he gasped, desperately trying to catch a breath.

Immediately after Luke's legs touched the floor, Fox took another step forward onto his right leg, lifted his left leg up and kicked down hard onto Luke's right knee. Another loud, musky crack rang out as Luke's leg snapped and inverted. He let out an intense, high-pitched scream as the pain immediately rushed through his body.

As Luke hunched over in agony, Fox swung his body weight round into a massive punch to his jaw with his right hand. Another cracking sound. Another badly broken bone. Mumbling and gargling, Luke fell to the ground.

Steven Norris now approached with Knight around three metres behind him. He had spent the last few seconds cautiously walking towards Fox, frantically attempting to slide the machete out from his jeans once more. He got it free and gripped it firmly in his right hand, just as Luke hit the ground in front of him.

As Norris closed in he leapt forward, thrusting the machete at Fox's chest in a stabbing motion.

The knife and Norris seemed to approach Fox in slow motion. He parried the incoming blade away with his right arm and took a stride to his left. As Norris' momentum continued to propel him forward, with the blade of the machete now beyond its target, Fox turned his left elbow hard into Norris' nose. It broke, and his neck jolted back violently from the impact.

Fox swung his body round to the right and sweep kicked Steven's legs from behind, throwing them out in the air in front of his body. After half a second of silence, he landed hard on his back, heavily winded. He let out an *"Oomph"* sound, spraying a mist of blood into the air.

Having spun around three hundred and sixty degrees from the motion of the kick, Fox pulled back his right hand and lunged down to the floor, slamming his clenched fist into Steven's chest.

Knight, who had been approaching to come to Norris' aid, stopped in his tracks. He felt the force of that last punch reverberate through the platform. How was that possible? A punch like that would surely be lethal. And it was. One of Steven's ribs had broken so violently that half of the bone had punctured deep into one of his lungs. The other half had pierced his heart.

Fox looked up at Knight from his crouched position on the floor. At this point he noticed that slightly further along the platform, Luke Weaver was attempting to crawl away, holding onto the wall of the waiting room building on the right as he dragged his badly broken leg behind him. He could hear the mumbled whimpering and only wished that the pain he had inflicted would last for as long as possible.

Having just seen his friend killed in front of him, Knight charged towards Fox with the cosh raised over his head. He let out an enraged and terrified shriek as he swung the weapon down towards Fox's head as hard as he could.

Without thinking, Fox rose up onto his feet and caught Knight's hands, mid-swing. The two men stood for a second, facing each other with their hands locked in the air above them. Knight shuddered and growled as he desperately tried to prise the cosh free from Fox's grip. Once again, Fox turned to the side and lifted his left leg, kicking down hard on to Knight's knee. It snapped violently. Knight let out an almighty, desperate scream.

Luke looked back in shock, still on his knees further down the platform. He turned to face forward, attempting to crawl faster and pick up the pace of his escape.

With Knight's grip now loosened, Fox snatched the cosh out of his hands. Knight dropped down on to his knees, shaking with the shock of the violent injury he had just received. As he looked up, Fox took a sharp, powerful swing of the cosh and brought it down hard on to the top of Knight's skull. It moved through the air with such speed that it made a whipping sound. The force of the blow instantly fractured Knight's cranium. He dropped to the floor, limp, having lost consciousness.

Fox turned his attention to a sound coming from further down the platform.

Luke Weaver let out a dull moan of pain as he reached the bottom of the stairs and looked up at his long climb to freedom.

The cosh clanged against the concrete floor as Fox immediately dropped it and began charging down the platform towards Luke.

Luke had dragged himself up three steps before he turned round to see Fox reach the bottom of the stairs. Trembling with fear and with a swollen, pale, bloody face, he extended his arm out in front of him with an open palm, begging for mercy. He mumbled something in a pleading tone from behind his badly broken jaw.

Without even stopping to acknowledge it, Fox walked up the three steps, raised his right leg up to knee level and stamped down hard on the side of Luke's head. The immensely powerful kick broke Luke's neck and killed him instantly.

Just then Fox heard the sound of a car screeching to a halt from beyond the top of the platform staircase. He had been too distracted to notice the approaching chorus of sirens that had been getting louder and louder over the last few seconds.

Fox quickly turned around and ran back in the direction of the far end of the platform, to where Julia's lifeless body lay. He stopped and knelt next to her. With the sound of sirens and boots thundering down the platform stairs in the background, he held Julia's head firmly against his chest as he sobbed uncontrollably.

Blue lights flashed from above, sporadically lighting up the night sky. Fox threw his head back and let out a piercing, primal scream that bellowed through the platform, up the staircase and through the station concourse. It was as deep and as terrifying as a lion's roar and at the same time, pierced the ears like the shriek of a trapped animal. All eight of the police officers that had now arrived on the scene froze for a few seconds as they heard it.

Although somehow breathing once more, Jay had in fact died on the platform that night, along with his hopes and dreams of a normal life. Something else now stood in his skin. Something stronger, faster and fitter than any human could naturally be. An abomination walking.

CHAPTER FIVE

Timothy Rolfe sat at the end of his single bed, staring down at a framed picture of his five-year-old daughter, Freya. He hadn't seen her or even heard her voice for almost a year — one of the many drawbacks of being on the run from the authorities as a leading member of an infamous hacking organisation.

Tim's ex-girlfriend, Joanne, had taken the decision to move away from London last year and had taken Freya with her. They now lived in a leafy suburb in Wiltshire.

Joanne and Tim had enjoyed a brief but romantically intense relationship. The two had met whilst working for the same security firm and hit it off after spending a few late nights in the office together. How simple things were back then.

The last week had been particularly rough for Tim, possibly the darkest in his life. The shooting of his best friend Michael Harding had turned his life upside down and sent him into a paranoid spiral. After partially getting over the initial shock and horror of the shooting, he had gone through a period of anger and resentment, desperately trying to find out what had happened to his friend and how he had ended up dead.

Together they had struggled through being framed for crimes they didn't commit and being hounded as a result of how dangerous the information they had uncovered had made them. But this had taken things to another level. Rolfe was a strong, extremely intelligent and at times even cocky character, but he was struggling to deal with the combined burden of being on the run and losing his friend in such a sudden, violent and unjust way.

The media had reported that Harding had gestured in a threatening way and that armed officers on the scene that day had believed he was reaching for something, potentially a concealed weapon. In the interest of preserving life, they had taken the split-second decision to take the shot and put Harding down. None of this made sense to Tim. In his initial trawling of the IPOC files on the case, he had quickly become aware that only one officer had felt the need to pull the trigger that day. S019 Officer Max Carter.

Tim had read multiple transcripts from witnesses at the scene that suggested Harding had behaved cooperatively after initially running. Mentions of 'reaching' only started to appear in later, revised statements. There were similar discrepancies in the reports filed by the police officers on the scene as well. Conveniently, all of the officers had their body cameras turned off for the entirety of the event.

What was Harding even doing in that area in the first place? The pair had been together in the days before and Michael hadn't mentioned anything that would explain it.

Rolfe was completely convinced of a conspiracy. Someone had arranged this 'hit' on Michael Harding. Someone had lured him out there under some kind of false pretences and had him shot down on the street.

Although he was driven by the desire to find out why Harding had been killed and who was really behind it, the intense pain and stress of the situation was testing Rolfe. He had grown weary, spending less and less of his days relentlessly trawling the web for answers, overcome with sadness and the realisation that he too would likely be the next target.

Who was he kidding? Did he really think that he would be able to find all the answers to this on his own? Even if he could, what was he going to do with this information? There would be very few people he could take it to that would believe him, let alone help him.

And Michael. It was too late for Michael. He had lost his life and no amount of proof was going to bring him back. On top of all of this, Tim had his daughter to think about. Even if he stayed in hiding for as long as he could and took no risks whatsoever, if these people were out there looking for him and they were willing to kill, there's every chance they could go after his family. He couldn't let that happen. He couldn't feel responsible for another death.

As he had contemplated the options he had left on the table, Rolfe had begun to come to the conclusion that the best way forward might be to hand himself in to the authorities, try to give his version of things and face the consequences that came with it.

"In other news, the Metropolitan Police are no closer to solving the shocking triple homicide that took place at Hackney South Train Station three days ago.

"A swarm of officers arrived at the scene just after eleven p.m. on Thursday night after several reports of a major disturbance. Multiple calls were made to police, with witnesses claiming they heard the sound of gunshots coming from the area.

"Officers arrived to what they described as a scene of utter carnage. Spread along the length of the platform were the bodies of two men and one young woman. A third man was found with severe injuries and remains in a critical condition in hospital.

"Police sources say multiple weapons were found at the scene and suspect that the incident may have escalated from a fight between rival gangs in the area. No comment was made as to whether any of the victims had been identified."

DCI John Fields shook his head as he stared up at the television in the cafeteria of Box Hill Police Station. He took another slurp from his teacup as he turned round to walk back towards his office.

"Fucking shambles that."

He glanced over at the small group of officers sitting at the cafeteria tables who were all watching the same TV. They exchanged a sarcastic smile as one of the officers yelled out a reply, "Yeah, shit CCTV, apparently!"

A few muffled sniggers went around the room as John continued his jovial walk out of the cafe and into the hallways of the police station.

John Fields was a fifty-seven-year-old detective constable in the Met. During his near thirty-year-long career he had experienced almost all aspects of police work. From being a bobby on the beat to undercover operations and even a stint in the armed response units, John felt like he had seen it all. He was a heavyset, six foot two, bald chunk of man who had 'let himself go' a bit in the years past fifty. On top of his well-built broad, muscular body there was a thick, ever-growing layer of fat. This was most evident in his large, rotund beer belly that hung forward off the front of his body like a large sack of water.

John had done very well in his career and had risen through the ranks in the police relativity quickly. In his heyday in the late eighties and early nineties, he had been part of what some would call a 'clique' within the upper circles of the Met.

Like any other organisation, especially during that time period, the Met Police had groups of friends in management positions that would look after each other in certain ways. Look the other way when they needed to. Look closer than they should if called for as well. John's ambitious and bullish nature meant he'd suited the mentality of this kind of organisational politics well. It also meant that over the years, he had engaged in some behaviour that was morally questionable at the very least.

It had only been five minutes since John had sat down on his office chair before there was a knock at the door. He sighed and finished typing the last sentence of his email before reaching forward to take hold of his coffee mug on the desk.

"Come in."

A stern, serious-faced Max Carter swung open the door and walked into the office.

Fields did a sort of double take as he looked up from his desk to see Max standing in front of him. He quickly got up and walked over to the floor-to-ceiling windows on the right-hand side of his office. With one hand on the pull of the blinds, he looked from left to right before pulling them shut, blocking the view into the room. He shut the door to the office before walking back over to his desk.

After a brief pause, Max followed over to Fields' desk and stood in front of it, waiting for the invitation to sit down. Fields reluctantly nodded at the chair opposite him and Max proceeded to take a seat.

"You know I don't like having these conversations in the station," Fields said.

Max Carter stood at six foot three. He was a chiselled, handsome young man with medium length, well-kept wavy black hair. He had earned the reputation as a bit of a 'bad boy' in his early twenties in the force.

Although he mostly kept himself to himself and was quiet by nature, whispers about Max's involvement in various instances of 'dodgy dealings' had surrounded him for years. Suspects coming forward saying their money had gone after he'd arrested them. Drugs going missing after being confiscated from criminals on the street. Countless arrestees claiming that Max had been too rough with them. He had a whole spectrum of allegations behind him.

Now thirty-two years old, although Max's tendencies hadn't changed, he was certainly a little smarter with the moves he made. Smarter, and far more serious.

Max had just returned from one of the several meetings that he had been forced to attend in relation to the shooting death of Michael Harding a week earlier. This was standard procedure for an IPOC investigation into an officer's decision to use lethal force in the field.

So far, the meetings had gone relatively smoothly. Carter's colleagues had stuck by their unspoken rule to have each other's backs in these situations and had aligned their stories accordingly. Some of them were not at all happy at having to do this and a few sleepless nights had been shared across the group. No one wanted to be the snitch in a situation like this though, and the fact that the CCTV footage from the two cameras covering the road outside the coffee shop had disappeared meant that there was nothing concrete proving anything to the contrary of Max's story.

Max stared down at the floor and sniggered before looking up to reply to Fields' slightly annoyed comment.

"I just need some assurances, John. They're asking a lot of questions in there."

John looked over at the office window and then back at Max before replying through gritted teeth.

"Everything is being taken care of on my side Max. The footage, the witnesses, internal affairs. All of it is going to go away as long as you just keep your head down and your fucking mouth shut."

Max sarcastically sniggered once more before replying, "Easy as that is it?"

John nodded, shuffling the papers on his desk. Max wasn't at all impressed.

"I bet it's a lot fucking easier when you're not the one who has to pull the trigger isn't it?"

John slammed the stack of papers down on to the desk, growling as he snapped back at Max.

"You think I haven't been that guy before? You think I haven't been in your position?"

The two men took a second to calm down, acknowledging where they were and how many people were on the other side of that office glass.

"I know you're stressed, Max. I know they're putting the pressure on now. But it will go away soon. They won't have enough of anything to discredit your story. Don't forget the guy was a fucking international terrorist — you'll be looked on as hero soon."

Max looked to the side and laughed.

"We both know no one around here is going to think of me as a hero, John."

The two looked at each other with a smirk.

Max continued, "I don't really care anyway. I just want my fair share in this. I don't want to end up being used as some kind of patsy."

John shook his head and replied in a mildly frustrated tone, "You just need to keep your head. You did well out there, son, and I'm going to look after you for it. You've done a lot of people a big favour... me included. But there's still more for us to do."

He gestured towards the door of his office. Max took the hint and slowly got up out of the chair to turn and walk to the door.

He stopped in his tracks as John addressed him once more.

"Oh, and Max... We're not having these conversations here. This time I'll pretend this meeting never happened."

Max looked back at John with a blank expression and nodded. He walked out of the office, closing the door behind him.

***

Dave Shilling stopped to take a deep breath and compose himself before he pulled down on the brass handle of the posh function room door. He had driven out to The Range Golf Club in Essex on the instruction of his friend Daniel Boulton. He'd been told the Fairfield suite to the rear of the clubhouse had been reserved for the family and that Daniel's father, Tommy, had specifically asked for Dave to attend.

Dave had only met Tommy Boulton once before. It was at a birthday party being held in a local community centre on the estate six years ago. He remembered that night quite distinctly because as the evening had drawn to an end, a huge fight had erupted that had spilled out into the car park out the front.

Several police cars had been called to the scene and five people were arrested. Amongst all the chair throwing, punch swinging and swearing, Joe Tyler, a fifty-three-year-old nightclub owner, had been stabbed to death. The rumours had quickly circulated that it was Tommy. Joe was a former business associate of his, and the word on the street was that the two hadn't seen eye to eye over an outstanding debt between them.

Needless to say, this one interaction coupled with an already notorious reputation on the streets had left Dave terrified of Tommy and, by proxy, his son Daniel.

Shilling nervously walked into the function room and scanned around the various tables for faces that he recognised. A thick smog of cigar and cigarette smoke lingered in the air. There were small groups of well-dressed men spread out across the room, engrossed in conversation. A long buffet table running across the length of the left wall was laid out with sandwiches and fruit juices. It looked like a wake of some sort.

Just then Dave recognised the angry, sombre-looking face of Daniel Boulton at the back of the room. He was standing just in front of the largest table in the room with his father Tommy sitting behind him at the top of the table. To his left, sitting with his head in his hands sobbing, was Jeremy 'Jez' Weaver.

Dave instantly felt sick.

He took a deep gulp and walked towards the Boultons, nodding to the left and right at the people he knew along the way.

Daniel walked to the opposite end of the table from where his father was seated and pulled a chair out, gesturing for Dave to take a seat.

As Dave sat down, Daniel took the seat next to him and the chatter in the room began to fade. Several other men, none of whom Dave had ever seen before, walked over and filled the remaining chairs on the eight-seater table. They all had stern, serious expressions on their faces.

Once everyone was seated, Tommy leant forward from his reclined posture and slowly removed the Cuban cigar from his mouth.

He blew a line of thick smoke along the table towards Dave as he laid the cigar to rest on the side of an ashtray, just in front of his glass of brandy.

"Dave, isn't it?" he asked in a deep, gravelly voice.

Many of the heads at the table turned sharply to face Shilling, sitting at the direct opposite end of the table.

He took another gulp before opening his mouth to respond.

"Yeah."

Tommy nodded.

"OK Dave. Everyone is gonna try to put their emotions to the side for a minute. We're all friends here. Why don't you tell us what happened the other night at Hackney South? You were there weren't ya?"

At this point, Jez Weaver lifted his head from the table and looked over at Dave with an enraged look in his eyes, which were red raw from hours of crying. Tears and snot covered his face as the man sat to his right continued to hold his arm around him to comfort him.

Dave nervously locked eyes with Jez for a couple of seconds before turning to face Tommy once more.

"Yeah... yeah, I was."

There was a two-second silence in the room as the other men at the table waited for Dave to elaborate. He reluctantly obliged.

"I was on my way home and I saw that cri... I saw a geezer from the estate that a few of us know with some bird. I told Luke they was there and he just got all pissed off and told me to stay where I was. Next fing I knew, Luke and a couple of the boys turned up wiv tools and all that and they walked down the..."

Dave paused as his voice became too shaky to continue. The emotion of the situation coupled with the pressure the men in front of him were putting him under was all too much. He managed to gather the composure to continue.

"They walked down the stairs on to the platform. I was just looking around you know, watching for anyone else coming or whatever. I thought they must be wanting to give him a doing for something… I had no idea about any of that shit with Colin… no fucking idea!"

He was beginning to raise his voice, desperate for the men surrounding him to believe him.

"I heard all this screaming and shouting… fings crashing into each other and getting broken… Then I heard the shots."

Tommy leant forward with his elbows on the table.

"Who had the gun, Dave?"

Dave looked back at Tommy with a pale, blank expression.

"I don't… I don't know…"

One of the other men on the table, two seats down from Dave, now also leant forward and barked out a question.

"And you didn't see anyone else come into the station? Was there anyone else down on the platform?"

"I don't… I don't think anyone could have got into the station without me seeing em… I suppose there could have been some other people down on the platform."

Several theories as to what exactly had occurred that night at the station had been exchanged between the men at the table already that day. Some thought that a disagreement with a rival gang may have got out of hand or that Luke may have finally rubbed the wrong well-connected person up the wrong way and paid the price. All of them had made the assumption that there had to have been multiple parties involved in this and didn't even seriously consider the idea that this kind of carnage could have been caused by one man, let alone a 'cripple' like Jay.

Tommy weighed in again.

"And you didn't think to go down there and see what the fuck was going on?"

"I… I couldn't."

This was met with grumbling and the shaking of heads around the table.

Dave continued, "I couldn't see what was happening from where I was. I stayed doing what I was supposed to do and then when the filth turned up, I did a runner."

Dave's voice took on a more panicked, hurried tone as he rushed to explain himself to his ever more suspicious audience.

This latest question had called attention to one of the elephants in the room. An altercation had taken place that had ended up leaving two of their associates dead and one in a coma. Dave Shilling was the only one who walked away from it unscathed. How did he manage that? And with his friends in such a dire situation, why had he not helped them? Dave became acutely aware of the fact that pretty much everyone in the room felt he was hiding something from them.

The strained conversation went on for another thirty minutes or so. The questions flew in; the answers yielded very little. Over the course of this, Shilling had been slowly coming to the conclusion that this situation was more than likely not going to end well for him. Nobody trusted him. Some thought he might have had something to do with the attack; some thought he was hiding something and others just thought he was a disloyal coward for not stepping in and doing anything.

The truth was that Shilling really *didn't* see anything. Given the fact that his associates had entered the station 'tooled up', he wasn't all that surprised to hear the screams and clattering sounds coming from the platform. He really *had* just continued to look for people coming and fled when the police had arrived. Perhaps even this would have been considered cowardly in their circle. In any case, he had started entertaining the thought of doing a runner.

The shindig at the golf club was not held for the specific reason of discussing the events that preceded it on the Thursday. Tommy Boulton held these Sunday afternoon gatherings once every couple of months to bring together some of his business associates and friends and discuss upcoming ventures and plans.

The following Friday, one of the fighters that Tommy was promoting was in action. Depending on the list of attendees, these Sunday gatherings would normally be a chance to raise investment for his promotion business and potentially even attract new clients. It would also be a good opportunity to handle the illegal betting operations and match-fixing, to ensure the right people got paid.

This particular gathering was a lot lighter on either of the two usual elements though, given what had happened on Thursday night. Only the trusted, immediate associates of Tommy and the family had been invited.

"The fight goes on this weekend, lads. We're not to show anyone any weakness. We'll find out who hit Colin and the boys and when we do, they will fucking get what's coming to them!" Tommy announced.

An enthusiastic, drunken cheer echoed round the room.

"I'd like to raise a toast to two members of our family that have lost their lives. To Stevie Norris and Luke Weaver. Bloody good lads."

An even more emotional and defiant cheer reverberated through the whole function room.

"We stay alert though. Anyone hears anything, you tell me directly. Anyone coming to the fight comes strapped or with a big fucking shank. We ain't taking any more chances."

Fight-night Friday. Shilling had decided that he had to be gone well before then.

CHAPTER SIX

The Friday night fights at Bristol Hall were a calendar event in the underground world of East London. Of course, there were casual fans that were happily paying the modest ticket fees to come along and watch a decent standard of boxing, but the event was known for attracting a large criminal attendance.

Many of the fighters themselves had ties with local gangsters and criminals. The fights were rumoured to have been used to launder money and as a general front for more nefarious activities. An illegal gambling racket was at the core of many of the monthly fighting events and Tommy Boulton was right at the centre of that.

Following the various 'undercard' fights, tonight's main event was a long anticipated twelve-round bout between two of the most promising fighters in the division: Joey 'Fighting Irish' Troy and Alex 'Scarface' Brace.

Joey was around five foot nine and had a relatively stocky but defined build. His nimble movements and impressive strike power had earned him a reputation and a winning streak that had lasted five consecutive fights.

Alex, at six foot three, stood a tall, towering 'brick shithouse' of a man. He sported a completely shaved head, contrasted by his overly hairy chest and back. He was big and muscular, but he was also visibly carrying some extra weight. Beers and curries most nights of the week had seen to this.

Alex was one of the most promising fighters to be signed to Boulton Boxing and tonight was going to be an opportunity for him to really put himself on the map. Having spent most of his early adult life hanging around on the estate with the likes of the Weavers and their crew, he also had a hard, mean reputation in the local area. This made him all the more suitable for Tommy's operation.

Eight of Tommy's crew had taken their seats at the very back row of the first tier, five rows from ringside. They chose this row because a one-row gap between the seating tiers meant no one was sitting directly behind them. Since the seating that they brought in for the boxing events was also inclined at an angle, their seats provided a good view. At a time where tensions were still running high from the murders of two of their close friends, this was especially important.

Many of the other groups were surprised to see Tommy and his gang make an appearance, considering recent events. It was clear that there was obviously some concern though, since they would have normally sat ringside for a fight like this one.

Understandably cautious, Tommy had multiple people among the crowd carrying weapons whom he had told to be alert and ready if anything 'kicked off'.

Tommy sat in the middle of his group with Jeremy Weaver on his immediate left and his son Daniel on his right. One noted absence, highlighted by a single empty seat at the far left of the row, was that of Dave Shilling.

Where before the group had exchanged ideas on whether they thought Dave was guilty of anything, the only conversation they needed to have now was who was going to 'do him in' and when.

The last fight on the undercard had come to a close and the eight men in the fifth row had shuffled along into their seats after a toilet break.

An excited buzz filled the room as the lights dimmed ahead of the fighters' entrances for the main event.

The strobe lights flashed and the deep, bass-filled, distorted music blared throughout the hall as the first fighter emerged out of the tunnel that led from the dressing rooms down to the ring. Jeers and whistles rung round, with Irish flags waving from the standing balcony area that wrapped around the upper level of the hall.

Tommy and his group had relaxed into the evening by this point and were exchanging smug laughs in reaction to the over-the-top entrance that Joey was making.

As the music and jeers faded ahead of the second fighter's entrance, the anticipation began to build in the room once more.

Tommy turned to either side to address his friends in the row.

"Here we fucking go, boys!"

The group extended their respective drinks to 'cheers' before all taking a swig.

The babble of conversations in the crowd continued for around thirty seconds with no sign of any second entrance.

After a further ten seconds, several organiser staff were on their radios repeatedly signalling for the next fighter to come to the ring, wondering what was taking so long. The odd heckle started to come from the crowd.

"Come on Scarface… you ain't bottled it have ya?"

Some laughs rang out in the hall. Mainly at how ridiculous the idea was of a hardened, fearless thug like Alex backing out of a boxing match.

Behind the scenes, one of the staff members was running down the maze of corridors to the changing rooms to give Alex and his trainer the heads-up that it was time for the ring walk. By now they should have already been waiting on the other side of the curtain. Jamie, a seventeen-year-old runner, had been sent to find out why they weren't.

Just then, a figure in an all-black hooded robe emerged from the tunnel and started walking down to the ring. No music, no flashing lights and no trainer. Many people in the crowd had just assumed that there were some technical problems and started cheering as soon as they saw him. The figure never lifted his head in acknowledgement, nor did he respond to the various event organisers calling out to him as he made his way down.

At the same moment, after knocking on Alex's dedicated changing room door a number of times, Jamie slowly and nervously pulled down the handle and eased the door open. As he did, he was immediately hit with the sight of Alex lying slumped against the lockers of the changing room, bruised and battered in a pool of his own blood.

Jamie reeled at the scene in front of him. He stood frozen in the doorway, holding himself up from either side as his legs had started to give way from under him. His face had turned a completely pale white.

After staring for a few seconds in shock, Jamie quickly realised that Alex's chest was still moving up and down. He was still alive. Badly hurt, but alive.

Jamie scrambled so fast that he almost fell over and began running through the hallways back towards the main event, screaming as loudly as he could for help.

The robed figure approached the side of the ring. By this time, several of the staff and the opposing fighter's team had realised something was off. From this distance, they could see that this wasn't the man they were expecting. Unsure if it was some kind of elaborate hoax entrance or part of the evening's entertainment in some way, no one challenged him.

As the figure reached ringside, he immediately leapt forward and took a dive under the ropes to slide into the ring. He stood up slowly and pulled back the hood of the robe with both hands to reveal the scarred face and blood-red eyes of Jayden Amare Fox. The bottom half of his face was covered with a bike mask and his long, sweat-soaked hair was draped over his head.

He started to turn in place, scanning the room for a particular group of faces. The crowd looked on in confusion as the babble of conversation grew louder in the hall. At this point, one of the event staff stepped over from Joey Troy's corner on the opposite side of the ring and extended an open palm at Fox.

"Mate, you need to get out of the ring please."

His comment was completely ignored as Fox continued scouring the crowd behind the bright ring lights.

The attendant took one more step forward and put his hand on Fox's left arm.

"*Mate*, you need to fuck o—"

Before he could finish his sentence, Fox had flung his left arm out violently to free it from the man's grasp. He twisted his body weight into a short range, snapping punch into the man's exposed chest. The man winced as the punch took him off his feet and left him on his back, close to the middle of the ring. The crowd let out a gasp, almost in unison.

As Fox stood up and turned to his right, he made direct eye contact with Tommy Boulton, sitting in his seat five rows back from ringside.

With less than a second passing, Fox took two long strides towards the right-hand side of the ring, pulling a small, sharp throwing knife from inside a pocket. He held the knife by the blade and pulled it up and behind his head, leaning back as he drew it. As he reached the edge of the ring, he swung his arm forward and threw the knife in the direction of the crowd, leaning forward over the ropes from the force of the throw.

The knife spun through the air, aimed and weighted perfectly to hit Tommy.

Jeremy Weaver had reacted instinctively to Fox's actions and had stood up and leant over to his right to put himself in front of Tommy, with his back facing the ring.

The knife made several complete revolutions in the air before embedding itself deep into Jeremy's back. The entire blade had penetrated, leaving only the small, black looped handle sticking out. Jeremy let out an angry, gargled roar of pain as he leant back to attempt to straighten up. The blade had pierced the bottom of his left lung.

A panic began in the immediate vicinity of Jez Weaver and quickly spread right around the hall.

In a state of shock and not giving even a milliseconds thought to anyone but himself, Tommy threw Jez off him, leaving him slumped over the seat on the left. He began clambering manically to get out of the row of seats, trying as fast as he could to push past his friends and anyone else in the way. A Mexican wave of distressed voices began echoing around the room in an anxiety-inducing bowl of sound.

In the ring, a full-blown melee was underway as everyone within distance had scrambled to try to detain the armed intruder. At the same time, news had just started to circulate over the event staff's radio that Alex Brace had been found 'badly injured' in his changing room. It was utter pandemonium.

Having managed to escape to the car park on the east side of the building, Tommy began frantically looking around for his son Daniel. He was panting heavily with his white Italian shirt ripped open and his designer glasses bent to the side.

Amongst the scattered herd of people running out of the fire exit on this side of the building, Tommy managed to pick out his son's startled face. Without saying anything, the two began running towards their black Range Rover at the rear-left of the car park.

Tommy, who was a few steps ahead of his son, jumped into the passenger side of the car and slammed the door shut. As Daniel approached the near side of the car and opened the driver's door, he heard a window smash behind him. He instinctively turned round just in time to see Fox flying through the air towards him.

Having leapt twenty-four feet from scaffolding at the side of the building, the full weight of Fox's body crashed into the side of the car door in a double-footed kicking motion. The door window shattered from the impact.

With Daniel's body sandwiched between the door and the rest of the car, he sustained massive injuries with multiple bones being fractured all over his body in an instant.

Fox bounced off and rolled back into a crouched position, facing the car. Daniel slumped to the floor, unconscious.

Unsure of what he had just seen and now in a complete state of panic and fear, Tommy began frantically searching for the door lever with his left hand, his wide eyes fixed on his son's limp body crumpled on the ground.

As Tommy finally flung open the passenger door of the Range Rover, Fox leapt into the air and slid across the bonnet of the car to arrive right in front of him. Tommy turned to try to run away, but Fox violently grabbed hold of his right arm and pulled him backward, slamming his body into the front left arch of the Range Rover.

Tommy stumbled round to the front of the car, promptly followed by his attacker, who then grabbed hold of his chin with his right hand and began to squeeze.

Tommy cried out in pain, something very few people had heard and lived to tell the tale.

Showing off his extraordinary strength, Fox lifted Tommy into the air by the chin with one hand before slamming him down onto the bonnet of the Range Rover. Fox vaulted up on to the bonnet and crouched down over his victim.

As Tommy began to roll slowly from left to right in even more pain, Fox grabbed hold of his left arm and held it down firmly against the car bonnet. With his free hand, Fox whipped another throwing knife from his pocket and lifted it high into the air before thrusting it down hard into the middle of Tommy's wrist.

A deafening shriek reverberated through the car park and all the way through the now nearly empty hall building.

The force of the strike was such that the blade completely passed through the wrist and embedded itself into the metal of the vehicle. Tommy's arm was now 'nailed' to the car in the most painful way imaginable. The blood was streaming from the open wound as he curled his body around it in agony.

Fox reached forward and took a firm grip of Tommy's right hand, slamming it down hard onto the other side of the bonnet. Once again, he held it down with his left hand, raised another knife into the air with his right and slammed it violently into Tommy's right wrist.

Tommy now laid spread across the bonnet of the Range Rover with his arms out to either side, nailed down crucifixion-style. He was shuddering as his body began to go into shock from the trauma of the sudden, massive injuries. His eyes rolled around in his head as his loud screams of agony started to turn into gargled, distressed mumblings. For now, though, he was still conscious. The blood poured from both arms, quickly forming two small streams that ran down the bonnet, dripping off the edge and on to the headlamps.

Fox stood looking at Tommy for a couple of seconds, breathing heavily as he took in the satisfaction of watching the life slip away from the man's body. He'd only seen Boulton a few times since the accident ten years ago and in all honestly hadn't planned on exacting any kind of revenge or retribution. But that was the old Fox. This 'new version' had thought of little other than revenge since the moment he opened his eyes on that train station platform.

Fox knelt down over Tommy's quivering body. This man had built up such a fearsome reputation over the years that no one would dare even look at him the wrong way. And yet here he was, in the most vulnerable and weak position imaginable.

"P-p-p-p... please... please don't..."

Tommy faded in and out of a dazed state as he attempted to beg for his life. It was far too late for that now.

Fox looked into Boulton's eyes, reached up and pulled down the bike mask covering the bottom half of his face.

Tommy's eyes widened in disbelief. The fearful look on his face intensified even more.

"*You*... it can't be... you're..."

Before he could finish his sentence, Fox reached forward and violently grabbed hold of him by his cheeks once more, squeezing even harder this time.

For the first time since his transformation, Fox spoke in a low, distorted and almost robotic gravelled tone.

"You and your comrades took everything away. You took everything from the person who once lived inside my skin... and left behind a *monster*!"

He shouted the last word so loud that it left Tommy's ears ringing.

"Hope... purpose... all of it gone. The only purpose that remains is revenge... after that... only the release of death that you too will enjoy very soon."

Tears streamed from Tommy's face as he began gasping for a breath. Fox gripped even firmer and moved his face in closer.

"... Two more."

The wailing sound of police sirens had been growing closer and closer once again. A line of officers suddenly came thundering out of the side entrance of Bristol Hall.

At the same moment, two Vauxhall Astra police cars came screeching into the car park, driving straight towards the left-rear corner to stop just in front of the blood-covered Range Rover. The headlights of the first car lit up the horrifying scene awaiting the officers. Two victims, a hell of a lot of blood, but no sign of a suspect.

Paramedics arrived moments later and battled to save Tommy's life, but it was too late. He had lost far too much blood and had gone into cardiac arrest before they had even got to him. They had spent a few moments contemplating how they would go about stopping the bleeding given the way he had been stapled to the car so violently with the sharp steel knives. No one had ever seen a knife used so brutally and with such force. How could a human being generate so much power as to thrust a knife all the way through someone's arm and then embed it into a metal bonnet? Was it even possible for someone to do that?

By the time the fire brigade had turned up to remove the knives from the car and free the body, Tommy had been pronounced dead at the scene.

Daniel had suffered multiple, devastating fractures to his ribs, hips and skull. His head and neck had been badly crushed in between the car door and the body of the car itself. He died a few hours later in hospital.

Based on both Daniel's injuries and the damage to the side of the car, the police and medical staff had correctly deduced that he had been sandwiched in the car door. They assumed, however, that the attacker must have driven into the side of the car with another, as yet unaccounted-for vehicle. Once again, the damage was far too extensive to have been caused by a single human being.

Back inside the hall, a police officer and then a paramedic had attended to Jeremy Weaver, who they had found lying motionless, bleeding heavily in the stairwell of the fifth row. It would later be discovered that the knife embedded deep in his back had badly damaged a portion of his spine and punctured one of his lungs. He probably could have been saved if he'd been found sooner but having been left to bleed out on the floor, he too was pronounced dead at the scene.

The fight nights had been public knowledge in and around the area for years. Fox had known he would find the group there together that night and waited to take the opportunity to exact his payback. Tommy was always going to be a target. His well-known position as the leader and mentor of the gang coupled with his prior run-in with Jay behind the wheel of that transit van all those years ago had sealed his fate.

Jeremy Weaver. His financier, mentor and boss, Tommy Boulton. Tommy's far-less-smart-than-him son, Daniel. They formed a list. The criteria were simple and absolute. It was all that Fox cared about and it consumed him every waking second. Anyone involved with what had happened that night on the train station platform had to die. And there were two left.

This was all that remained of Fox's perceived existence. He would not only happily have his life end on completion of this goal, but he *intended* for it to. Anyone else who got in the way, who would try to stop him or defend his targets, would be dispatched without a second thought.

Fox knew from overhearing news reports that of the three thugs on the platform that night, one had survived.

Neither Steve Norris nor Jamie Knight were all that well known to Jay. They were there as Luke Weaver's muscle and had a reputation around the estate for handing out beatings on the gang's behalf. Knight, being the only surviving attacker, had made himself number one on the list of the two remaining targets.

The second, equally loathed target was Mr David 'Archibald' Shilling. The joker of the group. The funny man. Since the very moment Fox had seen him running from the scene up on the road bridge, his destiny was set.

Fox had hoped that he would be able to find and kill all of his targets that night at the boxing ring. Under normal circumstances, everyone in the gang's circle would have been there. Having lived an extra night longer than he expected, Fox now switched his focus entirely to finding and murdering the two remaining men on the list.

He felt a slight increase in clarity and relief in the fact that some of the involved parties had paid with their lives already. The resolve, determination and anxiety behind finding these men was still incredibly overwhelming and he looked forward to the release of being able to end his own life when he was done with ending theirs.

CHAPTER SEVEN

Dave Shilling stared anxiously into the paper coffee cup that was on the dull white table in front of him. The coffee that filled just under half of the cup had long gone cold. He'd been too preoccupied to drink it. The door to the interview room swung open and the two 'suited and booted' police officers walked back in.

"Sorry to keep you waiting, Mr Shilling."

Shilling leant back and looked over to the solicitor on his left as he nervously sniggered. He was playing this cool and trying to come from a position of negotiation, but everyone in the room, including him, knew that he was really shitting himself.

The two officers took their seats on the opposite side of the table.

"So we've talked to some of our superiors and we think we can come to some kind of arrangement... if... you tell us more about what happened at Hackney South that night."

Shilling's facial expression went from pleasantly surprised back to drained and frustrated as he quickly huffed out a response.

"I've told you already... I don't know anyfing else."

The two detectives turned to look at each other. Shilling delivered the same short story that he had repeated at least twice already that day.

"I came off the train; the boys showed up; told me to wait up there on the bridge and when you lot turned up, I did a runner."

There was a pause as the detective on the left scribbled some notes down on the pad of paper in front of him, too small for Shilling to read. The detective on the right leant forward, waiting for Shilling to continue. Shilling obliged.

"I've told you; I don't know anything else about that night... but I *can* give you a lot of other stuff."

The detective on the left instantly stopped scribbling and looked up at Dave, who was now looking over at his solicitor for reassurance. He turned back to face the detectives.

"I… I can give you a shitload on the Weavers and that lot, Deshawn and his gang, even the elders on the estate like Roy Baker and Tomm…"

Dave's voice was shaking as he trembled in fear. He couldn't even say Tommy's name out loud any more.

The detective on the right leant even closer in.

"Tommy Boulton?"

Dave rocked back and forth in his seat, staring down at the floor, nodding reluctantly. The detectives exchanged another intrigued glance.

Shilling continued, "But I've gotta be honest, I don't know anyfing about the fight ni—"

The detective on the right immediately let out a sigh and leant back into his seat with an unimpressed look on his face.

Shilling had picked up on this and began talking in a far more distressed and desperate tone.

"Look I don't know about all these murders and shit. I was there at the train station yeah, but I don't know anyfing more than I've told you already… and I was already in a cell by the time this other stuff happened at the boxing match, so I don't know anyfing about that either. I'm fucking terrified with all this shit going on — I *need* some protection!"

He slammed his fist down on to the table in front of him, with tears now overflowing in his eyes.

The solicitor on his left immediately put his hand on Shilling's arm to try to calm him down. He took a second to take a deep breath before continuing.

"I can tell you everyfing about the gang. How we made money, how we split it, how we laundered it, who we owed and who owed us. I can hand you some big players off the street and give you some absolute diamonds of information."

The detectives began to look interested again. Dave looked each of them one by one in the eyes, appealing to them.

"But if I do this, I want the full works. Witness protection. New identity. I want to be a fucking ghost."

Shilling had ended up in the custody of Essex police after attempting to board a plane to Alicante two days earlier at Stansted Airport. His blurry face had been circulated on news reports of an individual seen running away from the Hackney South murders and several phone calls had been received identifying Dave as the man in question. His flagged passport triggered an alert and now, here he was.

The detectives who were interviewing Dave had made the trip over from London after being notified of his detention. Faced with an ultimatum involving serious prison time, Dave had quickly made the decision to cooperate.

Although he hadn't successfully executed his poorly planned and desperate attempt to flee the country, being in police custody was a lot safer than being out there on the street, in Dave's mind. With Tommy and the boys suspicious about his lack of detail on the night of the murders and unimpressed with the fact that he did not try to help his friends, he was convinced they would soon have beaten up, tortured, or even killed him. The news that someone had since killed Tommy at the Bristol Hall Boxing Club, as well as being an incredible and surreal shock, had actually come with a slight degree of relief.

Dave had lost several nights' sleep over what *on earth* had happened at the train station that evening. Who had done that to the gang? Where were they now? Did they see him on the bridge? What happened to Jayden?

The thoughts sent Dave's mind into an anxious spiral every single night.

The subsequent days' events had only reinforced Shilling's decision to attempt to run, even though it had ended in his capture. Realistically, the authorities were the only people that would have a chance of offering him protection from whatever the hell was going on.

***

As Dave Shilling's questioning continued in the interview room over in Essex, an uninvited guest walked through the glass doors at the front of Box Hill Police Station back in East London.

It was a nervous and physically shattered Timothy Rolfe.

Rolfe cautiously shuffled over to the reception desk on the left, his eyes darting wildly around as he made his way over. Two officers walked directly past him on their way out of the station. One turned around and did a double take as he thought he might have recognised him, but he couldn't place from where.

The eight or so steps from the front door to the reception desk seemed like a hundred. The female receptionist squinted as she looked up at him from behind the wide wooden desk. He stood in front of her with long, dirty black hair covering half of his face and a thick, black fuzz of a beard. The green hoodie that he was wearing had obviously not been washed for days. The receptionist's initial thought was that this was one of the homeless men that occasionally strayed into the station to make some bizarre request.

Tim took one more nervous look around the lobby, overwhelmed with paranoia that someone might try to kill him, like they did his friend.

"My name is Timothy Rolfe... I've come to hand myself in."

For a leader of an international 'terrorist organisation', this had been a very humble and drama-free way to be taken in by the authorities. After days and days of thinking about his options, though, Rolfe had come to the conclusion that this was the only path he could realistically take. Given the various attempts to frame his hacking cult and the recent killing of his best friend, he knew there were forces out there to get him that he just wasn't strong enough to face on his own, especially if it meant they might come after the people he loved.

The constant running and worrying, the grief, the anger, it had all become far too much for Rolfe to bear. This course of action was the alternative to the first option that he had considered: that of taking his own life. The thought of never seeing his estranged daughter again had prevented him from being able to go through with that, but he knew full well that handing himself over could result in the same eventuality.

Tim had deliberately chosen to hand himself in to a busy police station first thing in the morning, without any warning. He thought that would give him the best chance of surviving the process. After all, it would be difficult to convince so many officers and station employees that they had seen a non-existent weapon or threatening gesture. It would also be hard to 'lose' the footage from so many CCTV cameras in and around the building. It would be hard... but not impossible.

News of Rolfe's arrest travelled fast within the ranks of the metropolitan police. Given the gravity of the accusations against Tim, representatives of the government had also been informed. The media had, for now, been left out of the loop. Tim Rolfe was to sit in the cells at the rear of Box Hill until further notice.

One of the many officers that had arrived in for work that morning to the news of their high-profile guest was DCI John Fields. He had been stunned and sickened by this information but had played it off with a joke and a smile when he had been informed during his morning coffee run. This may have well and truly screwed up their plans. Michael Harding and Tim Rolfe were both supposed to end up dead and this was a massive hurdle in the way of achieving that goal. Given that Tim was now in custody at his station, Fields knew that his co-conspirators would expect *him* to 'take care' of the situation. His 'shooter', Max Carter, was not going to be of any use in this instance.

Fields spent almost every second of the morning whirring through the options in his mind. That went on until just after eleven a.m. when he was due to host a team briefing down on the ground floor of the station. This, of course, had completely slipped his mind given this morning's distraction. A concerned officer had interrupted his daydreaming by knocking on his office door to remind him, ten minutes after the meeting had started.

Fields stood in front of a large, grey evidence board that was mounted on the rear wall of the station briefing room. It was covered with printed maps, yellow sticky notes and police surveillance photographs. There were mugshots of Tommy Boulton and his associates pinned up next to pictures of the inside of Bristol Hall and other photographs from the various crime scenes.

The stressed DCI took a few minutes to one side to collect his thoughts and put on a brave face. He told himself that they would sort the Tim Rolfe situation out, just like any other problem they had overcome in the past. For now, he would put it to one side and focus on the work in front of him.

"As you all know we're here to review the known facts surrounding the triple murder at Bristol Hall on Friday night," he began. "I know none of us are going to lose any sleep over any of the victims. But we still have a job to do, and we still need to find the horrible bastards who did this… even if some of us would like shake their hands when we do find them."

A few muffled laughs went around the room in an agreeing tone.

Fields took on a more serious demeanour as he continued, reaching out to point to one of the more gruesome crime scene photos. That of Tommy Boulton's brutally injured body, spread out over the bonnet of the Range Rover.

"The level of violence that was on display that night is truly shocking and very concerning from a public safety point of view. We do not want to allow individuals who are willing to commit these kinds of hideous acts to roam around free on our streets."

A more sombre mood set in amongst the officers almost immediately.

"There's also a level of organisation to consider here. We are assuming several attackers, all of whom have managed to carry out these acts and flee the scene before we arrived. The only individual we can build any sort of profile on is our one masked suspect. We know this individual went as far as actually getting in the boxing ring that night."

Fields aimed his laser pointer to a grainy picture of Fox standing in the ring with the black robe on. The hood was still up, covering his head.

"Believe it or not, this photo is the clearest one we have of that suspect. We believe he is at least partially responsible for the severe assault on Alex Brace and the murder of Jeremy Weaver, found dead a couple of hours later in the aisles."

Just as Fields finished his sentence, the door at the back of the briefing room swung open. He paused as a few of the officers in the room turned round to see who it was.

A six foot four, skinny man with a receding blond-and-grey hairline, stood in the doorway. He had a long, pale bony face and a pointy nose. You could immediately tell from the smug resting expression on his face that he was arrogant and held himself in high regard. In contrast to all the uniformed officers in the room, he was wearing a tightly tailor-fitted black suit and freshly polished black shoes.

Just as Fields opened his mouth to ask the man who he was, Mary, a member of the police staff who worked on the reception desk, poked her head around the door frame and nodded at John, raising an awkward 'thumbs up'. All he could take from that was that the man in front of him was supposed to be here and was expected for some reason. Perhaps a detective from another station investigating a related case.

After taking about three steps into the room, staring directly at Fields with a cocky smile on his face, the man in question uttered in a sleazy sounding posh voice, "Please continue. Don't mind me — we can do introductions at the end."

He took the first seat that he came across at the back of the room. Fields, slightly unnerved by the man's presence but in no way wanting to show that, continued with his presentation of the facts surrounding the Bristol Hall murders.

The hour-long briefing covered the evening's events and the known guests at the fight. The information gathered from CCTV and witness statements was minimal as expected. The type of people who attended the fight nights at Bristol Hall would not have appreciated conducting their evening under the watchful eye of security cameras and the venue owners were more than aware of that. They were also not the type to be seen talking to the police.

Given the identities of the victims and how close together the two events had occurred, the idea that there was a connection between the murders at Bristol Hall and the triple murder at the train station a few days earlier had been discussed. The latter was being handled by a team of officers from a police station closer to the site of the incident. Both crimes were assumed to have been committed by multiple rival gang members.

The man seen walking with the murdered young girl that night near Hackney South had not been identified from the grainy surveillance images and none of the missing men in the area had matched his description. Unofficially, though, given the amount of blood found on the scene, most officers considered the as yet unidentified man missing, presumed dead.

As the briefing drew to a close, Fields rustled his papers together whilst the officers filed out of the meeting room.

After about five minutes, only one man was left in the room with Fields. The mysterious 'special guest' who had made a scene walking in to the meeting earlier, unannounced. He uncrossed his legs, got up and began a slow, strolling walk to the back of the room where DCI Fields stood.

"That was a very insightful overview, John. It reassures me to see that our police force is so proactive in getting to the bottom of these things."

Fields looked up from his paper shuffling with an unimpressed expression on his face.

"It's DCI Fields."

The mystery guest looked down at the floor with a smirk on his face. He raised his head to make eye contact with Fields once more.

"My apologies… DCI Fields, of course."

Fields now looked frustrated.

"And you are…?"

There was a pause as the man let the question linger in the air for a moment.

"My name is Creedy. Charles Creedy. I work for a… branch of the government."

As Creedy said this, he pulled a small wallet from the inside pocket of his blazer and produced a badge. Fields had seen one of these a few times in the past while working on cases that had national security implications. He knew it was associated with one of the security agencies, but he couldn't remember which one. He rolled his eyes and sighed.

"Are you here about the hacker then?"

Creedy sniggered and widened his smug grin even further.

"Oh, I've heard you've got a celebrity in the building, must be exciting. No. Our interests lie exclusively in what you have just been discussing."

Creedy gestured at the wall of information on display behind Fields. Fields turned around to look at it in surprise, as if part of him expected something else to be there.

He turned back to face Creedy.

"Oh right… OK."

Fields looked down at his desk and shuffled a couple of items around.

"Well, what exactly do you and your… people want to know about the case?"

Creedy looked down at his watch and replied, "The nature of both sets of murders in the area has piqued the interest of my organisation. The exact reasons for this are, unfortunately classified. For now, I would like to continue to join these meetings and observe the great work that you and your team are doing."

DCI Fields continued to pack the items away on his desk, looking down the whole time Creedy was talking to him. Creedy leant forward as he added, "With your permission of course?"

Fields looked up at Creedy and forced a visibly fake smile.

"Of course."

With that, Creedy turned and walked out of the briefing room, leaving Fields to pack away the rest of the aides from the morning session. As soon as he left the room, Fields stopped packing, took a long, deep breath and let out an exhausted sigh. What a mess. His focus now immediately reverted to the hacker in custody in his station — the briefing might as well have not just happened from his perspective; he barely remembered anything he had just said.

That day in Box Hill Station dragged like no other for Fields. He attended all of the usual meetings and heard the updates on the higher-profile open cases but was noticeably distant and less interested than usual. Where he would normally probe and encourage the back-and-forth conversation between officers, today he was shutting them down, minimising his involvement in everything that he could until the end of his shift. When that finally came around at just after seven p.m., he shut the front door of his brand new dark green Vauxhall Astra, started the engine and drove out of the police station car park.

After about five hundred metres of driving, Fields reached into his inside blazer pocket, pulled out his phone and clipped it on the wireless holder stuck in the car's air vents. He dialled a number into the keypad and put the call on loudspeaker.

The phone rang about twenty-two times but eventually, the automated conferencing system on the other end answered.

Fields hesitated for a few seconds before starting to talk in an obviously nervous and stressed tone of voice.

"All right. We need to talk about what's happened this morning. What are our options?"

A few seconds' delay followed as Fields could hear his voice echoing back at him from the other end of the phone line. Eventually, a response came in an obviously 'put on' male voice. As if lowering his voice slightly was going to protect him if this conversation was being recorded.

"*Our* options? Our biggest problem has just handed himself in to *your* station. Finish the fucking job."

Having pre-empted and dreaded this response all day, Fields began nervously laughing.

"Finish the job! How the fuck am I supposed to do that? I worked damn hard to get that shooter but what use is he in this situation?"

John's nervous and frustrated panting filled the three-second void before the response came.

"John, you need to watch your tone when you're talking to us. It was your idea to handle it like this in the first place."

Fields paused to take a couple of deep breaths and calm down as the man on the other end continued.

"These 'loose ends' need to be severed. We can't allow him to be interviewed; God only knows what he might say. He needs to be dealt with, immediately."

Fields knew all of this already and understood the urgency of the situation better than anyone. Everyone on the call had a lot to hide, but John took the biscuit with his long history of corruption and 'swept under the rug' affairs.

"OK… So has anyone got any ideas? As I've said, my main asset here isn't really any good to me," Fields said.

After another pause, a softer, higher pitched and more middle-class sounding voice came on the call.

"We've dealt with something similar in the past if you remember John. At some point tomorrow a 'doctor' will come into your station to visit Mr Rolfe. This doctor will 'assess Rolfe's mental health' and his suitability to be kept at Box Hill to be interviewed there. All you are required to do is ensure that this person is allowed to enter the station and then Rolfe's cell without any issues."

The first voice came back on briefly.

"...And make sure no interviews take place before then... preferably."

Fields opened his mouth to respond but no sound came out. He was stunned but quite frankly relieved with the proposal that was being laid out in front of him. It would be suspicious and he'd have to pull a few strings to make it happen, but it was a lot better than some of the other scenarios that he had been imagining himself in over the course of the day.

The voice came rattling through his phone's loudspeaker once more.

"Are we aligned?"

Fields nodded.

"We're aligned."

This group's interest had first been piqued when the 'blackNet' had publicly leaked hundreds of documents relating to questionable police and military activity during the Troubles in Ireland. Fields and other members of the Mason-like group of corrupt officials were on a list of names in one such document.

The document named several individuals who were alleged to have been involved in the illegal distribution of ceased weapons, including automatic firearms and explosives. This was supposedly compiled by an undercover informant working for a security agency at the time; his assignment being terminated when the Good Friday agreement was signed in 1998.

The leaked documents were eventually removed when the controversial website that hosted them had been forced to shut down by a court order. Not long after being exposed, they had made it on to the desks of several senior police detectives and prompted some serious questions from the anti-corruption divisions of various agencies. Ultimately, though, with the lack of detail or verification of the documents' authenticity, no further actions were taken.

This leak, like many after it, was enough to shake Fields and his comrades to the core. Those weapons charges would be extremely serious if ever brought to court and they were only the tip of the iceberg.

CHAPTER EIGHT

An abandoned makeshift shanty house under a Victorian railway arch in East London. It was cold, damp and extremely unsafe but for an illegal dwelling, this was as advanced as you would see in the city. It boasted insulated aluminium walls, internal dividers to create rooms and electricity wired in from the railway infrastructure above. Originally built and lived in by a pair of hard-working Eastern European railway labourers, the dwelling was now home to a tired, dishevelled and ever more rage-driven Fox.

The thirty-two-inch, thick LCD television that had been left behind by the previous inhabitants had been repurposed as a monitor in the wire-heavy computer set-up in the rear of the container home. It was now hooked up to an old stolen laptop which was wired in to the ethernet cables running along the underneath of the bridge. Fox had spent several sleepless nights here, trying to discover the location of the two men that he so desperately needed to kill.

Dave Shilling had become a ghost. His social media activity had ceased and both of his mobile numbers, which Fox had retrieved from a phone inside the pocket of a dying Tommy Boulton, were now disconnected from the network. It could easily be gleaned from some of Shilling's less intelligent family members and their Facebook posts that Dave must have been planning an escape to somewhere. His cousin Gemma, to name one, had written: 'Gud luck bruv we will have your back 100% whateva you do, whereva you go. We don't care what they fink about ya we're your fam and we love ya XXX'.

Apart from these hints, though, Fox had very little to go on. He needed access to less publicly available information like travel records and potentially even police databases if he were to stand a chance of finding him.

Locating Jamie Knight was of equal importance. It had been reported through several news outlets that there was a severely injured but stable 'fourth victim' from that night at Hackney South Train Station. Someone in the police had, very wisely, acted quickly and prevented the press from reporting anything around Knight's identity or his current location out of fear of reprisals. The level of violence shown in such a public place and the fact that no one had even been brought in as a suspect was a real and justified concern.

From his research, Fox had deduced that it was likely Knight was still being treated in hospital for his injuries, explaining his absence from the fight at Bristol Hall. Assuming this was the case, there were three potential hospitals that Knight could have realistically been taken to on the night based on their proximity to the crime scene. Attempting to contact them would be fruitless, since data protection laws coupled with the police's specific instructions to withhold this information would mean that no one would be at liberty to confirm he was in their care.

It was also quite possible that Knight might have been transferred to another hospital that specialised in dealing with certain aspects of his injuries.

Trying to find and interrogate Knight's family members might have been an option, but this was a far too lengthy and organised process for a man in the monstrous mindset that Fox was in. His rage and lack of patience would likely just result in him killing them before he could persuade them to lead him to his target, if they even knew where Knight was in the first place.

The only real option Fox could see through his haze of anger was storming each of the three large hospitals one by one to find Knight. He might end up dead before he could even get to him, but this two-man hunt was Fox's only remaining purpose and the way he saw it, if he died trying, so be it.

***

Thursday 2nd April, 12:01 p.m. Six days after the murders at Bristol Hall.

After a night of little to no sleep in the Box Hill station cell, Tim Rolfe sat on the edge of his cold, hard, unforgiving cell bed, once again clutching the crinkled and worn photograph of his daughter. He had promised no trouble and full co-operation when handing himself in at

Box Hill, on the condition that he would be allowed to keep this on his person in the cell.

During his stay, Rolfe had only been informally 'talked to' by a couple of senior-ranking officers, confirming his identity and his wish to co-operate with them wherever necessary. He did find it strange that no one had interviewed him yet but perhaps, given the magnitude of the allegations against him, it might take a while to gather all of the relevant information and form the right questions. A deep feeling of dread sat in the pit of his stomach ahead of these questions. He knew there would be some things he could admit guilt to and explain, but when the more serious crimes that he and Harding were accused of were brought up, it would be excruciating trying to persuade people that they were framed. He knew no one would believe him and the long, drawn-out process would more than likely lead to him spending the rest of his life in jail. If he had known what DCI Fields and his friends had in store for him though, it was an eventuality that he would have likely preferred.

At the front of the building, a tall, smartly dressed man in a beige overcoat and thick, black designer glasses came confidently bounding through the glass police station doors. He had smooth, slicked back black hair and a Clark Kent-like chiselled jaw. In his right hand he was firmly clutching a brown leather briefcase.

He turned to the girl working on the reception desk, the same young lady who had been surprised to look up and see Tim Rolfe the previous day. Once again, she looked up to greet today's guest.

"How can I help you sir?"

The man put on his best warm and polite smile and giddily gave his response.

"I'm sorry I'm actually a little late. I'm Doctor Marshall, here to carry out an assessment on someone you have in custody."

The lady at the desk looked confused for a moment before searching through the appointment files on the PC in front of her.

"Erm... I can't find any record of that, just give me a sec..."

The 'doctor', still holding up his ultra-polite middle-class veneer, cheerfully chuckled a reply.

"Oh, that's no problem at all, I'm not the only one who has to deal with less than adequate computer systems it would appear."

The girl looked up and smiled back before continuing to click and type away at the computer. After a few more searches and multiple shuffles through the tray of notes to her left, she looked up at the doctor once more, shaking her head.

"I'll just be one moment, sorry about this."

Marshall gave a single polite nod and stiffened his lips in acknowledgement. As the receptionist got up and walked away, a single, thick bead of sweat trickled down the side of his face.

***

Just over one mile away from Whitechapel Hospital, Fox was walking with his hood up and head down in the pouring rain. Once again, a bike mask with black mesh 'breathing holes' covered his face. His fists were tightly clenched inside the pockets of his soaked hooded sweater. A black biker's backpack was secured tightly to his shoulders by both straps. Of the several nefarious items inside, a loaded black 9mm Glock 17 pistol sat nestled near the top.

His intense, paced walk slowed gradually as he approached a pub that he used to often visit with Julia — The Sliding Doors on Haverley Street. It was a good old-fashioned no-frills pub and the couple had loved spending time there together. Now it was simply a window into a past life for him.

Fox stopped and stared through the thick, morphed glass at the warm glowing light coming from inside. A young couple, a group of colleagues having lunch, even the man sitting on his own at the bar reading the paper oozed a serenity that was now impossible for Fox to attain. He didn't even remember what normal felt like any more. What being human felt like any more.

Fox stood in a daze for a few seconds as the rain continued to bound off him, running down his face and onto the ground. Out of the corner of his eye, one of the large televisions at the rear of the pub caught his attention. The twelve o'clock news had just started, with the subtitles flashing up in bold white text against a red background at the bottom of the screen.

"The alleged leader of one of the world's most notorious criminal groups, 'blackNet', remains in police custody after stunning local officers by handing himself in at a London police station yesterday.

Thirty-year-old Timothy Rolfe is wanted in several countries including the UK and the United States on multiple charges relating to fraud, the breaching of high security computer systems and causing millions of pounds worth of damage to government property. He and his associate, the late Michael Harding, are also the prime suspects in the 2015 HP Stanthorpe mail bombing that killed six people and injured at least a dozen more.

Harding was shot dead by police marksman only weeks ago after being confronted outside a London coffee shop. Timothy Rolfe is understood to have voluntarily turned himself in to Box Hill Police Station where for now, he will remain."

Fox stood transfixed, staring wildly at the screen through the window as the rain continued to stream down it.

Suddenly it hit him like a bolt of lightning. This man could help him find the people he wanted so badly. He had sat for days and days at his computer in his pathetic little temporary home, desperately trying to find the information he wanted. He had almost wanted to die from the frustration of not knowing.

A man with those skills could get him access to everything he needed. Hacking the police and hospital databases should be a piece of cake for him and, in his current position, what did he have to lose?

If Fox survived the encounter, maybe the hacker could even help him understand who he was, where he came from, how he became like *this*. The thoughts were racing through his mind at a hundred miles an hour.

Just then the concerned young barman who had seen Fox standing there for all this time walked over to the old pub door just to the left of the window and pushed it open.

"You all right mate?"

He shouted over the sound of the pouring rain as the door swung open. When he leant his head out and peered round to the side though, there was no one there.

***

The 'doctor' had been waiting for just over two minutes before the flustered receptionist returned to her post behind the desk.

"Sorry about that sir. Someone will be through in a moment to walk you through to the custody office."

Marshall immediately relaxed, letting out a covert sigh but displaying only an expectant smile. The receptionist had checked in with her superior Karen Pritchard over the phone, who had confirmed that DCI Fields had told her to expect their guest at the front desk. No formal paperwork or informative email had been sent to anyone else, but that alone wasn't enough to rouse anyone's suspicions.

A short, stocky PC appeared on the other side of the electronically locked door to the main hallways of the station, just to the right of the reception desk. He nodded to the receptionist through the glass window as he pressed the button to release the lock and swing the door open.

"Doctor Marshall?"

Marshall smiled back and nodded.

"This way please, sir."

The officer held the door open in front of him, nodding back out into the hallway.

Marshall looked once more at the receptionist before following the officer into the station corridors.

An immediate right turn, a few steps, a left turn through a set of double doors into bland, blue-painted hospital-like hallways. A walk down the long, straight corridor that passed the sergeant's office on the left-hand side followed by a left and then a right to face another short corridor, at the end of which were the thick, locked double doors of custody.

The escorting officer had been talking to Marshall during their brief tour of the ground floor of the station, but his voice had been reduced to faint mumbling in the background. Marshall was taking in as much of the surroundings as he could, remembering the route. He paid attention to the distinctive features along the way, even counting the number of officers he passed.

The officer buzzed Marshall through to the custody reception and walked him through to the cells. He was then shown to the last of a row of four 'male cell' steel doors that lined the right-hand side of the custody suite. The officer leant forward and slid open the letter-box-sized hole at the top of the cell to peer inside. A dazed Tim Rolfe looked up from his 'head in hands' position at the side of his cell bed. His eyes were red and coated with a thick, deep glaze. Needless to say, Rolfe hadn't slept for more than ten minutes since his arrival at the station.

"You've got a guest."

The officer leant back from the cell door to address Marshall.

"You ready sir?"

Marshall looked at the steel cell door and then back at the officer.

"Yes."

Based on his size, demeanour and behaviour during his brief time in custody, none of the officers would have deemed it necessary to have Rolfe in cuffs for a visit to his cell like this. Marshall had secretly hoped he might have been but didn't want to create any sort of scene by making such a request. After a loud metallic crank and creak, the cell door swung open and the officer walked in.

"Doctor's here to see you, Rolfe."

Tim began to stand up as the officer raised his hand out in front of him, gesturing him to stop.

"Stay seated, if you don't mind."

The officer looked back towards Marshall and gestured for him to follow him into the cell. Marshall obliged and cautiously walked forward. The officer nodded.

"You all set?"

Marshall and Rolfe stayed locked in eye contact for a few, intense seconds before Marshall turned back to the officer with a polite smile.

"Yes, fine thank you; I'm ready to begin."

With that, the officer acknowledged his comment and walked around Marshall to let himself out of the cell, slowly closing the cell door behind him.

There was an awkward silence for a few seconds as the two men exchanged another intense stare inside the cell. Marshall managed to quickly snap back into his more positive demeanour. He forced out a smile and gestured towards the closer end of the cell bed.

"May I?"

Rolfe froze for a second in confusion as his tired, frantic mind took time to process the request. He looked over to the far end of the bed and shuffled along, allowing ample space for the 'doctor' to sit next to him. Marshall obliged and took a seat on the near corner of the bed. As he did, he swung his briefcase up to rest it on his knee, popping open the gold safety catches on either side of the top of the case. He turned to the right to face Tim.

"So I'm here primarily to assess your mental health and well-being. My job is to decide whether or not you are in a fit state, mentally and physically, to be interviewed by the officers here."

Marshall pulled a purse-sized black leather pouch from inside the briefcase, resting it on his lap before closing the case and placing it on the floor in front of him. Rolfe didn't like the look of this doctor. Something was off with his mannerisms. He seemed a bit nervous, a bit stiff. His overly gleeful expressions were forced, and Rolfe could tell.

Marshall continued, "I'll be asking you a series of questions which I'd like you to answer in your own time. There's no rush. I really want you to think about how you feel and answer as honestly as you can."

Rolfe said nothing. Aside from the fact that he was completely exhausted, he didn't really trust this man at all. Staying silent seemed the best thing to do.

"We'll start with a little relaxation technique. If you don't mind, I'd like to ask you to place your hands on your knees and sit up straight."

Rolfe paused for a moment before reluctantly obliging.

"Great. Now take a deep breath in and hold it for three seconds, slowly letting the air out of your lungs through your mouth."

Once again, Rolfe obliged, staring straight ahead with a blank, weary expression on his face as he performed the actions.

"OK good. Now I'd like you to close your eyes and repeat the breathing exercise a few more times until you can start to feel your body relax."

Rolfe closed his eyelids about eighty percent shut, still allowing the smallest slit of vision to creep through.

He entertained Marshall's wishes by continuing to perform the long, slow breathing exercises in his seated position on the bed. He could see through his blurred partial vision that Marshall was pulling something out of the leather pouch on his lap and passing it between his hands. The doctor was narrating each breath as Rolfe took it.

"That's it... in... and out... in... and out"

As Rolfe drew the fifth breath in, curious to see what the doctor was holding, he partially opened his left eye and slanted his head to the left. This was just in time to see Marshall pull back his right arm and aggressively drive a syringe towards him.

Rolfe reacted just in time to raise both of his hands up to the side and grab hold of Marshall's arm, stopping the needle centimetres from his chest. Marshall let out an angry grunt.

"What the fuck are you doing?" Rolfe yelped.

Tim Rolfe heard his own croaky, panicked voice for the first time since he had woken up that morning. He was now using all of the energy he could muster to try to fight off Marshall.

"Fucking let go and die, you little nerd bastard!"

The respectful middle-class doctor veneer had been lifted as Marshall swung his left arm round to punch Rolfe in the stomach.

As Rolfe winced in pain, still managing to hold on to Marshall's arm, he immediately realized that this man was here for one reason: to assassinate him in his cell.

CHAPTER NINE

The doors to the front of Box Hill Police Station swung open once more.

The receptionist looked up from her post behind the large, curved wooden desk. Standing in front of her was a man about six foot two, dressed in an all-black tracksuit with a black bike mask over his face.

After walking three steps into the station, he turned to face her, instantly making her feel uncomfortable as she looked into his deep, blood-red eyes. The sight was intimidating; he was easily the most unsettling figure she had ever seen walk through those doors.

She sat completely frozen in fear as Fox walked past the desk to face the door leading through to the station hallway. At that moment, two officers came bounding out of the door, laughing jovially at a joke one of them had just made.

The two officers stopped as they came face to face with Fox right in front of the reception desk. The officer on the left instinctively began to raise his hand up to the radio on his chest. His colleague, standing closer to Fox, began leaning back and reaching down to the right in an attempt to get a grip on his police-issue baton.

Fox lunged forward and threw the officer hard against the wall adjacent to the door that was still in the middle of closing.

The second officer had managed to press the button on his radio and had begun to let out the first sounds of a word before Fox reached out and grabbed hold of his throat. The officer gargled something quietly, looking dead ahead with a wide-eyed fearful expression on his face. Fox threw his head forward and headbutted the officer, immediately rendering him unconscious as he crumpled to the floor.

The receptionist jumped back from her post at the desk, putting her hands up to her face in shock and letting out a reverberating shriek.

Fox caught the long, silver handle of the closing door with less than a centimetre of an opening left.

As he stepped out into the pale-blue hallways of the station, the high-pitched bell sound of the station alarm began ringing loudly from every direction. After taking the immediate right then left, he turned to face a gauntlet of officers lining the long, narrow corridor in front of him, stumbling out from the various doors on either side.

Fox looked down at the floor for a second. This would be the biggest test of his strength so far. How far did these new abilities stretch? Could he make it to the other side of this? And then what exactly? Somehow, he knew without a shadow of a doubt that he would be standing on the far side of those men in a matter of minutes.

Marshall and Rolfe continued to struggle in the cell. By this time, they were rolling around on the floor as Tim barely managed to hold off the assault against him. Marshall was by far the stronger, fitter and better equipped man but Rolfe had the motivating factor that he was fighting for his life. The banging and clattering coupled with the occasional grunt and yelp coming from the cell had not been heard by any of the officers on duty in the custody area. The loud sound of the alarm ringing through the station and the panicked radio communications were understandably enough of a distraction.

Slightly battered and bruised, Fox stood halfway down the corridor that ended with the large steel double doors into custody. He was panting heavily from the exhaustion of fighting the twelve or so policemen that were now spread out along the corridors behind him. Some were rolling left to right, moaning in pain as they nursed a broken arm or leg; others were completely unconscious.

There were now only two officers between Fox and the custody doors. They stood about five metres in front of him, batons and CS spray in either hand in a readied stance. Both men were absolutely terrified but were trying their best to look as aggressive as possible. They bellowed panicked warnings down the hallway.

"Get back... get back!"

"Do not come any closer... get on the fucking ground now!"

The two of them were practically screaming over each other, making it difficult to even understand what they were saying.

Fox could hear the alarmed chatter of another group of officers approaching cautiously from the hallways behind him. He knew his time was limited.

He took a deep breath, put his head down and began walking towards the two officers in front of him. As soon as he moved, they instinctively jolted back, letting out the beginnings of another series of warnings in an even more panicked tone. They had an incredibly short time to react. Feeling backed into a corner, the closer officer on the right-hand side raised his CS spray and fired the long stream of high-irritant liquid at Fox's head. It wasn't the first dosage he'd had today and although he could feel it, the spray had little effect.

Leaning his head over to one side to avoid the incoming spray, Fox continued walking ahead, unimpeded. The officer took another step back. Just then his colleague took an impromptu overhead swing with his baton as he leapt forward from Fox's left.

Seeing it coming with time to spare, Fox waited until the last moment before suddenly moving to the left to avoid the incoming baton swing. Having lunged forward, the officer's momentum carried him a few more inches, so that he and Fox were now right next to each other. The officer was still mid-swing. Fox snapped a hard left hook into the officer's ribcage and then a right into his stomach. He raised his right arm above the back of the officer's head and chopped down on the back of it. The baton fell to the floor with a loud metallic clunk as the officer was immediately rendered unconscious, slumping to the floor with absolutely no resistance.

Fox immediately walked toward the last remaining officer, now standing right next to the electronic lock of the double door into custody. He could hear the voices of the other officers getting louder in the corridors behind him. He lunged forward and grabbed the officer by the throat, slamming him up against the wall. The young, five foot ten blond officer looked into Fox's eyes with a wild expression of fear — a look he was getting used to by now. The officer dropped both of his weapons as he gargled and struggled to breathe through gritted teeth and saliva. Fox let go of the officer's throat, grabbed hold of the black police lanyard that was round his neck and pulled it down hard, snapping it. He then turned his right elbow hard into the officer's chin, knocking him clean out.

Fox raised the white key card on the end of the snapped lanyard and held it up to the small, black rectangular panel on the right-hand side of the double doors. The LED light on the top of the panel went from red to green as it let out a 'beep' sound. The clank of the mechanical lock releasing on the door then followed.

As he pushed open the right-hand side door into custody, Fox glanced back to see a group of officers turn into the hallway in a formation behind him. He slid through to the other side of the open door and calmly allowed it to shut behind him. It took about two seconds, by which time the officers were almost approaching from the other side.

At the exact moment the door shut and the metal lock clicked back into place, Fox slammed his fist into the control panel on his side of the door. The panel shattered and sparked, letting off a puff of smoke. He reached in and pulled the wiring from the exposed release mechanism, setting off further sparks and a series of electronic 'popping' sounds.

A series of loud, booming thuds followed as the group of officers came crashing into the thick double doors from the other side. They had just missed their opening.

Fox turned to face the custody desk. He leant over to the right, peering at the white steel-barred gate that led to the male cells. The area appeared to be empty, but he could hear and smell the quivering officer cowering behind the desk.

PC Sandra Kynoch had only started working on the custody desk recently. The man who would normally be taking charge of this desk was the fatter of the two officers that Fox had just disabled on the other side of the double doors. Sandra sat curled up in a ball, shaking with fear behind the perceived safety of the thick custody desk. A few moments of silence passed before Fox vaulted the desk and stood in front of her.

She shrieked in fear as she looked up into his eyes. He froze. With her strawberry hair tied up in a bun and her azure-blue eyes, she instantly reminded him of Julia. For a moment, he was taken back as his mind once again wandered to better times from a past life.

Fox slowly kneeled down to eye level with the officer, their faces only about thirty centimetres apart. Slightly calmer, she was still quivering and muttering in fear with teary mascara running down her face in a stream of smudged black. The sound of the officers frantically booming their fists against the double doors rang out in the background. This was coupled with varying versions of "open the fucking door now!"

Fox calmly pulled the bike mask down, revealing his badly scarred face. He nodded towards the door to the cells, adjacent to the desk.

"I'm here to see the hacker."

After taking a moment to process the request, the PC frantically turned around and reached up underneath the corner of the desk to the large metallic ring holding the set of keys to the cells. As she turned back and extended her violently shaking hand out to Fox, she muttered, "Th-the big one... and then the small blue one."

Fox took the keys slowly, maintaining eye contact with the girl. He then gently reached out and touched the side of her face.

Boom!

The sound of the panicked officers weakening the double doors to custody echoed through the room, ruining the moment. Fox knew it would only take a couple more swings and they'd be through to this side. He pulled the mask back up over his face and leapt over the desk, heading for the door to the cells.

By this time everyone in the station was aware of the unfolding situation and a mass state of confused alarm had set in. The hallways leading up to the custody entrance were filled with police officers and staff, leaving a gap of a few metres for the small team of riot-gear-clad officers who were desperately trying to break down the thick, electronically locked doors.

Another team of officers had made their way around to the rear of the building. Their aim was to attempt to enter the custody area through the larger blue steel door off the end of the sloping walkway from the station car park.

Multiple calls had gone out over the radio, but the details had remained sketchy. At least one assailant had assaulted several officers in the station and was now barricaded in the custody area. Tens of officers were frantically speeding in their vehicles 'on blue lights' to get to the station as quickly as they could. This included officers from the Met's heavily armed counter-terrorism division. They were taking no chances.

Fox stood in front of the door to the last cell on the right of the custody corridor. As he inserted the cell key and turned it to the left to feel the steel lock release, he was surprised to hear what sounded like a struggle coming from inside. It changed nothing though. He loosened the straps and shuffled the thin, black backpack off his shoulders, swinging it round in front of him as he pulled the zip back to open it. He quickly reached in and pulled out the black Glock pistol, holding it in his right hand and the backpack in his left. As he did that, he raised his right knee into the air and kicked the door, forcing it to swing open.

The cell's occupants immediately ceased fighting to turn round and face the masked man standing in the doorway. They both had a look of complete shock on their faces.

Rolfe was on his knees at the far end of the cell with Marshall standing over him, forcing Rolfe's body backwards on to the bed as he tried desperately to get a needle into his neck. Both men were completely red, covered in sweat and had ripped clothing in several places. There were smears of blood all over the floor of the cell. You could see they were both exhausted, but it was Rolfe who was very nearly at the end of his ability to fight.

Marshall turned to look back at Rolfe, who was still transfixed on the mysterious figure standing in the doorway. Seizing the opportunity, Marshall raised his right arm above his head, clutching the syringe, and began lunging at Rolfe's head.

Without hesitation, Fox raised his right hand up, aimed the pistol at Marshall and fired three shots into his chest in quick succession.

Rolfe leapt backwards onto the bed in shock. It was just in time to avoid the lifeless body of the 'doctor' as he slumped forward onto the floor.

There was a brief, two-second pause as the smoke rose from the barrel of the pistol.

Fox stepped back, still with the gun pointed out in front of him and gestured out into the corridor.

"Out of the cell."

Suddenly, the loud boom of the officers finally breaking down the double doors that led into the custody section of the station echoed through the corridors. The previously muffled voices suddenly became sharper as the angry, aggressive rabble got closer and closer. Although startled by the crashing, chaotic sounds coming from down the hall, Rolfe sat frozen — physically exhausted and shuddering with fear.

"Out... now!"

As Fox bellowed out the second, more urgent command, he leant down and slid his backpack along the cell floor in a swinging motion. It clattered into the cell wall, in between Rolfe and the lifeless body of Marshall.

Terrified of what might happen next, Rolfe pushed himself off the end of the bed and ran the four steps out of the cell. As he reached the doorway, his legs turned to jelly and gave out from underneath him. He dived forward out of the cell with a last burst of energy.

As Rolfe fell forward out into the corridor, Fox aimed the pistol at the backpack settled neatly against the rear wall of the cell and fired two more shots. The second struck the tightly packed demolition-grade explosives inside the backpack, instantly triggering a massive explosion.

The force of the blast visibly shook the entire police station and stopped the approaching group of officers in their tracks. A bright flash and deafening sharp bang forced most of the officers to hunch over, closing their eyes and covering their ears with both hands. A thick cloud of dust and smoke instantly filled the corridor and began to drift out into the main lobby through the locked gate.

Rolfe, who had been violently thrown further out into the cell corridor by the force of the explosion, lay spread out on the floor with almost his entire body covered in a layer of dust. He mumbled and groaned as he came around from briefly losing consciousness. A loud high-pitched ringing was the only thing he could hear and the smell and taste of gunpowder was overpowering. As he turned round from his laid-out position, coughing and spluttering, he could see beams of light shining through the clouds of dust. They were coming from a newly formed two-metre hole in the wall at the back of his cell.

Having had less than a few seconds to recover, Rolfe felt a hand take hold of his arm and aggressively pull him up to his feet. He could see the silhouette of Fox in front of him, dragging him forward through the thick cloud toward the opening.

After a few hobbled steps, the blinding grey light of the outside pierced Rolfe's eyes as they emerged from the gaping hole in the side of the building out into the station car park. It took a couple of seconds for his vision to adjust. This was all too much for a normal human brain to process.

Rolfe felt Fox let go of his arm and instinctively turned to his left to see what was happening, raising his right arm above his head to shield his eyes from the daylight.

Two officers had been in the process of parking their BMW R1200RT police motorbikes when the explosion had ripped through the building. The closest bike was now on its side on the ground, with the uniformed rider lying on his back next to it. Flying debris from the blast had clattered into him, injuring him and knocking him off the bike. His helmet had saved his life. The second officer, slightly further from the explosion, had also dropped his bike but was now on his feet, attempting to steady it on its stand. He had taken his helmet off to get some fresh air and dropped it upside down on the floor next to him.

Just as the officer let go of the bike in its upright position and reached for his radio, he looked up to see the dust-covered, bloodied figure of Fox standing in front of him, pointing a gun in his face. The officer instinctively threw his hands up into the air and took a step back. Fox leant forward, reached down and pulled the officer's steel handcuffs out from the leather holder on the right-hand side of his waist. As the officer looked down to react, Fox turned his arm inwards and thrust his elbow into the officer's jaw, throwing him backwards and immediately knocking him unconscious.

Fox quickly walked back over to Rolfe, who had stood huddled over, watching in a state of shock. Once again Fox grabbed hold of him by the arm and began pulling him towards the bike.

The sound of police officers approaching was now coming from all angles, including a mixture of coughing and shouting from the other side of the smoking hole. The group of officers who were previously trying to gain access through the alternate custody entrance were also seconds away from coming into view from around the corner. From directly in front, one of the multiple patrol cars that had answered the emergency calls from the station came screeching in through the open car park gate, around thirty metres away.

Fox violently kicked the storage box at the back of the police bike, shattering the plastic that held it in place and breaking it off. This left a small dip behind the seat with exposed black metal bars. A second seat. He snapped one half of the handcuffs on to Rolfe's left wrist and nudged him closer to the bike. Rolfe looked nervously over at the stopped police car as the front doors flung wide open. His head quickly spun round as the other group of officers appeared from the left near corner of the station. Fox nodded towards the bike.

"Get on."

The fear-inducing tone of Fox's command immediately galvanised Rolfe into action. He didn't know what he was doing. He didn't really have any time to think or even process what was going on around him. He knew he had nearly been killed in that cell and that now, instinctively, he wanted to get out of there. Besides, Fox was the one holding the gun; there wasn't exactly much of a choice to make.

Rolfe placed both his hands on the bike and vaulted into a seated position in between the exposed metal bars. He took a firm grip of the bars behind him, looked back up at Fox and then at the incoming group of policemen, now only metres away. Fox turned around and pointed the Glock to aim about a metre above them.

He fired two warning shots into the air.

All of the surrounding officers stopped in their tracks and crouched down in shock at the sound of the shots being fired.

Having bought himself a few more seconds, Fox turned round and reached behind Rolfe to snap the other end of the handcuffs to one of the metal bars on the bike, cuffing him to the makeshift seat. He then jumped on to the front of the bike and started the ignition.

This was the first time Fox had even sat on a bike since the accident that had left him badly injured all those years ago. He should have felt nervous, scared, anxious. But he felt none of those things. Fear was something he hadn't felt since that night on the station platform. His senses, reflexes, strength and vision were all far better than they had ever been. The bike's engine rasped into life and Fox pulled back hard on the throttle, kicking the bike into gear.

As the bike accelerated rapidly, Fox weaved in and out of the parked cars to finally be faced with the gauntlet of police cars at the open car park gate.

He forced his head down into the wind and aimed for the narrow gap between one of the cars and the side gate. As they passed the car at almost 40 mph, the right rear-view mirror sticking out from the side of the bike smashed against the brick car park wall and came flying away from the bike's chassis. At the same time the plastic side panelling on the left scraped against the door of the squad car.

The bike wobbled and jolted violently, but it made it through.

CHAPTER TEN

Following the mass confusion and panic at Box Hill, one of the largest pursuits that any of the officers in the area had ever been involved in was now under way.

Several emergency buttons had been pressed on police officers' radios, meaning the whole of the Met had been listening to the confusing and chaotic description of what had been unfolding at the station. Pretty much every car in the area was now attempting to follow the stolen BMW police bike.

Although Fox's riding had been extraordinary and he had been successfully weaving in and out of traffic at unbelievably dangerous speeds, the vast number of police cars that had joined the chase meant that between them, they had managed to keep up with his movements.

Having narrowly avoided a police car that had attempted to swerve in front of him at a large roundabout, Fox had now taken a left turn onto a long slip road that led on to the North Circular Motorway. From there, he took the first exit leading onto the M11, travelling north.

The ride had become extreme for both rider and passenger, with the wide lanes of the motorway allowing Fox to open up the bike's acceleration fully. After a minute or so of more dangerous weaving through traffic, he put his head down into the wind to push the bike even further, racing down the 'hard shoulder' inside lane.

Rolfe leant forward into Fox, his eyes closed and his face scrunched up as he desperately held on to the bars at the back of the bike for dear life.

Travelling at over 140 mph, Fox was beginning to put some real distance between them and the pursuing police cars. Adding a complication, however, was the fact that India-99, the Metropolitan Police helicopter, was now flying at 1,500 feet directly above them in pursuit. Even the chopper was being pushed to keep up with them at these speeds. With the onboard cameras and their extensive access to maps, though, they would be keeping the bike in sight.

The dozens of police cars involved in the chase had been instructed to slow down and not attempt to keep up with the fugitives. The police were convinced that at this speed, given that neither rider was wearing a helmet, a fatal crash was imminent.

After travelling just short of seven miles north along the M11, Fox approached another junction. The police helicopter had been giving the rest of the officers in the area a running commentary of where the bike was over the radio, including an advanced warning as they approached each motorway junction in case they took the exit.

Although Fox waited until the absolute last moment, he slowed the bike slightly, leant his body off to the side and veered off to the left, taking exit twenty-three. Their ten-minute chase had taken them out of built-up East London and into the Essex countryside.

After taking the second exit at the roundabout and making a series of left and right turns, Fox opened up the throttle once more along a small, bendy country road with fields on either side. He glanced back to see the police helicopter still following them from above.

As Fox turned back round to face the road, the sight of an oncoming police car up ahead came into view. He slammed on the bike's brakes as the driver in the police car did the same, deliberately crossing over on to their side of the road.

As the two vehicles came within a few metres of each other, Fox pulled back the throttle and turned the bike to the right, crossing over to the other side of the road before smashing into the small grass mound at the roadside.

The front wheel of the bike jolted up and over the grass verge hard, sending Rolfe crashing into the back of Fox. Less than a second later, the back wheel followed, violently throwing them up off their seats. The bike stayed upright as it ploughed through the thick, green foliage and into the vast farming fields on the other side.

After wresting with the incredibly rough, bumpy ride and the erratic steering conditions, Fox was somehow managing to build speed on the bike as they hurtled diagonally across the fields. The bike was shuddering intensely and massive chunks of mud had wedged themselves in between the panels. The front light was cracked, the tyres were deflating fast and the suspension was badly damaged.

The driver and passenger in the police car that had very nearly collided with the bike had considered following them over the verge and into the field. As they had scrambled to line the car up and stared ahead at where they were about to attempt to drive, though, they decided against it.

India-99 was having even less difficultly following the pair now, as the speed that they could maintain over the field was limited. A normal rider wouldn't have even been able to keep the bike upright. Fox was constantly fighting back against the bike's sideways momentum with incredible upper body strength and co-ordination.

Given the green open space surrounding the chase, the pilot of the helicopter had decided to lower the altitude drastically in an attempt to intimidate the pair and force them to 'decamp' or jump off their vehicle and flee on foot.

The chase crossed a boundary into a third field as the helicopter reached an altitude of just below 200 ft. A wave of flattened grass surrounded the police bike as the downward wind battered the bike and its riders. Both men's hair and clothes were flapping around wildly; they could feel the power of the blades slicing through the air on their bodies. The noise was both deafening and incredibly intimidating. At this distance, Rolfe could even distinguish the sound of the helicopter's screaming engine and the whipping, chopping sound of the blades as they whirred round.

Still with both eyes closed, holding on to the bike for dear life, Rolfe let out a roaring scream, desperately fighting the urge to put his hands up to either side of his head to try to block out some of the noise.

Fox reached round into the back of his trousers with his left hand and once again pulled out the black Glock 17 semi-automatic pistol. He'd fired a total of six shots back at the station. The gun held nine. Three shots left.

Suddenly, as the bike lurched forward in a burst of acceleration, Fox took his other hand off the handlebars and leapt up into the air, twisting his body around to come to a kneeling position on the bike seat, facing Rolfe.

Feeling the sudden, strange movement, Rolfe opened his eyes in shock. Fox extended his arm out, took a second to steady his aim and fired three shots up towards the fuselage of the pursuing helicopter. It should have been near impossible to hit a target at that kind of distance with a pistol, especially in those conditions.

The first two shots whizzed past the body of the helicopter. The occupants were close enough the see the muzzle flash from the gunfire down below. They called out in shock, "We are being shot at by the suspects. I say again, the suspects appear to be armed and shots are being fired in our direction."

The third bullet skimmed the lower right-hand side of the fuselage, causing a small leak in the fuel tank. The metallic 'clink' sound heard inside the cabin was enough to let them know that they had been hit.

Detecting that fuel was being lost faster than usual, one of the onboard sensors screamed out a continuous, high-pitched warning tone as a red light flashed above the pilot's head.

"We are taking fire from the suspects, possible damage to the aircraft!"

The co-pilot turned around to exchange a nervous look with his navigator.

Fox tucked the gun away and spun back around into a seated position, immediately pulling back on the throttle to launch the slowing bike forward once more. At the same moment, the helicopter pitched up and took a drastic right turn as an evasive manoeuvre.

"India-99 to base, we are aborting this pursuit."

In a state of complete disbelief of what he had just seen, Rolfe turned around to watch the helicopter become smaller and smaller in the sky behind them as he continued to violently bounce up and down on the back of the bike.

After reaching the far corner of the field, Fox joined a footpath that tracked alongside some woodland and followed it for just short of three miles. He used the flatter and more stable ground as an opportunity to pick up the pace.

The last mile of the path ran through the woods and began to converge with the railway that had been visible in the distance from the field. With either side lined with dense trees and bushes, the pair were now riding through the path of an older rail line that had been removed years ago.

As they passed a rail maintenance shed on their right, Fox slammed hard on the bike's brakes. Rolfe's body was once again thrown into his rider's back and the bike slid from left to right across the gravelly path before coming to a stop.

Without saying a word, Fox kicked out the bike's stand and lifted his right leg over to dismount from the left-hand side. He and Rolfe exchanged a look of complete exhaustion.

Fox raised his left hand into the air to hold a fist above his head and snapped it down hard on to the top of Rolfe's forehead. Rolfe just had time to see it coming before it knocked him unconscious.

CHAPTER ELEVEN

The hours after one of the most sensational custody breakouts in the history of British policing were never going to be easy for anyone working at Box Hill Station. Dozens of officers had been injured, there was extensive damage to the building and a huge media storm was now brewing. Rumours of guns and explosives being used as part of this daring and unprecedented raid on a police station had made it front page news, nationally. The entire station was now cordoned off as a crime scene with only a select number of senior and investigative officers being allowed inside. News crews surrounded the area - shouting questions at officers as they came and left the station, sending drones up for aerial shots and interviewing locals for any piece of juicy information they could get. The full story had not yet become clear but what *had* been established and repeated in the headlines for the whole morning, was that Timothy Rolfe, a high-profile international 'cyberterrorist' had been apparently 'broken out' of his cell in the middle of a police station in London.

For DCI John Fields especially, this event had caused massive, massive problems. What on earth had happened?

Like many others that day, John had been called in to work urgently in response to the unfolding events. Having not been present at the station when all of this had occurred, working through the aftermath as the situation was pieced together around him was a nerve-wracking affair. After all, it was he who had given the reception staff the order to allow the first 'guest' into the building earlier that day. Was he partly to blame for all of this? What part did the 'doctor' play and more importantly, how quickly could it come back to Fields?

The 'doctor' was later determined to be the badly severed and burned corpse slumped next to the gaping hole in the wall of the cell block. Again, not good. But at least he wasn't being questioned.

Fields had spent the whole afternoon anxiously awaiting a call from his Mason 'friends.' Finally, just after six p.m., it came.

"John. Please don't even talk unless you have an improvement on the news being beamed around the entire fucking country right now."

Nervous but also frustrated, John closed the door to his office softly before taking a deep breath and replying, "An improvement? All I know so far is that fucking guy who was supposed to help get this shit sorted came into the station today and about fifteen minutes later, all hell broke loose!"

A pause.

"Someone else arrived after that though, I understand?"

This was the voice of the same man who had offered the help of the 'doctor' previously. Fields was slightly taken aback by the fact that the man had this information. He had thought that *he* was the only point of contact at Box Hill station.

"Yeah. That's right. He one of yours as well? Maybe he followed your guy in?" Fields asked.

The voice on the other end of the phone was quick to respond.

"No."

Fields replied, "Maybe a friend of that doctor or something? How else would h—"

"No!"

The voice had become more insistent and enraged, cutting Fields off before he could finish his next remark. There was another pause before they resumed.

"You had our target sitting in a cell in your fucking station. It's bad enough we had to send someone to finish a job that should've been your responsibility. Now it's turned into this, and you have the gall to try to point the finger in my direction!"

Fields didn't have anything to say. He bit his lip.

Now slightly calmer, the voice on the other end continued.

"We need to find out what happened and who's responsible. This mess needs to be cleaned up immediately. All loose ends need tying up... Just make sure that you are not one of them."

The line abruptly went dead.

After spending a minute or two just standing in silence in his office, Fields rushed back down to join the rest of the investigation team. By now, the wall of the briefing room was covered with stills of Fox's partially concealed, scarred face taken from various cameras throughout the station. The investigation was now focusing on who this man was, how it was possible for him to make his way through the station, where he might have gone and finally, his connection with their infamous prisoner.

Several theories were exchanged over the course of afternoon. Perhaps this was an organised hit made by someone desperate to see the hacker dead? Given more support than that was the theory that a 'terrorist' sympathiser of the blackNet group had done this, maybe even on the group's orders. Maybe Rolfe handing himself in and being broken out again was a sign of strength.

Regardless, the trail had gone cold at the point the police helicopter had been forced to turn back from the pursuit.

Given the high-profile and unprecedented nature of the day's events, some of the country's most senior figures in the police were either directly in contact with the station or on their way to physically join the investigation team.

Fields sat through session after session, in and out of a daydream as he stared at the images of Fox on the wall, transfixed. He had to find out who this guy was and where he had taken the hacker before anyone else did. But how was that even possible? Maybe he was already dead… or maybe the worst had already happened and the information that his co-conspirators had sought to protect by silencing Rolfe had already been leaked. His mind went round and round in a frenzy.

The nine p.m. 'round-up' session was John's to lead before calling it a night and ending his shift. Most of the officers involved were taking the opportunity to work the overtime that was offered, but Fields was finding it all a bit much. He needed some time to try to get his head straight, if that were even possible.

Having dragged himself though that final session, Fields promptly packed away his things and left the briefing room with several officers still left inside. With a folder lodged under his left arm and a briefcase in his right hand, he turned into the hallway and was immediately met with the sight of a well-dressed Charles Creedy leaning against the right-hand side wall. He once again had the smug 'I know something you don't' smile on his face as he stood cross legged in his tailored all-black suit.

"Another very inspiring meeting John… In a bit of a rush I see?"

Fields grumbled with exhaustion and snarled back at Creedy, "Listen I don't have time for this right now! Whatever questions you've got you can put it in an email or something."

Fields put his head down and started to march down the corridor, right past Creedy.

"It's the same person you know."

Creedy's voice echoed in the corridor behind him. Fields stopped walking.

"Those train station murders, the Bristol Hall debacle and now this… It's the same man… Just one man."

Fields turned round to face Creedy once more, sniggering back at him.

"One man…? All of that? I would love to know how you work that one out. I suppose you're going to tell me who he is next?"

He turned to face forward as if he intended to walk away again, but he was compelled to listen to what Creedy had to say. Creedy slowly walked a few steps towards him and continued in a quieter tone.

"Given what's gone on today, it would seem that the two of us definitely have a 'mutual interest'. Why don't we help each other, John? From where I'm standing it looks like you need it."

Fields turned to look back at Creedy with a concerned and frustrated expression. How and what did this man know about what he was caught up in? Could he even be trusted? Creedy stared back with that same, smug grin.

After a few seconds, Fields reluctantly gestured for Creedy to follow him and the pair walked through the winding corridors and up the wide staircase to the first floor of the station. Fields led the way into his office, leaving the door open behind him for Creedy to follow. The exhausted DCI walked straight over to his desk and put his files and briefcase down on the floor before settling into his leather office chair. Creedy carefully shut the door behind him and walked over to the chair on the other side of Fields' desk. He straightened his suit jacket from both sides before taking a seat.

Fields extended his arm out in front of him with an open palm to gesture for Creedy to begin talking.

"Well, I'll cut straight to the crux of it, John. From what I've come to know about you and your associates, I'm quite certain that we both have interests in today's events that lie… shall we say… *outside* the bounds of regular police work?"

Fields looked nervously down at his desk and back up at Creedy with a blank expression on his face. Creedy smiled once more as he continued.

"It's OK John, I'll keep your secrets if you can keep mine. As I said previously, I work for a particular branch of the government. My exact position isn't something I can go into today but let's just say I've taken charge of certain 'experimental projects' that are… out of the public eye."

Fields struggled to hide his intrigue, continuing to stare blankly ahead at Creedy.

"Based on our experience in this domain, we find ourselves drawn to the recent events in your jurisdiction and… well… we think there's something a little out of the ordinary going on here. As I've stated, we think that the suspect in all three of those cases is the same, single person. Not a rival gang at the station, not a group of well-organised thugs at Bristol Hall. One man. The same one man that managed to fight his way through scores of your officers, blow a hole in the wall and take off with a prisoner that I know you have… a particular interest in."

Fields once again attempted to show no reaction to Creedy's accusing comment as the pair spent a second staring intensely into each other's eyes

Creedy continued, "The point is I think we could be of assistance to each other's cause, John. I have a lot of friends in high places who would also love to see this hacker dead, just like the last one. Frankly though, as far as my business goes, I could care less. My focus is one hundred percent on the man who broke into this police station today. And to be clear, I would like him to be brought in alive, ideally."

Fields let out a nervous laugh.

"*You* want him alive? This guy is part of a massive police manhunt for fuck's sake! *If* and when he gets caught, and *if* there really is only one person doing all this — which frankly I find hard to believe — he is going to get taken into police custody and charged with all of it accordingly."

Creedy sniggered.

"And the same for the hacker?"

Fields leant back in his chair before muttering a painfully obvious lie.

"Of course."

Creedy leant forward on the desk with his hands clasped in front of him.

"Look John, I know you're close to retirement and I know that deep down you will want to do what's best for you and your officers. For you and your family even. Sandra, your son Michael, everyone."

Immediately, a look of anger and concern came over Fields' face. Creedy certainly had his full and undivided attention now if he hadn't had it before.

"If you just stay focused on finding the hacker, that should inevitably lead us to our man and we'll both be happy. You seemed to have little trouble finding and 'dealing' with the first one so I have no doubt you will do the same this time. I just want your co-operation that's all… a little professional courtesy."

Fields looked down at his desk. Creedy pushed his chair back and stood up, once again straightening his jacket.

"The higher-ups have pulled some strings and placed me on this investigative team, John, so we'll be seeing a lot more of each other."

Fields looked up again at Creedy — the unwelcome surprises kept coming. Creedy offered some parting words.

"Keep in touch."

Creedy turned around and calmly let himself out of Fields' office, closing the door behind him as he left.

John Fields sat alone in his office once more, deep in thought as to what his next move was going to be from here. After about five minutes of procrastinating, he pulled out a set of keys from his right pocket and leant down to reach for the bottom drawer of his large, dark wooden desk. He unlocked and pulled open the drawer to reveal several folded pieces of paper, a laptop hard drive and a cheap mobile phone. He grabbed the phone and pushed the drawer shut, holding the power button down on the top of the handset until it flashed into life. After letting the phone boot up, DCI Fields dialled in Max Carter's number. It rang five times before there was eventually an answer at the other end.

"Hello?"

Fields let the silence linger for a few moments.

"This you John?"

Fields eventually confirmed it was as he replied, "Max. I need to keep this brief..."

Having spent the whole day curious as to what the hell had happened at the station, Max had been anxious to hear from anyone involved. As is standard practice, while he awaited a verdict from the IPOC investigation into the Michael Harding shooting, Max had been temporarily relieved of his duties as an armed response officer and had been spending a few days at home.

"John what the fuck happened up there today?" Max asked.

Fields sighed into the phone, far too exhausted from the car crash of a day that he'd had.

"We'll talk about that later. Are you ready to finish this thing? To do the second one?"

Another awkward pause.

"This is a right fucking mess... But you know I need that money John. I'm not settling for halfway... half the pay... it's far too late for that now," Max replied.

Fields was relieved to hear this.

"Good. I'm going to get you on this investigation team, once we—"

"But I can't, they've fucking susp—"

"Never mind about the suspension. I'm going to sort it out; just trust me. I'm going to get you on this team. I want you coming in to the station every day from tomorrow... That clear?"

Another pause before Max reluctantly responded.

"This isn't really what I signed up for... but I'll get it done... I want an extra ten grand."

Fields hung up the phone, held down the power button once more and dropped it into the open bottom drawer of the desk. He kicked the drawer shut and leant forward with his elbows on the desk, massaging his temples and taking deep breaths in an attempt to de-stress.

CHAPTER TWELVE

As Timothy Rolfe slowly started to regain consciousness, a blurry picture of his surroundings started to come into view. Starting as tunnel vision, the black surrounds slowly faded to the side to reveal a little more of the image. The muffled metallic grinding sounds of a train passing somewhere very nearby were becoming sharper and louder. The painful lump on the top right-hand side of his head seemed to pulsate with every heartbeat. He was drowsy; his mouth was dry, and the overwhelming smell of damp made him feel immediately sick.

It was very dark but from his position, sitting on a cold concrete floor with his hands cuffed behind his back, Rolfe could make out most of the room that he was in. It was a small 2m by 3m box of a room with basically nothing in it. The pale silver walls looked like the kind you would see in a metal shed and the 'window' on the far right was just a see-through sheet of fibreglass. Wherever this was, it was a shithole.

Rolfe was sitting in the rear middle of the room and directly in front of him, standing in the doorway facing outward from the little shanty building, was a six-foot-two figure dressed in all black. His shape was just about made visible by the faint light coming from in front of him.

"I apologise for the rough ride."

Fox continued to stand with his back facing Rolfe.

Wondering whether all of this was some kind of elaborate dream, Rolfe looked down at the floor, trying to prepare himself to talk. After about five seconds of blinking his eyes and taking a few gulps, he managed to get something out.

"Are you… are you going to kill me?"

Rolfe closed his eyes in anticipation of receiving the answer. It came quicker than he expected it to.

"No."

The first, inevitable question was out of the way.

"Then what…who do you work for? Are you with the…government? Some kind of… agency?"

Silence.

"What do you erm… why am I here?"

Fox let out a short sigh as he dropped his head and looked down at the floor just behind him.

"I need your assistance."

Rolfe let out an exhausted, nervous and surprised laugh before responding in his drowsy, slurred voice.

"My help…? After everything I've just seen… *you* need *my* help…? What for?"

Rolfe didn't *really* want to know the answer to that question. From his perspective, though, this was all still very much in the territory of 'it might not be real'.

"I need to find someone… two people. I injured one badly so it's likely he's in a hospital somewhere. The other… I'm not sure," Fox replied.

Rolfe looked even more concerned and confused. Considering the audaciousness of the breakout and Rolfe's high profile in the media, what kind of people could this man be looking for and why would he ask *him* for help? Was this all part of some kind of trap? His hacker mind was telling him it might be, but his gut was telling him it wasn't. There was something very different about Fox; he had an aura that Rolfe had never come across before.

"You want me to help you find a couple of people? I mean… what kind of… who are these people?"

"Low lives. Scumbags. They aren't important to anyone else except me. All I need is for you to find them and tell me where they are and that's it… we'll be done."

Rolfe looked down at the floor again in confusion. There were a million questions whirling around inside his head. *What had he just witnessed today? How was it possible that this man could do these things? And was he really this 'lone soldier' that he made himself out to be? Could he really only want Rolfe's help to locate a couple of 'low lives'? Why go to such an extreme to get him?*

Fox continued, "I apologise if your options are a little limited after this. Hopefully, they could see who was holding the gun today."

Rolfe sniggered.

"It won't make a difference — they were going to throw the book at me anyway. Once they extradited me to the US and threw that 'patriot law' shit at me it would have been a hundred years plus. Besides, that 'doctor' that they sent into my c..."

Having fully come round to consciousness, it suddenly dawned on Rolfe. It was the first moment he'd had time to comprehend it.

"I think you... you saved my life today... thank you!"

Fox hadn't given it a second thought either. Not even really being capable of an emotional reaction, on reflection it did intrigue him as to what exactly he had walked in on in that cell earlier. In the moment, all he had known was that he needed Rolfe out of the cell and the other man had looked like he was going to get in the way of that. Enough reason for him to die.

The two men sat pondering for a few moments. Rolfe broke the silence by beginning to do some of the thinking aloud that Michael Harding had suffered for years.

"I mean how... how the fuck did all of what happened earlier today... actually happen? That was like something out of a fucking film! I can't remember how many times I thought I was going to die out there. The guy in the cell, the gunshots, the explosions, those moves on the bike... you..."

He looked up from the floor to face the back of Fox once again with a wild and curious expression on his face.

"How can you do all that stuff...? How can that be possible? I mean I've seen videos of elite soldiers and enough classified war footage to make a grown man cry but that shit... that was unlike anything I've ever seen... *how?*"

Fox continued to stare down at the floor. If anyone else had asked, he wouldn't have answered at all.

"I don't know."

Rolfe didn't know why, but he believed the man. He looked around the room nodding as he contemplated that answer.

"OK... Well... thanks again... I owe you my life."

Another six-second silence passed.

"So what do you need to get started?" Fox asked.

Rolfe took a second to think before responding. If he was going to try to help this man, and frankly he didn't see any other option, there was only one place he could safely do it from.

***

In the months following the intensification of the pursuit of blackNet, Michael Harding and Tim Rolfe had been forced to live completely 'off the grid'. Living in a conventional home, no matter how remote, was practically an impossibility. The classification of the group as 'terrorists' meant they were subject to the advanced tracking techniques that the several government, media and criminal organisations who were after them had at their disposal. Facial recognition on CCTV cameras, voice recognition on phones, pictures being distributed in the media. They could be careful, but their options were severely limited. Having a landlord would not be ideal in any scenario.

Among the many discoveries made during their fruitful career in breaking into computer systems was a list of the locations of underground bunkers, built across the country in the 1950s and sixties during secret preparations for the escalation of the Cold War. Many of the locations of the larger bunkers had long since become declassified and even turned into tourist attractions or 'museums' of the Cold War era. Several of the smaller sized bunkers, however, were never released from government ownership and were repurposed for various other uses. Some of them simply ended up being left completely abandoned, with no one having a particular use for them. One such bunker had the codename 'Epping-255'.

Epping-255 referred to a location within a small woodland near Epping Forest in Essex. In the middle of said woodland, just in front of a hill, a small, white, brick-built two-bedroom house stood randomly amongst the trees and bushes. Although badly deteriorated and almost entirely reclaimed by nature by this point, the shape and main structural features of the small house were still intact. There were holes for one window and a door downstairs and two windows upstairs. The space for the front door was boarded over with several layers of thick, mostly rotten wood and the windows were covered horizontally with sheets of corrugated black plastic. The original, decayed wooden beams of the roof were still there, but whatever tiling had once covered it was long gone.

Over the years, several enquires related to this house had been submitted to the local council, usually met with a vague response. The only instruction that had been issued repeatedly was to ensure the building was boarded up and that development/demolition options were to be 'considered.' The most recent of the checks related to it had been carried out back in 2010.

Several curious dog walkers and mischievous teenagers had poked their way around both the exterior and interior of the building over the years. Spray painted 'tags' and a few smashed bottles were left behind as evidence.

As you got closer to the house, you could see that large chunks of rendering had fallen away from the building. Even on the inside, the plaster had decayed away to the brick in many places. The ceiling had holes in it, to the point where you could see into the rooms upstairs — the most extreme example of which was a ceramic bathtub resting diagonally against the back wall of the house. It was originally in the room above and had fallen through the ceiling as it had decayed over time and eventually buckled. The floors in each of the rooms were covered in dirt, wild growth and debris.

Amongst the unsightly mess there were some faint remnants of 1960s décor to be seen. At the bottom of the badly rotten stairwell at the front of the house, there was an old red plastic beer delivery box that read 'Beers at home', written in a curly sixties-style typeface. An old-style light switch dangled from one of the walls with the electrical wiring exposed around it. At the end of the short hallway, four and a quarter tiles of the original yellowy backdrop provided a vague glimpse into what used to be the kitchen. The whole house looked decrepit and haunted and it was a dangerous place to even stand in.

One feature that had not been discovered by any of the 'random' visitors over the years was the thick metal hatch buried under the floorboards of the smallest room at the front-right of the house. The only room that had no windows in it. It wasn't clear how this hatch was originally disguised during its use, but as part of the building's decommissioning, it had simply been welded shut and floorboards laid over it. That was until this house at Epping-255, for a time, became the 'lair' of one of the most notorious hacking groups in the world.

Over thirty years after being sealed, the steel entrance hatch was once again accessible underneath a newly installed, lockable wooden trapdoor. This had been cut into to the floorboards in the top-right corner of the small room, with a large hinge that opened outwards. Opening the metal hatch underneath with a key and twist combination exposed a vertical circular borehole with a red ladder extending 30 ft straight down into the ominous pitch-black interior. You could feel the cold air and hear the echoed sound as soon as it was opened.

The long, dark climb down the ladder led to the bottom-left corner of a 1000 ft^2 concrete box of a room. A densely encased underground bunker. Sealed off from the wind and rain of the outside world, the continuous grey concrete floor flowed seamlessly from end to end with little to no dirt or dust on it at all. The walls and arched ceiling above were of the same harsh colour and texture as the floor.

As Fox slid down the ladder after Rolfe's slower, more careful descent, the jaded hacker reached over to his left and flicked a switch on the wall, dramatically revealing the rooms contents.

Dim 'warm yellow' lantern-style lights that had been placed at near equal lengths apart along the walls of the room beamed into life. The exposed cabling between them was stylishly draped across the wall, creating a surprisingly pleasant aesthetic.

Standing with the ladder directly behind him, Fox took a second to visually scan the room, panning from right to left. The area directly to the right was a five metre by five metre square in the corner of the room that was being used as a gym. There were a series of three mirrors on the wall, dumbbells lined neatly beneath them, and an old, worn, thick punching bag hanging near the right corner.

The area to the immediate left of that, stretching to the far corner of the bunker, was what could best be described as a large living room with makeshift sofas arranged in an L-shape in front of a huge one-hundred-and-twenty-inch projector screen, mounted on the right wall. A large tapestry of Persian-style rugs nicely softened the harshness of the concrete floor underneath the patched-together seating. There were random pieces of old, mostly damaged furniture spread around that area:

dark wooden coffee tables, some old lamps, small boxes and other trinkets. Several large pieces of thin fabric with colourful patterns on them had also been spread across the walls.

Directly behind the seating area was the centrepiece of this underground bunker. A large, black desk with six widescreen monitors suspended above it and two 'gaming-style' chairs parked in front. Two tall servers sat to either side of the desk, with thick cables running out the back of each of them.

A door on the left wall behind the computing/living area led out to a small, narrow corridor that ran the length of the bunker. There were four equal-sized rooms off it. Two living quarters, a kitchen area and finally at the end of the hall, a bathroom.

The original configuration of this bunker had been designed to house up to ten people. It was fully plumbed-in and still had running water and of course, electricity. At some point, dividers in the main area of the bunker had been removed, creating the main open space.

For the first time in a while, Fox smirked to himself at what the hackers had created.

"Impressive."

Rolfe looked back at him and smiled as he walked towards the large computing rig setup behind the seating area.

"Make yourself at home."

He extended his arm out towards the seating area as he passed it, gesturing for Fox to take a seat. The sofas were a dark grey colour and relatively firm. They were in fact, self-assembled flat pack garden seating covered in layers of foam padding and thick fabric in an attempt to make them a little more comfortable and 'homely'.

Rolfe bent down to reach behind the black metal server on the right-hand side of his desk and flicked on the switch for the power supply. A green LED on the motherboard was now visible through the Perspex window on the left of the tower. Rolfe was relieved everything still worked. He pressed the power button and the server began to make a series of mechanical noises as it started to boot up. The five large blue LED fans inside whirred into life, creating a spinning spectacle of light on the ceiling above. All six monitors immediately came on, each of them displaying the infamous blackNet logo. Rolfe smiled to himself as a tear came to his eye. The sight of this logo now invoked a complex range of emotions.

Rolfe slid his chair over to the right and opened his mouth to start to ask Fox a question. He stopped mid-breath when he was met with the sight of Fox sprawled out asleep on the adjacent sofa. The first rest he'd had in weeks. Rolfe looked down at the floor and laughed before sliding his chair back over to this workstation, cracking his knuckles and settling in to do the one thing he knew he was good at.

***

Hours had passed by the time Fox opened his eyes again. Sleeping wasn't something he was used to recently and he spent the first few seconds confused as to where he even was. He'd adjusted himself into a seated position with his head in his hands when Tim Rolfe walked out from the corridor holding two mugs.

"Good morning! Good sleep?"

Rolfe had always been the type to remain jovial in the strangest and most testing of situations. Although this side of his personality had been waning recently, he somehow managed to find some level of amusement in the circumstances.

Fox let out a grumble in response as Rolfe placed a mug of what looked like green tea on the small table in front of him. He was immediately hit with the strong aroma emanating from the cup.

"It's cannabis tea," Rolfe quipped as he sat down on the neighbouring sofa, leaning forward to take a sip from his cup at the same time.

Fox reached for the cup, raising an eyebrow, intrigued. Rolfe had something else to share.

"So I found the first one by the way."

Fox immediately looked up at Rolfe, shocked and surprised by how quickly he had done his job… if that was what he meant?

"Knight? … Where?"

Rolfe took another sip from his mug.

"The Royal Open Hospital in North London. I've got it written down over there. The ward, the bed, the doctor who's looking after him. From the notes that they've entered in the system, it doesn't look like he's regained consciousness since he's been in there. The police have visited a couple of times to talk to him as well."

Fox reached forward and put his mug down on the table before getting up and walking around the sofa that Rolfe was sitting on to inspect the desk. Next to one of the keyboards was a small notepad with the information scribbled on it as promised.

Jamie Knight
32 years old
Royal Open Hospital
Admitted for 14 days
In care of Doctor Miles Foster
4th Floor ICU
Section G Bed 17

Fox ripped the page away and held it up in front of him to read it. Rolfe finished another sip of his tea, stood up and turned around to face Fox with a semi-smug look on his face. He was always going to get a kick out of this. Breaking into the computer systems of the NHS and the hospital itself was his bread and butter.

"Finding the other guy is going to take a little longer though. The trace goes cold pretty quick for him. From what I've seen he was wanted by the police for his alleged involvement in that triple murder case at the train station in Hackney. There are a couple more potential avenues for me to go down after that but like I say, it'll take time."

Fox stood frozen for a couple of seconds. The sudden, casual mention of the event had caught him off guard.

He scrunched the paper up in his hand, turned and began walking across the room towards the red ladder. Rolfe scrambled around the side of the sofa and walked towards him.

"Wow, wow… where are you going?" Rolfe asked hurriedly.

"To the hospital…"

Rolfe wiped some spilt tea away from his mouth.

"Now?"

Fox said nothing and continued walking, marching a few more steps before grabbing hold of the rungs of the ladder and beginning his ascent up towards the outside world.

"Do you even know how to get there…? What are you going to do?"

Fox reached the top of the ladder and swung open the hatch, taking a brief look down before he pulled himself up into the derelict house above.

"Be careful, yeah?" Rolfe shouted.

The hatch slammed shut behind Fox. Rolfe continued to look up in amazement. He felt a little silly with that last comment, but it felt like the right thing to say in the moment.

As well as the lockable trapdoor in the floorboards, Harding and Rolfe had introduced another level of security in the form of a new customised door to the small room in the house above. They had moved the best conditioned door left in the house and retrofitted a thick steel panel on the inside layer to make it more difficult to break through. They had added a thick, heavy lock that could be opened from within the room with a lever but required a key to open from outside. Rolfe also had several cameras in and around the property, inconspicuously disguised as random objects like rocks and bricks and then hidden in the nooks and crannies of the old, decrepit building. This meant he could view the surroundings at any point and could therefore watch for Fox's return on his several monitors. If he was even coming back of course.

CHAPTER THIRTEEN

The Royal Open Hospital in North London was one of the few hospitals across the capital that was in the middle of a massive refurbishment. Some of the older buildings on the complex were being demolished to make room for completely new, modern structures. Others were simply being 'patched up' and renovated. This meant that the site itself was covered with construction equipment and many of the buildings were surrounded in cages of scaffolding. In terms of navigating your way around, the place was a bit of a mess. Temporary metal fencing and plastic signage guided visitors through the maze of dirt piles and closed-off entrances. The ICU building was one of those that was being refurbished — the fairly pleasant looking period brickwork of the building was all but completely obscured by the floor-to-roof multistorey scaffolding that was erected in front of it.

Lying in the northeast corner of the fourth floor in a curtained-off bed, true to Rolfe's information, was the unconscious, tubed and wired-up body of Jamie Knight.

There had been a five-day period of twenty-four-hour surveillance of Knight in the immediate aftermath of the brutal 'Hackney South Train Station Murders.' Several sporadic police visits to his hospital bedside had followed in the days after. Now that two weeks had passed, given Knight's lack of any sign of improvement and the fact that no one of any significance had even been to visit him, the police had all but lost interest and thought it unlikely that he would be a useful line of enquiry. They wouldn't think that for much longer though.

As 07.00 a.m. rolled in and the reddish dawn sun filled the sky, Dr Foster began the first of his many daily rounds on the ward. After turning the corner on to the north side of section G, he noticed that one of the large windows at the far end of the ward had been lifted slightly open. The light breeze was blowing the thin white blinds further in and then out of the room. As his eyes scanned down, he could see large pieces of broken glass and white-painted wood fragments from the window frame on the floor below. He immediately began picking up the pace to walk over and investigate further, skipping his checks of the other patients that he passed on the way.

As Foster came within five metres of the broken window, the curtain cordoning off the beds just beyond it suddenly flew up into the air. A bloodstained, tall man dressed in all black with a bike mask covering his face emerged from the area. The doctor stood frozen in fear as he stared into the man's blood-red eyes. The curtain slowly draped back into place behind him.

Foster backed away a few paces and glanced over his shoulder to see if any other staff could see what was happening in front of him.

"Security!" he shouted.

Fox ran a couple of steps forward before darting off to the side and diving out of the window, crashing through more glass and wood.

Dr Foster turned his head, shouting once more, *"Get someone up here!"*

He ran forward to the window, crunching over the broken glass with his last few steps. As he approached it, he leant left and right to try to see which direction the assailant had run off in. There was no one in sight.

Foster looked over his shoulder as the reassuring sound of two security guards running towards section G came echoing down the corridor from the other end of the ward.

Backing slowly away from the window, he turned his attention to the curtained-off section in the corner of the room to his right. He could hear the ominous droning 'flatline' tone from the life support monitor getting louder and louder as he approached. As he edged towards the curtain, he gestured to one of the security guards running in from behind to head towards the broken window. Foster took the last couple of nervous steps, leant forward and pulled the curtain over to the left. He gasped at the sight in front of him.

An eight-inch blade had been violently thrust into Jamie Knight's chest, with the handle still protruding up from the open wound. Blood was visibly pouring out on either side, creating a thick, red pool in the bed below him.

Dr Foster and his team tried valiantly for almost an hour to save Knight's life, but to no avail. Given that the blade had pierced his heart, there was little that they could have done. He was pronounced dead at 08.17 a.m. on April 3rd.

***

The Royal Open Hospital had very quickly become one big crime scene, which was difficult given the nature of a hospital. Many of the patients located close to Knight's bed were moved to create a sealed-off section of the ICU. Several police sniffer dog teams had swept the area around the building but had found nothing. A group of forensic officers in the full 'white suit' getup were working by the blood-covered bed, brushing for fingerprints and footprints and looking for any sign of a source of DNA that might have been left behind by the assailant.

The head of the forensic team was Detective Josh Linsall, a heavyset bald man with hair around the circumference of his scalp and large, nineties-looking glasses on his forehead. He was talking to one of the nurses who had been close to the scene, just on the other side of the taped off area of section G. About five minutes into their conversation, he noticed a figure walking towards them from down the hall. It was the smartly dressed, smarmy-looking Charles Creedy.

Creedy strolled down the hallway and into the ward, stopping a few metres away to lean against the wall where one of the moved beds would have been. He glanced over to the pair several times, making it obvious that he was waiting for them to finish their conversation.

Eventually, overcome with the awkwardness, Linsall excused the nurse, thanking her for her time and for answering the questions he'd had. Creedy watched her walk out of the room and into the hallway and then turned to face the not-so-impressed Linsall.

"Can I help you?" Linsall asked.

Linsall addressed Creedy with a degree of impatience in his tone. He wasn't sure who this man was and why he was at this crime scene, but he immediately didn't like the look of him. Admittedly, most people didn't like the look of him, and getting to know him usually led to a confirmation of the negative assumptions they had initially made.

Creedy glanced over at the team working behind Linsall on the other side of the police tape. He had his eye on one of the officers who was taking a very close look at a particular pane of jagged glass, still held within the window frame. Blood. Creedy could see, even from where he was standing, that there were small droplets and smears of blood left stained on the glass. He couldn't hide his slimy smile at the sight of it.

"I believe you can, yes."

Linsall turned to see what Creedy was staring at. He quickly turned back to face him once more.

"I'm sorry — who *exactly* are you? This is a crime scene."

Creedy smirked as he pulled his ID from his inside jacket pocket and displayed it to Linsall. For the first second or two, Linsall didn't know what he was staring at and he was simultaneously relieved to see that a couple of other senior police officers were on their way down the hall towards them. They could deal with this guy, he thought, whoever he was.

Just before Creedy put his wallet back in his pocket, though, Linsall suddenly remembered where he had seen the name on the ID before.

A court order had been sent through to his department a few days earlier, requesting that several of the items taken into evidence from both the Bristol Hall incident and the assault on Box Hill Police Station be released to a Charles Creedy for 'further examination'. Detective Linsall's team had been specifically instructed that the request was on a 'need to know' basis only.

Linsall instantly took on a more co-operative stance, nodding once nervously. As Creedy tucked his identification back into his coat he kept his intentions brief, aware of the incoming officers from the sound of their footsteps behind him.

"The samples from the window over there. Any blood you find... any at all... gets packed up with the others. I want them coming to my team *first* for analysis. Is that clear?"

Not wanting to meddle in affairs of this kind, Linsall once again nodded, glancing back at his team. Creedy smiled once more before abruptly turning and walking back down the hallway past the two other policemen. They both looked at him suspiciously as he smirked and nodded back at them with his usual cocky demeanour.

***

Having seen the initial reports about the hospital murder online, Rolfe sat glued in front of the one-hundred-and-twenty-inch projector screen, anxiously watching for updates from a twenty-four-hour news channel. The headline recaps endlessly repeated the limited amount of known information, showing various clips of the hospital and a long-distance shot of the broken window.

Although Rolfe had expected something like this to happen when Fox had left the bunker, it was still very surreal to watch it all actually unfold in front of him. More surreal even, was the fact that the story was only second in the line of 'top stories' behind the previous day's unprecedented and daring prison break.

Over two hours had been and gone since the first report of the incident on the news and Rolfe was waiting both nervously and curiously for any sign of Fox's return.

He had initially been passing the time by focusing on getting the place back into working order. The old 1960s fridge in the kitchen still worked, but of course didn't have any food in it. The vintage microwave was also working, and he had used it to heat himself up a bowl of soup, one of over two hundred cans that were left down here from the hackers' 'emergency supply' that they had built up.

Rolfe had been in and out of a daydreamed daze, still in shock at the events that had led him here and the dizzying thoughts of what the hell might happen next. At the forefront of his mind, before even the concern for his own survival, was when he might be able to see his daughter again. If he ever would.

Just after the headlines had been repeated for what must have been the twenty-fifth time, two of the motion sensors from Rolfe's CCTV system wailed into life at almost exactly the same time. By the time he had scrambled up from his seat and round to his computer, the third and fourth had also gone off.

After frantically keying in his security codes to access the computer, the multiscreen surveillance interface came up on the display. One of the screens near the top left showed the ominous all-black-clad figure walking towards the front of the house. It felt strange to see such an intimidating sight and for the plan to be to 'open up' for him to come in — but that was what Rolfe ran over to the ladder to begin to do.

CHAPTER FOURTEEN

DCI Fields felt like he couldn't catch a break. The pressure was building from all angles. Not only did he have the stress of finding the escaped hacker that he had failed to 'take care of', but the eyes of the country were now on his station as the result of the breakout. Media statements, the press taking pictures outside, it was all becoming a little too much for one man to bear.

After attending the daily briefing regarding the assault on the police station, he set off to retire to his office on the first floor. It had given him some sense of comfort to see his 'shooter' Max Carter now attending these meetings as requested. At least he knew he was now 'in it with him' to some degree. Countering that warm, fuzzy feeling was the sporadic attendance of Charles Creedy in the same meetings. His presence made Fields even more uneasy. All he knew was that Creedy was with a government outfit that was clearly able to pull certain strings, obtaining court orders for example, and that he had a vested interest in some of the recent events in Fields' jurisdiction.

As Fields turned the corner into the corridor leading to his office, he was once again met with the sight of Creedy standing outside his office door. Everything inside him wanted to turn and walk the other way, call it a night earlier than planned. What was the use though; this guy would probably be here again tomorrow if he wanted to speak to him.

Fields sighed as he continued walking towards the office with his head down.

"John… You could at least *pretend* to be happy to see me?" Creedy said.

Fields laughed sarcastically as he walked straight past Creedy and turned the key to open his office door.

"It's been a long day Creedy. You were in the briefing earlier weren't you? What more do you want me to tell you?"

As Fields walked through the door to his office and straight over to his desk on the far left, Creedy slid in behind him and once again turned round to close the door.

Fields sat back into his seat and opened his laptop as Creedy took a few, slow steps over to stand in front of him with his arms crossed.

"There wasn't much mention of the Royal Open Hospital murder today was there?" Creedy asked.

Fields looked up from his desk, surprised.

"That's in another borough… it's another constabulary's case."

Creedy nodded in acknowledgment.

"Yes, I understand that… but the man killed, he was involved in the train station murders was he not? The only survivor found on the platform, in fact."

"Yeah… he was. That information came in earlier. I covered it briefly when we went over the open and active cases. Obviously, this 'break into the police station and steal a high-profile prisoner' case is taking the priority at the moment — you know what I mean?"

Fields had somewhat dropped the ball on most of his other open cases. He had been so consumed by the pressure to find and recapture this hacker that his ability to even pretend to do his job properly was beginning to suffer.

"John. We've been over this before. You need to fast-track the idea that you are dealing with the same criminal. He's returned to finish off the last of the people he murdered at that train station… and take a wild guess how he found Knight?"

Fields' facial expression turned from a sarcastic disgust to one of intrigue.

Creedy continued, "Your hacker. He's helping him. For whatever reason, he's helping him. At least that's what our intelligence would lead us to believe."

Fields laughed and shook his head.

"How do you know that? The hacker could be fucking dead, for all we know! Someone turned up at the hospital and killed your boy. So what? He was in with the Weavers and them… balls deep in organised crime!"

140

Fields slammed his fist down on the desk with frustration. Creedy let a moment pass before calming the tone a little.

"Look at the CCTV images of the person who came in through that window. If we want to stand a chance of getting these men, we need to get a step ahead instead of lagging behind all the time..."

Creedy glanced over his shoulder, as if to check if anyone outside of the office could hear them.

"I'm aware that... your *primary* concern is the hacker, John. And you know that mine is our prime suspect in these very serious incidents that have taken place on your patch. I thought that we were working together on this?"

Fields sat back in his chair, breathing heavily as he took in what Creedy was saying.

"He killed those people at the train station, three more at Bristol Hall, broke into this police station and now he's gone back to finish off one of his survivors... But there was at least one other person at the station that night, wasn't there, John?"

Fields looked over at Creedy. He had all but forgotten the existence of Dave Shilling.

Over the past few days Shilling had been busy giving statements that implicated his friends and fellow gang members in a wide variety of crimes. He was settling in to his new 'safe house' digs in the Essex countryside as his entry into the witness protection system was being processed.

Fields nodded with a thoughtful look on his face. Creedy elaborated on his thinking.

"Our man is clearly after associates of that gang and he is bound to have an interest in Shilling. Now we can let them find him on their terms... or we can lead them to him on *our* terms."

Fields leant forward, waiting for more information.

"Go on..."

Creedy replied, "They will be looking for a trace, the use of a credit card, a mobile phone in Shilling's name, something like that. Let's put him somewhere of our choosing and then... give them what they want. You can arrange for some... assets... to be at the scene to take care of things when they arrive."

Fields looked around his desk as he thought through what Creedy was suggesting to him. It was an improvement on the random mush of thoughts that had been going round in his mind since all of this mess started. He hadn't even sown the smallest seed of a plan before this conversation and his teams of officers had virtually no leads on where the hacker or their mystery guest had gone after their spectacular breakout. Maybe this was worth entertaining… after all, what did he even have to lose?

Creedy lowered his voice and leant in over Fields' desk with a menacing look in his eye.

"If there ends up being another 'accident' like with the other hacker, I'm sure no one will care, John. I'd be behind you one hundred percent in that, you do what you have to do. But the other one, the killer, I want him alive… preferably."

Fields looked at Creedy with suspicion. Was this some kind of trick to get him to admit his involvement in the Michael Harding shooting? What were this man's intentions truly? He had no way of knowing, but given his situation and the limited options, he would probably have to at least partially trust him.

"OK Charles. Let's say we go down this avenue then. Let's say you're right and the hacker *is* helping that nutter who broke in here last week and that he *is* coming after that rat Shilling next. Who's going to set this whole thing up? Me? Using this guy as some kind of live bait… it'll take some work."

Creedy smirked as he leant back from the desk.

"I'm glad we're at least talking the same language now. If a 'credible threat' against Shilling were to come in over the next few days and a decision is made that he needs to be relocated for the sake of his safety… do you think you could put yourself in a position to influence the location that he's moved to?"

Fields sat and thought for a second. Given Shilling's involvement with various crimes that his officers were investigating, it wouldn't be beyond the realms of possibility for Fields to stick his nose in and wield some influence. However, with the level of information that Shilling was providing relating to organised crime, there were now several departments of the police interested in his testimonies. Taking control of what happens to their informant might not be without its difficulties.

"Let's say I try… then what?"

Creedy continued to be prompt with his answers.

"Then someone that we place at his new location makes a 'mistake' and it becomes easier for the hacker and his new boyfriend to find them."

Creedy used air quotes to display his sarcasm. Fields was looking more and more uneasy.

"I assume you mean we don't make the part of the plan where we slip his location 'official' then?"

Fields returned the use of the air quotes in a passive-aggressive manner before continuing to voice his concerns.

"You know that if the assumption that all of these crimes are connected is correct and this killer that we are trying to lure turns up, we'll be putting the lives of our officers and members of public at risk by doing this? You know what will happen if people fucking found that out?"

Once again Fields' tone became more aggressive and his voice louder. Creedy remained unphased.

"John. Come on. They'll be at less risk than they are now. He's out there as we speak doing God knows what… at least this way, we'll know exactly where he's going to strike and we can have the assets there waiting. No response time."

Creedy made a fair point. If all of the assumptions were correct — and that was a big 'if' — this could put them in a position of having some idea that something was about to happen in a particular location, rather than running after the faint breadcrumbs of evidence left behind.

***

Fields spent the evening mulling over everything that he and Creedy had discussed in his office earlier. His wife was talking to him over dinner; the television spoke to him after that. He took barely any of it in. This was a lot to think about. It was a big gamble to even be talking as openly as he was with a mysterious character like Creedy. This might well be

143

the only shot they had at getting the hacker, though, and his ability to retire and live without looking over his shoulder depended on that.

Fields started the daily briefing the next morning, focusing on the links between the recent murders and the station break-in and what they knew about the suspects in each of those cases. Ultimately of course, this was not much at all. Jayden Fox had still not even been identified as one of the men on the platform on the night of the train station murders, and there was no one close enough to him to report him missing. His boss at work had expected him to be 'going away' for a while, so nothing was suspicious on that front. Julia's grieving family had never even been told about Jay and they had no idea who she was with that night. Investigators had also quickly discovered that there was little to no quality surveillance around Hackney South station and outside of Shilling's testimonies, the only way they could deduce who was on the platform for sure was by counting the bodies.

Across the various incidents, the police had singled out only one individual suspect. Again, they assumed him to be one of many and were frustrated by the lack of evidence. The only features that they had to go on with this suspect were some distinctive scars on the top half of his face, his height and what he was wearing. That and mostly low-quality CCTV footage that showed him acrobatically fleeing and seemingly disappearing before officers arrived at any of the crime scenes.

Creedy sat at the back of the briefing room that day, smiling the whole time. He would occasionally look over in the direction of Max Carter, enjoying imagining DCI Fields giving him the low-down of what was coming next in his grumbling, panicked and aggressive tone. This fat old man and his shooter had better bloody do what they were told.

CHAPTER FIFTEEN

Max Carter's home life had suffered under the pressure of the IPOC investigation into his behaviour. His wife Sarah, who over recent months had been growing less and less patient in dealing with his snappy temper and generally grumpy mood when he came home from work, had finally reached the end of her tether. Two weeks ago, she had left home with their three-year-old daughter Charlotte and gone to stay with her sister in Gloucester.

Although somewhere underneath his hard exterior Max was sorry that his daughter was no longer with him, he was relieved to not have to answer his wife's questions or listen to her nagging about him being down or 'lost in thought' all the time with work. Besides, he could use the time to pander to his ever-growing vain side, chiselling up that six-pack and perfecting his jab, jab, hook combinations in his garage gym at home.

This latest IPOC enquiry was by no means the first investigation that had come Max's way over the years, but it *was* the one that had put him under the most scrutiny. Aside from the fact that falling foul of a guilty ruling would jeopardise his freedom, Max was particularly anxious for it to go away as soon as possible for other reasons. He needed to finish the job that had been handed to him by DCI Fields and collect his money. After all, the upcoming divorce that had been on the cards for almost a year now was likely to be expensive.

Max Carter had had delusions of grandeur and high expectations from day one of joining the police. He came into the force via the cadet programme at eighteen years old with glamourised visions of policing in his mind. A few years of the high-speed chasing, drug-busting life before moving up to take a high-flying detective position earning the 'big money'. Not to mention a whole load of debauchery and fun along the way.

And the guns. He couldn't wait for the day that they let him carry the guns.

The reality of the life was something that had hit Max hard. He spent his first couple of years on the streets of East London earning his stripes as a 'bobby on the beat', mostly dealing with shoplifters, drug addicts and general low-end crime. On the rare occasion that he did come into contact with a criminal who was a little more 'big time', he'd more often than not be frustrated by a lack of evidence to pursue them any further. Some of the drug dealers in the area were driving brand new cars, covered in thick gold jewellery and Rolex watches. As far as he could see, they were getting away with it a lot of the time as well. Day after day they dangled their wealth and enjoyment in front of Max and his 25K starting salary. He grew more and more angry at the procedures, paperwork and legal limitations in the way of him being able to put these people in their place. He didn't feel the justice system was catching up to them quickly enough and even when they did, the sentences were far too lenient. Needless to say, he'd prefer a more 'direct' method of judgement.

Even when the guns finally came, they once again disappointed Max in comparison to the movie-style image his younger self had dreamt up. Training, drills, paperwork and rules. Years of simulating certain scenarios and answering test questions were doing nothing to fulfil Max's desire for some action. Years of having his finger on the trigger without being able to pull it.

The money certainly wasn't turning out to be what Max had hoped for either. He'd always fancied himself in one of the nice, detached houses out in the Essex countryside with a couple of decent-looking sports cars on the drive. The closest he had got to that was the semi-detached house in the built-up residential area of Ilford that he later had to sell and split with his ex-fiancée, Maria. She'd found the second phone that he kept in the glove box of his Ford Focus, used primarily for contacting the several other women that he had 'on the side'. The worsening relationship with his current wife was looking to be a potential case of history repeating itself.

Max had never fully accepted his financial expectations being shattered and had spent most of the last ten years or so living well out of his means. Expensive watches, designer clothes, nice new cars bought on finance and luxury, over-the-top holidays. His negative balances on credit cards and short-term loans had grown and grown to the point where they were becoming a problem. There was always the subconscious thought in the back of his mind that 'one day' he would sort everything out. 'One day' something would come along that would let him clear his growing debts and continue to fund the kind of lifestyle that he felt like he deserved to be living. As is the case with most things in life, Max didn't become a 'bent copper' overnight. His morals slipped gradually, piece by piece.

It started with the shift from arresting shoplifters to instructing them to "Stop fucking nicking things on *my* patch," even pointing them in the direction of an area where they could operate and *he* would no longer have to deal with them. He started to look the other way when certain crimes happened that he 'couldn't be bothered' to fill out the paperwork for, turning a blind eye to some of the persistent A-class drug dealing in the neighbourhood. If a suspect were drunk or drugged up enough and Max had experienced a particularly stressful week, he would physically assault them. Usually this was tactfully done by winding them up, nudging against them aggressively during their initial questioning in the hope of getting a reaction from them. When that reaction came, ordinarily in the form of a push, Max's retaliation would be one of extreme violence.

In the moments where he was beating down on someone with his baton, crashing the steel bar into their legs or their ribcages as they held their arms up in defence, there was a sort of release for Max. It was a brief relief from the frustration and helplessness he had building up inside him from what was turning out to be a disappointment of a life.

***

By the time Max had moved to the armed police, his moral line had shifted significantly. Given that he was now carrying a loaded weapon every day on his shift, this was always likely to end up in a deadly situation. The regulated and scrutinised nature of the job made it a little more difficult for an officer to be able to break the rules and get away with it though. Cue his introduction to DCI John Fields in 2015.

Fields had been a known hard-ass since Carter had joined the force. People knew not to mess around with him. He had the reputation of being very firm and having little patience or sympathy with any of the officers or suspects that he interacted with. He was also very private and kept very much to himself. He excluded himself from most of the social events that were organised and rarely let anyone 'in' on his personal life. His colleagues knew that he had a wife of many years and that for whatever reason, he didn't talk about her much at all. Professionally, he had a very successful and decorated career in the force. Like Carter, Fields had attracted some controversy over the course of his much longer term in the job, but no one could argue with his numbers. Some big crime figures had been taken off the street under his watch… others, of course, had been deliberately left in place.

The pair were first thrown together when it was decided that armed officers were to guard Fields' home temporarily in June of 2015. Fields was leading an investigation into an organised crime element in London that had links to A-Class drug distribution and firearms smuggling. The police had received intelligence that his name might have been leaked to affiliates of the organisation, and hence took the precaution of posting Max and one of his SO19 colleagues at Fields' plush, gated, five-bedroom detached house in a small Essex village. For Max, this was a welcome break from the normal routine of patrolling a train station or driving around in an armed response vehicle waiting for something interesting to happen, usually in vain.

Carter had always admired Fields and his no-nonsense reputation in the force, and getting an insight into how he lived made him look up to the man even more. Fields and his 'Mason' friends were always open to finding new people that they could rely on to do their dirty work in exchange for some quick money. These two factors were the building blocks on which the two men's relationship was built.

Now, weeks after murdering one international criminal in broad daylight on the streets of London, Max sat with a gun on his lap in anticipation of murdering a second and finishing the job.

Fields had pulled strings to allow a rare 'exemption' for Carter to be able to return to the field, his IPOC verdict still outstanding. After Charles Creedy had come through on his end of the deal and made a call to an 'old friend' with government connections, the recommendation to move Dave Shilling from his current location had come down from the top of the police rankings.

Given the ambiguity around where the threat against Dave Shilling had come from, the police needed time to decide on a new location to move him to and ensure it was safe going forward. In the meantime, two flats across the hall from each other in a newly built apartment block in East London were to be used as a temporary 'safe house'. Not fully finished and part of a development that was not yet on sale to the public, they had been hired for another, completely unrelated surveillance mission by DCI John Fields.

Fields had ensured that he was involved in this decision-making process, wielding his influence as one of the senior officers looking into the connection between the Bristol Hall and train station murders. It was met with some resistance given the various different departments now involved in Shilling's testimonies, but after some heated debate, the decision was eventually settled upon.

The first flat facing out to the city streets would house Dave Shilling, who was to be accompanied by at least one officer at any given time. The opposite flat, on the other side of the corridor, would have armed officers filling a 24/7 posting there to protect against any threats. Their orders had been simply to patrol the hallways to make sure everything looked OK and wait for further instructions, occasionally checking in with the officer(s) based in the room opposite. Security guards were also posted at the front and rear of the apartment building. Since it was otherwise uninhabited, the only people being allowed to come and go from the building were police officers and the various takeaway food deliveries that they were ordering to the property.

***

Meanwhile, life at Epping-255 had settled into a sort of routine for Tim Rolfe and his new house guest. Rolfe had left the compound twice to get essential food and drink supplies, walking a few miles through the woods to a mini supermarket in the nearest village of Galden. His face had been plastered all over the news for a week now, and being at the centre of such a high-profile jail-break story meant being recognised was likely. He wore a thick, dark-blue baggy tracksuit with the hood pulled over his head and a cap underneath that dipped down over the top of his face. Paired with the muddy, worn Caterpillar boots, he donned the 'labourer' look and kept his head down as much as possible when passing anyone in the street.

Fox had been using the modest 'gym' area in the bunker to its full potential. From the moment he woke up in the morning, he would start his gruelling routine of hundreds of press-ups and sit-ups followed by weight training. Of course, the 25kg dumbbells were not heavy enough to be a challenge for him to lift, but he improvised. Rolfe was always astounded watching him shadow box with the weights in either hand — he had never seen anything like that kind of upper body strength and control. Fox's knuckles were permanently red raw and bloody from the hours of hitting the punching bag that had now been partially filled with rubble to give it a heavier and of course, much harder feel. He alternated between hitting that and the cold, solid, concrete wall behind it.

At the end of each day, Fox would have one conversation with Rolfe to hear the updates on his progress before retiring to his room. They spoke very little outside of that and ate separately most of the time. Rolfe had found this arrangement very awkward at first but had got used to it as time went on. He would spend almost the entirety of his day at his workstation, focusing on the job he had been tasked with.

A board on the wall beside Rolfe's screens had been used to create a makeshift 'crime family tree' for the Weavers' gang and their associates. Rolfe had printed several sheets of information about everyone involved. This included their names, addresses, family details and criminal history. If they were dead, their printed mugshot had a red cross drawn through it and notes below addressed the details around the circumstances of their demise. The board was littered with other, smaller news print-offs and sticky notes with details about the gang's interactions and allegations. Lines and arrows illustrated the relationships between the various parties, slowly building a comprehensive picture of the organisation and its operation.

Fox hadn't asked for this, but Rolfe had felt like it was useful to build a visual representation of the information that he was uncovering, not least to help *him* visualise everyone involved and how they were all connected. It made it easier to match things up as he unearthed more information along the way. Logs of phone calls, text message records, social media postings, vehicles that members of the gang had owned, phrases they had googled from their computers, bank account information, medical records and of course, the information that the Metropolitan Police had on file. All of this was being trawled through by several of Rolfe's advanced algorithms that could execute in parallel with a very minor risk of being detected.

This mass of information was being transferred through the Ethernet cables that led out of the back of Rolfe's supercomputer and up the bunker wall. It joined with the electricity cables that fed through a channel all the way up to the decaying house above. A one-metre-wide satellite dish at the rear of the top floor of the house transmitted the data to and from the outside world. Rolfe and Harding had cleverly devised a way to do this that avoided virtually all modern detection methods. The information being sent and received from the two-way dish was being cleverly disguised as other 'legitimate' packets of data normally sent by satellite (digital television programmes, for example). After being transmitted it was then bounced between a variety of servers all round the world before being sent back to another satellite broadcasting service to beam the information back down to them. To retrieve the data being returned you needed the correct equipment, knowledge and corresponding 256-bit encryption key. Over the years several of the blackNet's exploits had been detected and even stopped, but they had never been successfully traced because of the complexity of this technology.

Rolfe was extremely curious about what exactly the men that Fox was looking for had done to warrant his pursuit. There was too much to choose from in terms of the gang's involvement in crime. They had been linked to several murders, serious assaults, robberies, the list went on.

Since the conversation wasn't exactly flowing between him and Fox, he didn't want to start asking those kinds of questions.

Tim had managed to identify at least one 'pay as you go' mobile phone that most likely belonged to Dave Shilling. This was deduced from a combination of SMS messages that had been sent to it from phones that he knew belonged to other gang members, and the cell mast location data. The late-night 'booty call' messages sent from the phone to Shilling's ex, Sophie and her responses of 'Fuck off Dave' were also quite the giveaway. Rolfe could track this particular phone using a backdoor into the same systems that the police and other agencies use to triangulate cellular devices. Its most recent communication was a text message sent around a mile from Liverpool Street Station before it was switched off and never turned back on again. Rolfe's next move would have been to try to gain access to some of the local CCTV from around the time that the phone became inactive, but he didn't have to.

One of the recent numbers Shilling had dialled was the customer service department of a low-cost airline, and a subsequent location and breach of their database revealed Shilling's Alicante booking. Rolfe could also see from the same database, however, that the ticket was never actually used. From that point on, all the usual indicators of a person's activity had gone cold. Up until then he could track activity on Shilling's bank accounts and social media but they both seemed to suddenly cease.

After a long-running search against the Metropolitan Police's CRIS database had finished executing, another interesting piece of information surfaced. Shilling was listed as having a warrant out for his arrest after having been identified as a person of interest in the Hackney South train station murders. One of the more recent entries on the file had flagged him as a 'flight risk'. This would have meant that all of the ports in the country would have been notified and sent an image of Shilling. Coupled with the fact that all his activity had ceased soon after that, the idea that he could be in police custody was now on the table.

As Fox worked out furiously in the background, Rolfe put the pieces in place to set up a breach of another set of databases to further his search. Just then, another one of his advanced queries running in the background popped up with a result. One of Shilling's credit cards had just been used in an online transaction. A £23 order from a Chinese takeaway to be delivered to an address in East London. The name given to the restaurant on the order confirmation was 'Shilling'. Rolfe was immediately suspicious, but after checking and double-checking, he leant back in his chair and looked over at Fox.

"I've erm…"

His first attempt wasn't loud enough; the noise of Fox furiously unloading super-fast punch combinations into the cement easily drowned him out.

Rolfe cleared his throat and sat up a bit straighter in his chair.

"I've found something…"

Fox threw one last punch and left his hand extended out in front of him as he panted heavily from the workout. He slowly turned round to face Rolfe.

"Shilling?"

Rolfe nodded nervously as Fox began slowly walking over to him.

"Where…? Where is he?"

Rolfe clicked away frantically at his computer as he tried to explain his findings.

"It's a food order. For twenty-three quid… a Chinese food order. But it's very odd. I mean there's been no activity for days on here and all of a sudden this pops up. I'm running a scan for any mobile phone activity close to the address listed on it now, looks like a brand-new block of flats. One of those ones they're advertising in the paper… It's called Wapping House."

Fox wasn't really interested in the details; once he had the address, he would go directly there. Whoever was there when he turned up could 'fill in the blanks'. He walked back over to the corner of the room and wrapped a thick black belt around his waist. He had crafted this to hold multiple throwing knives in notches carved all the way around. Two diagonal loops in the back of the belt would hold the larger knives he had been sharpening for the occasion. He reached behind his back from both sides and tucked the long, thick knives in before walking back over to Rolfe's desk.

Rolfe was displaying multiple views of the apartment complex in question. There was a 3D floorplan from the estate agents' website, a satellite view of the location and several angles from Google Maps, amongst other technical information about the building.

"Right erm… the order is to flat 106. That's at the north-west of the building up on the tenth floor. According to the estate agent's website, none of the flats are even ready yet so I don't know what he's doing in there or who he might be with."

Rolfe continued typing as Fox leant in closer over his shoulder to read through the information that was being displayed on the six screens. He scanned around the various views of the complex, visualising where exactly in the building the apartment was.

"This is weird… I don't know what the hell this means," muttered Rolfe.

Fox turned to the left, pulled the same black bike mask up over his face and began walking towards the ladder at the far end of the bunker.

Rolfe noticed this out of the corner of his eye as he continued frantically typing commands into his mechanical keyboard.

"Wait… just wait a sec!"

As Fox reached the bottom of the ladder and put his foot on the first rung, Rolfe blurted out another piece of information that he had just discovered.

"The Met! Two flats in that apartment complex have been rented out by the coppers. This rental agreement is with 'Blue Line plc'. They use these fake company names when they rent places out like this; I've actually seen that same company listed before on a few places. It's the pigs, for sure."

Rolfe had breached the security of the estate agent's network and accessed the rental agreements they had on file in a matter of minutes.

Fox froze for a moment at the bottom of the ladder as Rolfe stared nervously at him from across the room.

"Where is the other apartment?" Fox asked.

Rolfe looked back at his monitor.

"It's the one directly opposite."

Fox continued to climb the ladder. Rolfe's voice became more panicked.

"This could be deliberate you know! They might have figured out that we were looking for Shilling and that we would catch that. They could be waiting for you, man!"

Fox looked down from the top of the ladder and nodded back at Rolfe.

"You did good, Tim. Thank you."

Rolfe could tell immediately from the tone of Fox's voice that he thought he might not be coming back. Maybe this was it. All Fox had wanted was to find this person's whereabouts and Rolfe knew that something bad was about to happen when he got there. Maybe he should have spent more time researching this location and establishing who else was there before he opened his mouth. Rolfe began focusing all of his attention on this brand-new apartment complex near the docks in East London.

CHAPTER SIXTEEN

The view from the flat assigned to the armed officers was far less appealing than that of the one opposite. Instead of a sweeping London skyline, the officers in flat 107 were staring out at the tenth floor of a 1980s-built multistorey car park.

Max Carter and his colleague Joe Power had just finished their sweep of the hallways and were back in the apartment where they would stay for the next hour of their shift. Not much was happening in the way of communication; neither man really liked the other and they were keeping themselves to themselves. Max was sitting back on the sofa staring down at his police-issue tablet, scrolling through the various 'boring' emails he'd received. Joe was over in the open-plan kitchen area boiling the kettle to make a cup of tea, for himself only, of course.

Both men's Heckler & Koch MP5 submachine guns were propped up against the wall near the door of the apartment with the safety catches on.

It was just after five p.m. and one of the two officers in the apartment across the hall with Dave Shilling was preparing to change shift. Neither of these officers were armed; they were in the room to make sure Dave stayed there and to facilitate the continuation of taking statements as part of his immunity deal. Dave and one of the officers were sitting on the sofas, glancing out at the views in between talking shop. The officer about to go off shift stood behind them looking at his watch, awaiting the arrival of his replacement. Both officers were plainclothes, wearing suits to blend in with the city types as they came and went from the apartment complex.

At that moment, out of sight of anyone in the building, a figure leapt from the tenth floor of the car park, across the five-metre gap and onto the wrap-around balcony of Flat 109 in the Wapping House complex. A second after that, a loud boom echoed through the building followed by a series of shattering noises.

Carter immediately leapt out of his seat and dived over towards the door of the apartment and his gun. Startled and slower to react, his colleague Joe began to follow suit behind him.

The front door of the neighbouring apartment burst open, with wood chippings and dust flying into the air from the force of it slamming against the corridor wall. Out came an extremely focused, all-black attired Fox.

Fox immediately ran and shoulder barged the door to Flat 106 open. It swung wildly and crashed into the hallway wall of the flat, taking out a chunk of the newly-plastered wall in the process.

Standing right in front of him as he entered was the skinny, bald, pointy nosed six-foot police officer in an all-grey suit. Having heard the noise, he had begun to make his way out to the corridor to see what was happening.

Without hesitation, Fox continued his momentum and charged into the officer, pushing him about two metres down the apartment hallway before throwing him hard against the wall on the left.

Fox stopped as he entered the open-plan living room of the flat. Dave Shilling froze in fear as he looked directly into those blood-red eyes.

The remaining officer stood just to the left of Dave, trembling in shock with his hands out in front of him.

"Get... get back...! Don't do anything stupid now; we're the police!"

Suddenly a strange sensation came over Fox. Time seemed to slow down to an almost complete standstill. He could feel a sense of danger from something behind him and instinctively started to duck down and turn around to see who or what was there.

Standing in the hallway with his Heckler & Koch MP5 aimed into the flat was a masked and goggled-up Max Carter.

At that moment a bright red flash followed by a loud, booming clap came from the end of the gun as it discharged a single shot. The bullet skimmed Fox's right shoulder as he dived further into the room.

As he slid across the laminate floor of the apartment towards the kitchen area, another shot rang out from behind, embedding itself in the floor. Only about a second had separated the shots — Fox had moved at a speed too quick for Carter to even follow.

As Fox came to a rest on the apartment floor, Dave Shilling stood up from his seated position on the sofa and leant over the countertop to grab one of the large kitchen knives from a wooden holder. Fox stood up about a metre from him as Dave drew back the knife and held it trembling in front of him.

"Please… just fuck off!"

Shilling backed away, glancing over towards the hallway waiting anxiously for the armed officers to come bursting into the living room. By this time, the cowardly officer who was already in the room was lying face down on the floor with his arms at either side for fear of getting shot in the crossfire.

Having run down the short hallway to the entrance of the living room, Carter, followed by his teammate Joe, slowed down and raised their weapons once more, ready to turn the corner into the room and face the situation in front of them. For all they knew Fox could have a gun by now and have it trained on the doorway, waiting for them.

"Help me, for fuck's sake!"

The primal, panicked cry of Dave Shilling came from inside the room as Fox continued walking towards him. Shilling was now backed up against the clear, floor-to-ceiling bi-fold doors that led out on to the flat's balcony. As he felt himself run out of floor, he gripped the eight-inch knife firmly by the handle and thrust it forward in the direction of Fox's chest, letting out a terrified battle call. His last stand.

Fox caught Shilling's wrist with both of his hands and stopped the motion of the blade. Before Shilling could even look down, Fox pulled and twisted hard on his wrist and violently broke the bone.

Max Carter spun round into the room, facing the scene from behind the sights of his MP5 machine gun. At the same moment, Shilling began to screw his face up and let out an almighty wail of pain from his broken wrist.

Fox could hear Carter entering the room from behind and launched forward to throw Shilling and himself into the bi-fold doors. This was done with such force that it propelled both men through the thick glass doors, creating a deafening shattering sound as the glass appeared to explode out on to the wooden decking of the balcony.

The sensory overload of the sight and sound of this threw Carter off for a split second as his sights lined up with the pair, tumbling as one mass out of the apartment. He fired another shot in their direction, about a metre too high.

"Jesus, Max!"

Max could hear the muffled voice of Joe behind him through his ear protectors. He was shocked at Max's wild shooting.

The two armed officers ran towards the partially shattered door as Fox and Shilling rolled around on the balcony floor, fighting for control of the knife.

Fox very quickly gained the upper hand and held Shilling down underneath him, facing back towards the building. He pulled the knife out to the side and violently thrust it into Shilling's neck as what had started as a plea for his life, turned into a ghastly gargling sound.

Fox looked up from his kneeling position over Shilling as Max Carter raised the barrel of his rifle once again. The two men stared eye to eye for a few milliseconds before Max pulled the trigger once more.

Again, time seemed to slow down in Fox's mind.

He rolled off to his left as this time, the bullet from Max's gun scraped along the skin of his forearm.

Fox jumped up and ran to the right edge of the balcony. Two more shots rang out, one embedding itself into the wooden decking, the other striking and shattering one of the glass panels that lined the outside of the balcony.

Fox leapt into the air and disappeared over the edge of the balcony.

Officer Joe Power immediately ran forward and turned his attention to the badly injured Dave Shilling lying on the floor in front of him. Having holstered his weapon, he leant down and began attempting to apply pressure to the gaping wound in the right side of Shilling's neck. The knife handle was still sticking out to the side and the blood was pouring out on to the balcony floor. Shilling continuously gasped for a breath. Power knew it didn't look good; he reached for the radio on his chest to begin calling it in.

Max immediately ran over to the side of the balcony and peered over the edge. He was just in time to see Fox run out of sight behind a metal maintenance shed on the roof of a neighbouring building a few storeys below.

He raised his gun and fired two more shots down in that direction. Joe looked up from attending to Shilling with a confused and angry expression on his face.

"What the fuck are you doing Max?"

Max completely ignored the outraged call from his colleague. He looked down at the metal fire escape that snaked down the side of the building. Without hesitation, he jumped over on to it and began bounding down the steps as fast as he could.

In seconds Max was level with the neighbouring building and made the two-metre leap to get on to the barren, stone-shingle-covered rooftop.

With his MP5 held steadily in front of him with both hands, Max began running across the rooftop towards the maintenance shed that he had seen Fox run behind. He would have to get lucky to see where his target had run to next, but he wasn't going to let this opportunity slip by him when he was this close.

As Max ran past the end of the shed, approaching the end of the rooftop, he felt a massive impact on his chest that instantly took the wind out of him. He was stopped dead in his tracks while his arms, legs and head were flung out in front of him with the momentum. It was like he had run into an invisible wall. As he stumbled back with his eyes and mouth wide open in shock, he looked up to see Fox with his arm extended out to the side.

Fox walked over and grabbed hold of Max's MP5, held in place on his chest by a shoulder strap. He pulled down on it hard, ripping it away from its holder, and then threw it off to the side.

Max instinctively reached down to the holster on his right hip that held his Glock 17 semi-automatic pistol, pulled the gun out and began raising it up in front of him.

Slightly surprised by Max's speed, Fox karate-chopped Max's right arm, sending the gun flying out of his hand. He then swung a hard right punch into Max's ribs and threw himself forward, headbutting Max in the face. Max's nose instantly exploded with blood as he threw back his head and let out a yelp of pain.

Fox then reached forward and took hold of Max's thick, black, bullet-resistant vest and threw him up against the metallic wall of the maintenance shed, pinning him in place. Max was struggling to get his breath back from the impacts that had broken two of his ribs. His face was now completely covered in blood.

Fox leant forward to stare intensely into Max's eyes. He had recognised Max's face as soon as he had walked into that apartment with his gun drawn. It was the same face he had seen on Rolfe's monitors several times over the past few days as he'd dug deeper into the man who had killed his friend Harding.

"You seem particularly keen on shooting me today, Officer."

Max grunted with frustration at the compromised position he was in and struggled for a second to try to get free. The grip was too firm. His vision was covered in a haze from the hard strike to his nose.

"I wonder why," Fox rhetorically added.

Fox could see out of the corner of his eye that a number of officers were now gathering on the neighbouring rooftop over to his left, pointing down in his direction. He knew there was likely to be several more officers on their way up through the offices below them.

Fox brought his right arm up and forced his forearm hard against Max's neck, pushing it against the metal wall behind him. Max immediately began choking and struggling even more to catch a breath.

Fox continued, "I'm sure you have your reasons... whatever they are, they will only lead you further into the darkness."

Max showed no reaction and continued to stare into Fox's eyes intently. Fox had only one more thing to say.

"If I see you again... I will kill you."

He let go of Max's neck and took a step back. Max instantly began to take large gasps of breath, hunched over.

Fox turned away and once again ran to the edge of the building, leaping out of sight.

Max stumbled forward in the same direction. His vision was getting worse as his face began to swell more and more. The pain from his injuries was intense and overwhelming, pulsating through his entire body. He struggled to balance and lurched from side to side as he lunged forward.

As he reached the edge of the building, he leant to peer over the side to see if he could get sight of his fleeing target. As he did this, his knee wobbled and buckled from underneath him. He lost his footing and slipped.

Max fell ten storeys down to the ground, bouncing off several fire escape staircases before crashing into a skip in the alleyway separating the buildings.

***

It was to be national news the next day. A double murder taking place in the middle of East London. One of the victims, an as yet unnamed suspect who had been taken into police custody for questioning. The other, a decorated police officer serving as part of the armed division of the Metropolitan Police.

Charles Creedy could already hear the headlines in his head as he stood over Max Carter's hospital bed the night before. Over in the corner of the room was a distraught DCI John Fields, sitting on a visitor's chair with his head in his hands.

Max had broken over sixty percent of the bones in his body during his violent tumble to the ground. Coupled with his already broken nose, fractured skull and cracked ribs from before the fall, he was in a very bad way. Having not been found for over thirty minutes, it had taken a while for him to receive any medical attention. By the time he had arrived at the hospital, the doctor's prognosis was not good. Max was deep in a coma and it was looking less and less likely that he would be waking up from it. Even if he defied the odds and managed to open his eyes, it was overwhelmingly likely that the brain damage he had sustained would mean he would never fully recover.

Creedy stood and stared in contemplation for over thirty minutes in the private room that they had assigned Max that evening. The situation was getting desperate, but this latest development may well have opened an opportunity up for Creedy and his shady outfit.

After DCI Fields had left the room to reluctantly go home to his wife, Creedy closed the door to make a call on his phone.

"Have the preparations been made?" Creedy asked.

"Yes."

"So we're back where we were six months ago then…? We have a lab again?"

"That's correct, sir."

Creedy smiled and turned to look over his shoulder at the lifeless body of Max Carter lying on the bed, covered in tubes.

"Get all of the equipment and the samples ready… I'll be bringing a subject in shortly."

"A subject? You mean a human subj—"

Creedy cut off the call before his colleague on the other end could finish asking the question.

Later that evening arrangements were made to transfer Max Carter into the care of a 'specialist' medical team following a police-approved order from Charles Creedy. After some disagreement between the hospital staff, he was carefully lifted into an unmarked ambulance and whisked away to an unknown location.

Less than twelve hours later it was reported that Max Carter had succumbed to his injuries and had been pronounced dead.

The news reported it just as Creedy had hoped. The seemingly disastrous day at the apartment complex had confirmed that the hacker was still alive and working with his 'person of interest'. This was now looking more and more like it was leading to a series of events that could very well play into Creedy's hands.

CHAPTER SEVENTEEN

Tim Rolfe had been very surprised to see his new 'friend' return to Epping-255 the previous evening. He had heard the hatch opening in the middle of the night and peered out into the main room to see an obviously exhausted Fox climb down the main access ladder. Although he was extremely intrigued to know what had happened at the apartment complex, it didn't feel like a good time to approach Fox for the gossip. His instincts had told him it would be all over the news in the morning and his instincts were correct.

Tim had walked out of his room in the morning to find Fox already awake, stood with his arms crossed watching the morning headlines roll out on the projected image on the far wall. Rolfe instantly slowed his pace of walking as the news of another 'lone wolf' double murder was laid out in front of him. Fox looked to the side and behind him as he heard Tim enter the room and then looked back at the screen.

"That policeman... I assume you recognise his face?"

Just as Fox said this, the huge image of Max Carter's police photograph was displayed on the screen alongside a less than complimentary mugshot of Dave Shilling.

Rolfe was stunned.

"I erm... yeah, I do."

"I know he's the man who killed your friend. He was determined to put a bullet in me as well. I didn't let him but..."

Fox lifted his black T-shirt slightly and pointed to the two scars on his shoulder and elbow from where the bullets had scraped him. Rolfe winced at the sight of them. Fox nodded back towards the screen.

"When I left him, he was alive. I hurt him... but he was alive."

Rolfe didn't know how to feel. There were so many emotions and thoughts running through his mind at the same time. Part of him was relieved that the man who had killed his friend had now received such instant justice... but it seemed too good to be true. There were still so many unanswered questions as well. Was Fox telling the truth about Carter being alive when he left? What had happened to him after that? Why *had* Carter killed Harding? Was it a massive coincidence that he happened to be the person guarding Fox's last remaining target?

As the details of the news story kept rolling on at low volume in the background, Rolfe had to ask one other question that had popped into his mind.

"And the other guy…? The witness?"

Fox turned to look at Rolfe once more.

"I killed him."

Another shocking fact. Another complex soup of emotions in the pit of Rolfe's stomach. By now things were all so surreal that his ability to reason about what was going on had been somewhat lost. From where he was standing, though, he didn't exactly have much choice in the matter. Besides, for some reason he trusted the scarred and battered man in front of him; these guys had probably deserved what was coming to them. He certainly felt that way about Max Carter.

***

Max's estranged wife Sarah had been given the awful news on the Saturday morning over the phone at her sister's house. Even though things hadn't been working out between them recently, she was devastated at hearing of his condition the night before and inconsolable with the confirmation of his death. She had cried her eyes out on her sister's shoulder for hours that Friday night but since it was a three-hour drive to the hospital, she had taken the advice of the doctor to leave visiting until the following morning. Somehow, even at that stage, she had the overwhelming feeling that she would probably never see her husband alive again.

The rest of the weekend was understandably a struggle. More than anything it was going to kill Sarah to have to explain to her happy little daughter that her daddy was never coming home again. She had decided to let Saturday and Sunday go by without burdening herself with that responsibility. It was the half-term school holiday the following week and she'd decided to pick a day then to sit her down and tell her. At least

165

she wouldn't have to worry about people talking about it in school before she had the chance to say anything.

That Sunday night Sarah spent a little longer tucking her daughter into bed before she went downstairs to check everything and lock up her sister's house. She could see from the hallway that the security light at the back of the garden was on, which was strange. After peering out of the patio doors off the kitchen and seeing nothing, she assumed it must have just been a fox or a cat and began to head upstairs to bed.

As she got halfway up the stairs, a loud bang coming from the back of the house stopped her in her tracks. She froze for a second in shock. Her sister Connie called out from one of the bedrooms upstairs.

"Sarah?"

Sarah walked a couple of steps back down the staircase and leant over to peer into the kitchen.

A tall, broad, masked man pushed out the last chunks of glass before stepping through the smashed kitchen door.

Her fear turned quickly to blind panic and her heart immediately began racing. She could feel a wave of adrenaline run through her body. For a second or so, she stared in complete disbelief at the sight in front of her. By the time the figure took a step inside the building, gripping the banister firmly, Sarah let out a terrified shriek and began running up the stairs.

She came face to face with her sister at the top of the staircase, who had left her room to see what all the commotion was downstairs. Sarah grabbed hold of Connie and pulled her into her daughter's room, slamming the door shut behind them.

They could both now hear the terrifying sound of the masked intruder jogging his way up the stairs towards them as Sarah desperately held on to the door handle.

Connie ran further into the room and pulled her mobile phone out from the pocket in her dressing gown. Her hands shook violently as she frantically dialled 999.

The police would arrive at the house eight minutes later, batons drawn. The pair of officers sent round to the rear of the house found the smashed back door and let themselves in. They cautiously walked up the stairs, shouting and identifying themselves as police officers after almost every step.

"Police! Is anyone in the house?"

Upon reaching the turn at the top of the stairs, the first officer up could see that the door to the bedroom on the immediate right was slightly ajar and signalled for the officers behind him to hold their positions. They began creeping forward once more.

"This is the police! Make yourself known."

None of the policemen were prepared for the sight that would greet them on the other side of that door.

The dead bodies of two women in their thirties and most tragically, that of a three-year-old girl. All three had been shot at close range.

A search of the surrounding area was immediately put into effect but ultimately, no suspect was found. The forensic team that would later show up quickly confirmed that the shell casings found in the room were discharged from a 9mm semi-automatic handgun. The only other piece of strong physical evidence that was found at the scene was a note that read, *"I came to finish what we started on that rooftop. Your family paid the debt in your absence."*

***

DCI Fields faced yet another difficult morning that Monday in Box Hill Station. He'd only just got used to the idea of mourning his dead colleague Max Carter when he had come to learn of the brutal murdering of Max's wife, daughter and sister-in-law. All over the same weekend as well. This had stunned, shocked and terrified him beyond belief. What the fuck was going on?

The Gloucestershire Police had contacted Fields, since the deceased were close relatives of an officer based at his station. The two teams had then discussed the possibility that the murders were carried out by the same man who had broken into Box Hill and later murdered Dave Shilling whilst in police custody. They had nicknamed him 'the lone wolf' for the purposes of referencing him across their investigations, a moniker that had also made its way into the vocabulary of the mainstream media. The ominous note and the fact that the shell casings found at the home were from the same type of gun used during the break-in at Box Hill made this the most obvious theory, but Fields was sceptical. Why would someone feel the need to do this when Max Carter himself was already dead? That just didn't seem to make sense.

Other officers would hypothesise that the killer might not have realised that Max was already dead before he carried out the murders. The tone of the note even suggested that he originally thought Max might have been at this house with his wife and daughter. Maybe this lone wolf was just sick and hell-bent on a twisted idea of getting 'even' in some way, or setting an example to any of his other 'targets' that might be out there. In any case, the lone wolf was considered suspect number one in these latest murders.

Fields finished work that day seriously considering doing a runner from his open cases, his job and his friends in the Masons. Things were spiralling beyond his control. Since ordering the illegal hit on Michael Harding, he had gained and lost custody of his second target as part of a sensational front-page prison breakout and now experienced the death of his colleague, friend, co-conspirator and 'shooter' in Max Carter. Not to mention Carter's wife and child. The blood on his hands was getting harder and harder to wash off.

As he closed the front door in his car and looked down at his phone, he saw he had two missed calls from a number that Charles Creedy had previously used to contact him. What did that prick want?

Fields was pretty upset with Creedy at this point. He hadn't trusted his slimy, mysterious aura right from the beginning. Now, after convincing Fields that using Dave Shilling's credit card as bait was a good way to lure out the lone wolf and therefore hopefully the hacker, an important police witness and a policeman were dead with neither suspect being caught.

Fields let the phone ring for about thirty seconds before reluctantly swiping right on the screen to answer.

"You've got some fucking nerve, Creedy."

A few seconds' pause followed.

"John, I apologise. I couldn't make today's briefing."

"Of course you couldn't — I wouldn't have shown my face in there either today. What a complete fucking disaster. I got nothing out of your little plan but more bad news."

"Now hold on, John. It didn't exactly work out for me either did it? My lone wolf got away and we lost that witness. That's on me too you know."

Creedy didn't sound anywhere near as cocky or confident as he usually did on the phone. Fields found this both relieving and concerning at the same time. Relieving in that Creedy appeared to understand the gravity of the situation. Concerning as it served to confirm how bad everything really was. What he didn't know was that beneath this act of compassion and understanding, Creedy was feeling as excited and cocky as ever.

Fields continued, his voice beginning to wobble under the emotion of the situation.

"Yeah, well this was your bloody idea and now Max is *fucking dead*... and his family... I mean Jesus Christ! His little girl!"

Fields broke down and began crying down the phone. He sobbed and sniffled for a good twenty seconds before either of them talked again.

Still with a put-on and exaggeratedly sincere tone in his voice, Creedy broke the silence.

"I know it's... it's a tragedy. I must admit that it did come as a great shock. Were there any clues at the scene? Any proof that it was our lone wolf that went after them?"

Fields managed to pull himself together before answering Creedy's question, sniffling a few times more.

"Yeah... they were shot with the same type of gun used in the station. There was also this note as well. Everything points to our man. Sick fuck. I don't understand why they had to die as well. Max was already fucking dead; why would you feel the need to..."

Creedy could hear Fields' voice was beginning to wobble once more.

"Listen John, I'll leave you for now. I won't be able to make the briefings for a while. I've got some other business to attend to that's taken priority. You look after yourself, and good luck with the investigations. You're a bloody good copper; I know you'll sort it all out."

Creedy didn't wait for a response before he ended the call. He hung up and turned around to address his head scientist, thirty-nine-year-old Alexi Ivanov.

Alexi stood at around five nine, and he was dressed in a scruffy, ill-fitting green shirt and black suit trousers. He wore a pristine all-white lab overcoat over the top with a set of pens tucked into the right pocket.

The scientist pushed his glasses back up onto his nose and flicked away some of the curly, dirty-looking mousey brown hair that hung down to his shoulders. He was staring at Creedy in anticipation of what he had to say.

"They bought it. Our man is the main suspect in the murders of subject's family."

Alexi smiled as he excitedly chewed his gum. He wasn't really the talkative type — his work in the laboratory was his form of self-expression.

Creedy continued to gloat.

"So predictable, aren't they? Just dangle a bit of circumstantial evidence and they'll bite if it makes their lives easier. Alexi, go and check on our subject. Let's make sure he's stable and get him ready. We can start the testing first thing tomorrow morning."

Alexi nodded and quickly left the 4m by 3m meeting room that the two men were standing in. He walked down to the end of a hospital-like corridor and opened the last grey door on the right. This led into a room, roughly the size of a studio flat. It was long and narrow and contained one large, mechanically adjustable hospital bed in the corner by a small window. The not so impressive view was out to another corridor on the other side of the room.

The bed was connected to a variety of high-tech equipment, some of which was commonplace in a modern hospital: an ECG and ventilator on the left, a dialysis machine and IV drip on the right. There were other, more unusual apparatus spread around the area, the most prominent of which was a tall black tower on the right-hand side of the bed with thick translucent tubes connected to it. You could see rows of small vials of multicoloured chemicals through various little fibreglass windows near the top of the machine. All of this equipment was electronically wired to a large computer terminal around two metres to the right of the bed. The thick, reinforced cabling was spread messily across the floor from the bed to the terminal, with two large monitors displaying a stream of scrolling statistical information.

Alexi walked over to the terminal and immediately began clicking and typing away, analysing the various data points that the machines had been monitoring in his brief absence. He smiled, pleased with himself and his subject since everything was looking in order. After double-checking the stats one more time, he walked over and looked down at his patient, resting his hand on the side of the bed.

"You've got a big day ahead of you tomorrow my friend. I hope we are both ready for it."

Of course, there was no response. The man lying heavily sedated, connected to the various machines through an inordinate number of tubes and wires, was the supposedly 'dead' Max Carter.

CHAPTER EIGHTEEN

Very soon after hearing the news of Dave Shilling's death, Tim had started to wonder what would become of the arrangement in Epping-255. The two people that his guest had been hell-bent on finding had been found and both of them murdered. What now?

Less than forty-eight hours had gone by before Fox had approached Rolfe at his desk and given him the news that he would be leaving the following morning, on the Monday. No mention of where he would go or what he would do next but given his prior admission that killing these two men was the only thing he was living for, Rolfe didn't have a good feeling about him leaving.

Once Tim was on his own again in this bunker, he'd be back to square one... square *minus* one, even. He would now have even more crimes to add to his growing sheet, including one of the most controversial custody breakouts in modern times and the involvement in several murders. At the same time, he knew that without Fox's initial intervention at the police station, he would be dead anyway. In any case, he didn't like the thought of being left alone again, no matter how unsettling and, frankly, surreal the existing company he had was.

Rolfe was the first one up that Monday morning. He had poured himself his usual milky bowl of Coco Pops and sat down in front of his computer. As he cycled through the various searches and hacker chatter that formed part of his daily routine, he was distracted by a breaking story from one of the major news sites.

"**The identities of the three bodies found by Gloucestershire Police in the early hours of this morning have now been released. Thirty-four-year-old Connie Brooks and her thirty-two-year-old sister, Sarah Carter, were found dead along with Sarah's three-year-old daughter. Police are now reporting that all three appear to have died** from gunshot wounds, but the official coroner's report is yet to be carried out.

"The authorities are looking into a potential, disturbing link between these murders and recent events here in the capital. Sarah Carter is the estranged wife of Met Police Officer Max Carter, who was himself of course tragically murdered on Friday. PC Carter was protecting a high-profile suspect who was being held under armed guard at an undisclosed location.

"DCI John Fields, part of the team looking into the murders, was quoted as saying, 'This is an absolute tragedy for all of us working in the police force. We are still coming to terms with the loss that we are all feeling and remain one hundred percent committed to finding those responsible.' When questioned on the potential link between the murder of Officer Carter and that of his wife and child, Fields admitted that 'It seemed far too much of a horrific coincidence for the two events not to be connected.' He went on to add that it was still very early days in the investigation."

Tim's appetite for his breakfast was immediately extinguished. He felt nauseous and deeply uncomfortable. He put his cereal bowl to one side and drew his chair in closer to the computer screens, scouring over the information once more to make sure that he had *really* just read all of that.

Behind him, Fox wandered into the room with a small black duffel bag packed, ready to leave the bunker. He was topless with a black T-shirt thrown over his shoulder. Without saying anything to Tim, he walked over to the far corner of the main room, dropped his bag and began inspecting his bullet-wound scars in the large mirrors on the wall.

Rolfe clicked away, reading the same information from various news sources, feeling sadder, sicker and angrier every time he did. He glanced over at Fox several times, gritting his teeth in frustration.

Just as Fox turned around and held his T-shirt out in front of him, about to pull it over his head, Rolfe stood up from his computer and threw his chair back in an anger.

"I'm not having any part in this kind of shit! A fucking kid! What could she have possibly done to deserve that?"

Rolfe stood staring furiously over at Fox, pointing at his computer with one finger extended from his tightly clenched, shaking fist.

Fox stopped what he was doing and threw his T-shirt back over his right shoulder. He calmly walked over to Rolfe, who instinctively took a couple of steps back. Rolfe's outrage in the moment meant he wasn't as terrified of Fox, but the sight of the badly scarred, insanely muscular torso bounding towards him provoked a primal reaction to move away.

Fox stopped about a metre in front of Rolfe and turned to look at the computer monitors. He spent about ten seconds reading the information on the screens before turning back to face Rolfe. The old Jay would have been shocked and appalled to read this information, but his ability to feel compassion and empathy had been severely compromised. Granted, this was a tragedy, and one that appeared to be connected to events that he had been directly involved in. But his humanity was all but diminished and his sense of purpose was no more. He was spent.

"Looks like someone wanted to tie up a loose end," Fox said mutely.

Fox began to turn and walk away.

Rolfe exploded.

"They are saying this was you? *Was* this fucking you? I can't be helping someone to do this kind of shit. I have a daughter that I want to someday see again for fuck's sake. This is completely *evil*!"

Fox immediately swung back round, walked over and grabbed Rolfe by the throat. Rolfe instantly raised both hands and began trying to prise Fox's hand off his neck, gargling as he struggled to draw a breath.

Fox's eyes seemed to turn an even deeper shade of blood red as he drew himself closer to Rolfe. The two men stared at each other, wide-eyed and with a ferocious intensity.

"Not that I have to justify myself to you. But I have not left this place since I came back from killing the scumbag you helped me find. I asked you to help me find two people. You have, and now they are both dead. I am finished now."

Fox gestured towards the computer screens.

"Anything further, you're going to have to figure out on your own."

With that, he let go of Rolfe, who immediately hunched over and gasped for air.

Fox turned away once more and began walking towards the far corner of the room in preparation for leaving the bunker for good. What he had said did make sense. Rolfe's systems would have alerted him to the fact that Fox had left the bunker and even if Fox had managed to somehow cheat them, was it even possible for him to have gone all the way out to that location, commit these murders and come back in the time frame? And *why* would he have done that?

It was then that Rolfe saw it for the first time. The tattoo of the outline of a fox on Jay's left shoulder blade. For a split second, he couldn't remember where he had seen it before. But then it came back to him. His eyes widened and his jaw dropped as the shock settled in.

Fox walked about three more steps before Rolfe called out to him, "That tattoo... is that how you can... do those things?"

Fox stopped walking instantly. He had never known anything about the origins of that tattoo. He turned back to face Rolfe once more.

"What exactly do you mean?"

Rolfe didn't know whether to be cautious about what he said next. Did Fox really know exactly what he meant and was this perhaps a test to see if he could leave him alive? The two men stared at each other awkwardly for a few seconds.

In a quivering, sheepish tone, Rolfe replied, "Never mind... I shouldn't have... I didn't mean anything by it. I thought it was something else."

Fox took a couple of more steps back towards Rolfe, intrigued by what he was obviously hiding from him.

"Do you know something about that marking? Have you seen it somewhere before?"

Rolfe nervously shook his head. Fox continued to stare dead into his eyes.

"My earliest memories are with that marking already etched into my skin. I have no past to couple it with it, no explanation for it being there. Are you telling me you know what it is?"

Rolfe was confused but again, his gut instinct was to believe what this man was telling him. Fox really *didn't* seem to know where the tattoo had come from. He really *didn't* seem to know how or why he was the way he was.

Another moment or two passed before Rolfe walked over to his computer and took a seat, glancing back over at Fox as he took every single step.

Within a few seconds of clicking and typing, Rolfe had a high-definition version of the logo on Fox's shoulder blade up on the screen. The logo on his body had faded and stretched significantly over time but the one on screen was fresh and sharp, revealing colour and detail that previously couldn't be seen. Much like on his body, the logo displayed the outline of a fox's head as if viewed from the front. The fox was a light grey in colour and had been drawn with sharp edges, lacking any facial details or even a mouth. Its eyes were also shaded a deep black, adding to the overall morbid and aggressive tone of the image. Another detail that was not included on Jay's tattoo was an inscription in Russian written below the image on the screen:

'За чем пойдёшь, то и найдёшь.'.

Fox's eyes widened. This was the first time in his life that he had seen an image that even closely resembled his mysterious marking. He pointed to the Russian text under the image.

"What does it mean?"

Rolfe looked down at the floor as he effortlessly translated the words on the screen without having to look anything up.

"As you sow, so shall you reap."

Fox turned to him in surprise, acknowledging that he must know a lot more about this logo.

"What does this logo represent? An organisation? A person?"

Rolfe was once again quick with the answer.

"An army."

He sighed as he pulled Michael Harding's old chair out from under the other side of the desk and gestured for Fox to take a seat.

Fox declined.

Rolfe looked once more at his workstation and then back up at Fox.

"Are you sure this isn't some kind of test? If you want to find out what I know... you can assume I know everyth—"

"Just continue... please."

Fox raised his voice, cutting Rolfe off mid-sentence.

Rolfe took another deep breath and swung his chair back round to face his workstation. He began reading from a selection of notes on his screen.

"The logo is from a small division of the Soviet Army that existed in the late eighties. It was given the moniker 'лиса' which is, of course, 'fox' in English. They were an exceptional group of soldiers put together as an elite unit to handle high-risk missions, often 'off the record'. They were like a sub-division of the SAS or the Royal Marines in this country.

"Anyway… in 1988, the unit was deployed to Afghanistan for the third time as part of the Soviet intervention in the Afghan civil war. The first two times their missions were a success, with only one reported casualty.

"Unfortunately, the third time they were sent out was to be their last. Some speculate that there was an intelligence leak, others think that they just got unlucky. In any case, they were ambushed by a group of heavily armed Mujahideen in the middle of their extraction. Officially, no one from the Fox Unit survived the attack that day and the remains that were later recovered from the site were buried as part of a military funeral for all of them at once."

Fox was focused on Tim's every word as the hacker alternated between reading his screen and turning to nervously look up at the man he was delivering this information to.

"But — and this is where it gets interesting — leaked documents and silenced testimonies from the time appear to tell a different story. That story is that, although incredibly badly injured by machine-gun fire and grenade shrapnel, two men from the Fox Unit actually survived the attack on that final mission. They were flown out of the conflict zone and spent a few days in a military hospital before being transferred to an undisclosed 'specialist facility' in the Soviet Union, apparently somewhere near Georgia.

"Now, this specialist facility is the subject of a massive number of conspiracy theories. Michael and I gave this place a good few months of our attention back in the day — I can tell you from what I have seen with my own two eyes, at least *some* of the crazy shit they say about it is probably true.

"Images obtained from US spy satellites in the eighties show a number of buildings in the area that are unaccounted for, and there's divided opinion as to which one is our 'facility'. One thing we do know is what it was built *for*.

"There were a lot of 'races' going on during the Cold War between the East and the West: the first to get to space, the first to the moon, who could build the biggest supply of nukes… those are the ones everyone saw play out on their television sets, served with a side order of 'anti the other side' propaganda. But on top of those, there were more secret, experimental and downright crazy projects being pursued on both sides. And one of them…"

Rolfe paused once more to look over at Fox before he continued. By now his heart was beating so fast he could feel it in his throat. He could hear his own voice begin to shake and his mouth felt completely dry.

"…one of them was the pursuit of chemical and biological human enhancement. They looked at steroids and injections that could give muscles and the metabolism a boost, all the way through to the holy grail: altering human DNA and the genome in the pursuit of creating a sort of 'superhuman'. The vision was that of a soldier that could be faster, stronger, smarter, impervious to chemical attacks even. We've heard of this kind of shit before in comics and bad action movies, but this was the real deal and the first of its kind that has any credible evidence associated with it —"

"What evidence?"

Fox, although captivated by the information being dictated to him, was starting to grow a little bit anxious and interjected.

Rolfe took another deep breath.

"The consensus is that those two badly injured soldiers from the Fox Unit were taken to this facility and heavily experimented on. The reality is that they *should* have died from their injuries, but they were kept alive and pumped full of all manner of chemicals, exposed to radiation and brought in and out of comas as part of the procedures. It was more than the human body was supposed to be able to take.

"The first man, slightly younger than the other at around nineteen, apparently died after three weeks of this experimentation. There're all sorts of rumours online about how many times they resuscitated him and whether he might have tried to escape but the understanding is that he was definitely dead before the second one… before the fire.

"Sometime in early 1989, supposedly around six months after these men were brought to the facility, something went horribly wrong. Maybe an explosion, maybe arson or maybe even a deliberate attempt to cover up what had been going on there — in any case, there was a very big fire. According to the classified documentation of the time, the vast majority of the scientists, soldiers and administrators stationed there died in that fire, along with their last surviving test subject from the Fox Unit.

"…and this is where it gets even more… disturbing.

"Around a week after the fire that destroyed the testing facility, a team of soldiers were sent to a village in the north of modern-day Chechnya."

Fox looked up from the floor as a shiver ran down his spine. Rolfe noticed this and paused for a second before continuing.

"This was apparently the village that their second test subject had once called home. According to the small number of villagers who weren't too scared to talk about the events of that spring day in 1989, the soldiers searched every house in the small settlement, including the home of the test subject's wife. Things had remained pretty peaceful for the first few hours of the search, but as the day drew to a close, the gunfire started. The official files state that a number of villagers were unhappy with the compulsory searches of their properties and attacked the soldiers, catching them off guard.

"Six soldiers were killed along with a single, unidentified man from the village. Again, the documentation around this is limited; it's hard to know what actually happened. But people who've read the files and joined the dots on this — and I include myself in that group, think that the second test subject actually *survived* the large fire at the facility. He survived and returned home before being located by this search party of soldiers a week later and when confronted, he put up a fight. He took a few of them out in the process but ultimately, with their automatic weapons at hand, they overpowered and killed him right then and there. The fact that he was shot over thirty times gives you an idea of how hard this guy was to put down. After they had… you know… done whatever they did to him in that lab…"

Rolfe paused to take a deep breath once more before delivering the final piece of information.

"It's erm… it's never been corroborated anywhere officially and there's no actual proof of it. But there is a myth… an idea… that the test subject's wife gave birth the following year. I honestly don't know if that's true; maybe it was much later on with someone else or maybe she never had a baby at all but…"

Fox was overwhelmed by the information being laid out in front of him. It was the first time since that night on the platform that he had felt any real emotion other than pure, unfiltered rage. There were so many questions left to answer… but the timelines seemed to match up perfectly. He didn't know much of the detail of his early life or even who his biological parents were, but as surreal as it all seemed, this was starting to look like the foundation of that story. This was potentially a shocking and chilling explanation about how Fox had ended up the way he was. His unnatural-looking blood-red eyes, his extremely muscular and skeletal appearance, the 'dead grey' colour of his skin and of course, his seemingly inhuman capabilities. With the extent of his injuries, he should have died that night on that platform, but something had awoken inside of him.

This hacker had been brought in to serve a very specific purpose and up until now, Fox had thought that purpose was fulfilled. Fox turned and walked a few steps away from Rolfe to digest the life-changing information that had just been delivered to him.

Rolfe couldn't help but continue.

"Or maybe she *did* give birth. Maybe she was overwhelmed with the fear of someone coming to look for that child one day and decided she had to give him up. Maybe she left a mark on the child so that no matter how far he ended up from home, he would still bear the mark of his father and his sacrifice wouldn't be forgotten."

Fox lowered his head to look at the floor.

"I wonder if she knew he would grow into such… a monster."

Rolfe looked on awkwardly from his seated position at the computer. What on earth could he say in this moment? This all seemed so far-fetched but at the same time, it kind of made sense. Rolfe didn't know much about Fox or his backstory, almost nothing in fact. Within minutes of meeting him at the police station that day, however, he knew there was something far beyond normal going on and the various stories of human enhancement that he'd read over the years had almost immediately come into his mind. No normal human could possibly do the things Fox could... or even look the way he did and still be alive. Judging by the logo imprinted on him and his reaction to the story behind it, this was starting to look like the biggest and most important discovery in blackNet's history.

If only Harding were alive to see this, he thought. *This would blow his fucking mind.*

The two men spent the next few minutes in silence. Fox stood staring down at the ground with Rolfe at his computer behind him, nervously typing away. Until just a few minutes ago, Fox had nothing else to focus on, no reason to live. Now with this bombshell of information coming to light, there simply had to be more digging.

He turned back round to face Rolfe.

"What do you know about the soldier?"

Rolfe spun round in his chair once more with an apologetic look on his face.

"Unfortunately, not all that much. I've seen a bunch of different code names thrown around, as you would expect, usually incorporating the word 'fox' after the unit name."

Fox had an immediate follow-up question.

"And the boy's... my mother... is she still alive?"

Rolfe looked down at the floor, in shock at the way the question had been phrased. He couldn't look Fox in the eye.

"I'm sorry I have no idea..."

Fox grunted and looked over at Rolfe's screens, where online discussions around some of the information he had been unveiling were on display.

There were so many questions running through his mind that it was hard to form a cohesive thought. For some years as a young man, he had wanted to trace his family origins and plug in some of the gaps in his history, curious about his early life in the east and who his biological parents were. Even the couple that brought him to this country were something of a mystery. As time went on, though, he had accepted his adopted mother Sonya as his 'mum' and decided that he might want to just leave the past in the past. Besides, none of those people seemed to have wanted him, right? So why waste his time?

This information changed the context of everything and he *needed* to find out more.

"Were there any more of them? Any more... test subjects?" Fox asked.

Rolfe thought for a moment.

"Well... I know there were equivalent projects started in the US, China and here in the UK all around the same time. They were all trying to spy on each other, all racing to be the first ones to achieve something ground-breaking. There's nothing to suggest that any of them achieved any success... but there was a rumour of a project in the UK, dubbed 'Free Spirit' that may have eventually got close. It was supposedly started a lot later, in 2001, and by then these shadowy organisations had got a lot better at covering their tracks digitally."

Another awkward silence followed the inconclusive answer. Rolfe wanted Fox to know that he was equally keen to find out more.

"Listen, give me a little time on this and I'll do some more digging for you, OK? A few days' worth of looking around, running some searches, I might be able to fill in some more blanks. It's what I do best."

Rolfe looked over at Fox and cracked his knuckles with a serious expression on his face. There was still a part of him jumping up and down inside with the childish excitement of having another project to work on.

Fox turned away once more.

"I can't offer you anything... not even your safety after this..."

Rolfe replied, "Hey, I haven't forgotten that you saved my life back there at the police station. I can't give you any guarantees either, but I can promise you that I will try to get this information for you. You deserve to know more about all of this... and it's the kind of thing that Michael and I got in the game for in the first place."

Fox simply nodded and began walking over to the 'gym' area of the bunker.

Rolfe suddenly remembered how this long conversation had started.

"Listen... about that other stuff before, those murders. I'm sorry that I didn't just ask you first, instead of blindly believing what they were saying on the news. I didn't even take a second to think about it and I was out of line."

Rolfe paused for a second.

"...But this copper... and then his wife and child... some sick bastard has done this and from the looks of things, tried their hardest to make it look like it was you. Why would they do that?"

Fox stopped in his tracks in reaction to the question.

"I don't know. But the man who shot your friend had bad intentions, I could see it in his eyes. He wasn't doing the work of a policeman. We might want to find out who he was *really* working for."

Rolfe looked around, nodding as he contemplated Fox's words. He started to think aloud once more.

"They killed Michael, damn near killed me and then the same policeman who shot my friend is sent to try to take you out. Then he and his family are murdered. There is some next-level shit going on here, I can feel it. I need to get to the bottom of it all."

Fox acknowledged with a nod.

"Do whatever you have to do."

Rolfe returned a serious, stern frown in agreement.

"Right. I was prepared to let Michael die in vain because I was too much of a coward... The blood trail has got a hell of a lot thicker and I don't know if I can look myself in the mirror if I do the same now."

Tim had never wanted to give up on finding out who was behind Harding's murder in the first place, but the fear of being on his own and messing with the kind of people who were prepared to kill was far too daunting. The seemingly safer option of handing himself in to the authorities had led him straight back into the same chair. This time, however, he had more information and reassurance in the fact that if someone came looking for him now, they would likely have to go through Fox.

Rolfe turned back to face his computer, stretched his neck on either side, and began working once more.

CHAPTER NINETEEN

The heavily guarded 'Research and Development' building stood about half a mile from the A1(M) motorway, just outside North London. It was surrounded by well-maintained open fields at the front and sides, with a private access road running round to the back. Tall trees and an intimidating, thick, spiked fence ran around the perimeter of the surrounding fields, with a manned security post near the beginning of the long road entrance.

The building was divided into several, well-segregated sections. A portion of it was being used for government-funded research, such as the testing of vaccines on animals, for example. This and other 'above board' uses of the building gave the section that Creedy and his team had been assigned some cover.

These types of buildings were naturally secured and employees were continually reminded to not speak openly about the nature or location of their work. Creedy's team inhabited a rear quarter of the building which, like the other sections, was completely contained with its own private entrance, car park and staff accommodation.

A solid week of invasive experimental procedures had now been carried out on Max Carter's body at the private facility. Creedy and his team had started with the use of some of the better-known chemicals in their inventory to speed up tissue recovery and increase Max's muscle strength and metabolism as he lay unconscious in the hospital bed.

The first risky procedure had been the infusion of plasma taken from one of their previous test subjects who had shown the most promise — 'most promise' being a relative term, since all the previous test subjects that had entered this facility under similar circumstances to Max Carter had died.

Max responded very well to all the treatments and only days into the 'trial', the team were ready to move on to the use of the main experimental substance. This complex chemical compound had been given the shorthand name 'Indigo2020' in reference to its deep, vibrant colour and the year of this latest iteration.

The pursuit of a test subject that could survive this infusion was one that had taken the team years. Tweak after tweak had got them closer and closer, but to their frustration and disappointment, never quite close enough.

This time was a little different though. This time they had the blood samples collected from the broken window at the Royal Open Hospital and an additional sample from the balcony of the East London apartment complex. The blood of someone who had drawn the attention of Charles Creedy and in doing so, inadvertently reignited the flame under his 'Free Spirit' project that was on the verge of having its funding pulled. The blood, of course, belonging to the long-lost son of the 'Fox Commander', Jayden Amare Fox.

Studying the cells from the blood samples and how they interacted under different conditions in the laboratory gave the scientists some new ideas on how to tweak their substance. This led to them finding new ways to both increase its effect along with the chance of their patient surviving. The information in those blood samples made up for about another ten years' work. They couldn't believe what they were looking at — in terms of what they had been trying to achieve as part of the Free Spirit project, it was the ultimate assist.

Max was given dose after dose of Indigo2020 in gradually increasing amounts as they monitored his body's reaction. Part of the activation involved exposure to levels of radiation that would normally be lethal to a human being. Quite a few of the early patients had died at this stage, Max breezed through it.

The end of the first week signalled the completion of the first phase of the process. This was officially the furthest anyone had made it in this programme and it was by the far the fastest the team had moved through the various procedures.

As a result of the accelerated recovery time the Indigo2020 had enabled in Max's body, the broken bones were healing rapidly. Moreover, his spine damage was no longer detectable and the bruised and battered muscles were repairing and rebuilding at a rate that was 'off the chart'. Although he had been placed in an induced coma for the duration of his time at the facility, Max's brain scans were showing massive signs of improvement as well. His resting heart rate was up at 80 bpm, another by-product of the DNA-alerting substance.

Creedy once again stood watching over Max's peaceful looking sleep as his 'number one', Alexi, gave him the overview that he had dreamed of hearing for years.

This was poetic. Just when things had been on the verge of collapsing and his so-called 'old friends' in the security organisations had turned their backs on him, this breakthrough had come to save the day. Prior to this, the project and the department itself had been slated for complete disbandment, partly due to moral concerns and partly in favour of other, more modern pursuits. Robotics and AI were far more fashionable areas now and the 'super soldier' idea was becoming a little bit outdated, especially considering the years of research without any concrete results.

Once Alexi had finished giving him today's low-down of the tests and their results, Creedy wasted no time in barking out the next orders.

"Very good. Let's continue to monitor him and get him awake as soon as possible — I suppose I can take care of giving him the awful news about his family... better make sure he's properly restrained when I do eh?"

Creedy leant over to Alexi, sporting another one of his unsettlingly slimy smiles. Alexi nodded and laughed giddily. He was one of the few people that actually enjoyed Creedy's sick sense of 'humour'.

"So we wake him up, check everything's OK, have a little chat with him and then put him back under for the final round of chemical treatments, correct?" Creedy asked.

Alexi nodded once more.

"And at that point I assume we will know for sure whether all of this is working and having... the desired effect?"

Again, Alexi nodded, grinning widely from ear to ear like a child. He added in a nasally, mousey tone, "I think we can be quite confident of that already sir."

Creedy was on cloud nine.

"This could be a momentous occasion, Alexi. We just might have made history here. After years and years of struggling, being told it can't be done, being told we have to give up. We might have finally cracked this bloody thing after all!"

Creedy's fists were clenched tight behind his back as he gritted his teeth, almost trembling with excitement. He turned once more to look at Max. Tomorrow morning they would wake him up and take this operation to its next, even darker phase.

"Right, I'm off. I've other business to attend to. Well done, it's wonderful to see everything going to plan here. Remember though, we are to keep all of this to ourselves, yes? I trust the others understand the importance of doing so. We don't want this getting anyone too excited before we know we have something concrete."

After another acknowledging nod from Alexi, Creedy walked through the long, winding hallways of the facility and past security to let himself out. All the way, he pondered the intricacies of how exactly he was going to play his next move.

Given the lack of support and the need to fight for his project's existence, Creedy's faith and morals had gradually been 'recalibrated' over the years. He had come into this initiative as a middle-aged general from the army, relishing the opportunity of being assigned to an exciting, new, potentially world-altering project. He was selected because of his no-nonsense approach to leading a team and his proven track record in the army of getting results where he needed to, without compromise. His superiors also knew they would need to select someone who was particularly suited to working in a top-secret environment and unlikely to have any reservations about some of the more 'questionable' activities that went on there. Charles 'Hard and Sleazy' Creedy had always fitted that bill.

Now, after almost twenty years of being involved in the project in one way or another, he was acutely aware of the fact that his time in this position was likely nearing its end. Eventually the new 'movement' would probably get what they wanted and either can this project entirely or remove it from under him. A combination of his bitterness and his relentless drive to succeed was not going to let that happen without there at least being some repercussions. This was now about putting himself in a position that he and the few associates that he had left could take advantage of.

Step one was still achieving the core aim of this project, to make a genetically altered 'super soldier'. The focus was then going to have to immediately return to locating and capturing this 'lone wolf' character that had both complicated and improved Creedy's professional life.

The blood had offered some clues and helped his scientists make quick progress, but they would need to *really* study the subject to understand exactly what was going on inside his body.

The witness statements from the murders at Bristol Hall had been sent to Creedy by an old colleague shortly after they had been taken by police. As soon as he had read them and put them together with the Hackney South crime scene photos from days earlier, he knew there was a chance that he was looking at a real-life example of something many considered to be a myth. The subsequent events at the police station that he had himself visited only solidified a belief that the blood samples later confirmed to be true.

The 'lone wolf' and his presumed accomplice would need to be found as a matter of priority so that the many outstanding questions Creedy had could be answered. Where was he from? Were there others like him? Who had perfected the technology to get there before Creedy and how had they cracked the human genome? Those were just the starters. Regardless of who else was involved, he would need to study this man further and then 'get rid' of him before anyone else got their hands on him.

***

It was an early start for everyone on Creedy's team the next day. He was the last to arrive at the facility at just gone seven a.m. on that sunny mid-April morning.

After the morning 'stand-up' was completed and the day's goals discussed, Creedy and Alexi headed over to the kitchen area of the building. They poured themselves a cup of coffee each and made small talk during the walk down to the large room that held their only patient. Two of the more trusted technicians were in the room, adjusting the bed so that it was inclined and Max was sitting up straight.

Thick, metal clamps were screwed on to custom-fitted metal bars at either side of the bed to hold Max's arms and legs firmly in place. These were strong enough to hold thirty men down; they certainly weren't taking any chances. One technician went round them all, clicking them tighter and tighter into place on a ratchet system like a roller-coaster safety harness.

As the technicians steadied Max up and made sure he was held firmly in place, they began carefully removing some of the various medical devices connected to his body, starting with the oxygen mask over his face. Having brought him out of the coma, they had been slowly reducing the amount of anaesthetic being pumped through his blood and he was now breathing completely on his own.

Creedy and Alexi stood directly in front of the bed for a few moments, letting the men do their work while taking the occasional slurp from their paper cups. This would be the first attempt at trying to talk to Max since he had arrived at the facility.

Creedy was getting his speech ready.

"How long until he comes round do we think Alexi?"

Alexi looked at his watch and then over to the terminal at the side of Max's bed.

"Shouldn't be too long at all now. Maybe five, ten minutes. We have reduced the dosage slowly to bring him out nice and calm."

Creedy nodded.

"Let's make sure we can put him straight back under if we need to, eh?"

Alexi sniggered in agreement.

The next five minutes were quiet but the tension in the room was overwhelming. The technicians quickly left after completing their duties, leaving Creedy and Alexi staring in silence at the marvel in front of them.

Max Carter was now a very different-looking man. His skin had taken on a dull-grey tone from head to toe, to the point that he looked either seriously ill or dead. He also looked like he had lost an extreme amount of weight. Every part of his body was lean and extremely toned. His cheeks dipped in at the sides, giving him an almost malnourished look. The veins in his arms and neck seemed to protrude from the skin and had taken on a darker, purplish tone. His whole body looked like it was constantly perspiring, covered with a sort of wet-looking glaze. This man did not look well at all. Of course, the statistics from the latest round of tests suggested otherwise.

Eventually, his darkened eyelids began fluttering open and his head rolled left to right as he murmured and grunted into consciousness.

"Leave us, Alexi," Creedy said.

Creedy's chief scientist looked at him with a concerned expression, surprised and slightly disappointed at being asked to leave the room at this crucial moment. He certainly didn't want to argue, however, and after a few seconds he obliged and walked out.

Max spent another twenty seconds or so fully coming round to consciousness. The ECG provided the soundtrack as the beeping increased in frequency with Max becoming more and more awake. This only added to the intensity of the moment. Creedy could feel his own heart start to race, something that did not happen frequently at all.

Max suddenly locked his eyes open, staring directly ahead at Creedy. His bluey-green irises had darkened to the point where they now looked black, blending in with his pupils.

His vision was still adjusting and for the first few seconds, the room wobbled and blurred in and out of focus. His hearing fluctuated between very clear and heavily muffled as it eventually began to align. His brain was now calibrating to a new, greatly enhanced version of the senses and it hurt, almost immediately.

Still starting directly ahead, Max began panting and clenching the muscles in his body as he tried to make sense of his surroundings. With his upper body completely exposed, Creedy could fully appreciate the striking definition and size of Max's muscles. They no longer formed the same pattern as 'regular human' muscles and were unsettling and intimidating to even look at.

Exhausted from the effects of waking up from a week-long coma, Max managed to pant out his first words through heavy breathing.

"Whe… Where am I?"

Creedy put on his best 'sincere smile' before answering Max's question.

"You are in a safe place now Max, a hospital. We've been looking after you here for a little while. How are you feeling?"

"I feel… I feel drained."

"That's only natural; you've been through a number of life-saving procedures. I understand you must be tired and a little confused… Do you remember what happened to you?"

Max looked down to the left and right, closing his eyes and frowning as he tried desperately to recall the last thing he remembered before waking up in that bed. Brief flashing images began to paint a very faint and patchy picture. Creedy would happily be filling in the blanks.

Max responded, "I was… I was chasing someone on a rooftop… we started fighting and then… then it all goes black."

"That sounds about right. You were assigned as an armed guard for a very important witness. He was in the process of giving the police some crucial statements relating to organised crime in East London. Do you remember that?"

"I think so… I think I remember we were waiting for someone to com—"

Max cut himself off as he realised he might have been revealing a little too much information about the nature of his orders on that day. Creedy was quick to reassure him.

"It's OK Max. I'm a friend of DCI Fields' — he's told me all about the details of his operation and the relationship that the two of you have."

Creedy cut to the chase.

"I think it's best you know the details. You were attacked, Max. As a matter of fact, you were savagely beaten. You were thrown off the top of a ten-storey building and left for dead.

"After you had heroically chased down and attempted to capture a murderer who had just killed a witness and injured another officer, the bastard caught you off guard. As far as we can tell, the two of you fought and he got the upper hand; seems you'd been injured quite badly before you even fell all that way down."

Max looked down at the hospital bed in front of him, visibly hurt by the information being given to him.

Creedy continued his impassioned explanation.

"He showed no mercy; he could have stopped, but he wanted to finish the job and add you to his list of killings. Those people at the train station, the Bristol Hall murders, the Royal Open Hospital murder and then this…

"When the other officers finally found you, your pulse was faint and you were on the verge of death. To be honest, it was a miracle that you had survived the fall in the first place. When they took you in at the hospital and started examining you, it would have been quicker to count the number of bones that *hadn't* been broken in your body. On top of that you had a punctured lung, spinal damage and a head injury that looked like it might have caused permanent, severe brain damage. You were in a coma, Max, and without something drastic being done, there's no way you would have woken up."

Max looked up at Creedy, slightly confused by his last statement.

"Something… drastic?"

At that point Max held his hands out in front of him, as far as the restraints would let him, and for the first time saw some of the changes his body had undergone. The pale, cold, damp skin on his arms wrapped with the thick protruding veins looked almost alien to him. He looked down further to his equally pale but also thinner and more defined torso. The shock of it all made him instantly feel sick.

Creedy continued, "Yes. You see this is a very 'specialised' facility. The doctors and scientists here focus on some very *experimental* treatments that some might go as far as to call controversial. You were past the point of regular care Max; you were almost certainly paralysed and you couldn't breathe on your own. They were ready to switch the life support machines off before we stepped in."

Max began to look more and more agitated and uncomfortable with what was being explained to him.

Creedy reached into his inside jacket pocket, pulled out a small tablet PC and began swiping and tapping it. He walked over to the bed before turning it round so that the screen faced Max. He began swiping through image after image of the badly injured officer in the hours after he had initially arrived at the hospital. The images were shocking for anyone to look at, let alone the person depicted in them. Even from the first couple of photos, taken from a few metres away, he could see the extent of his own injuries.

As Creedy continued to swipe, the images being displayed became more and more graphic. In one of them, a thick plastic neck brace was holding Max's massively swollen head in place and two thick tubes were lodged into his throat to aid his breathing. The next two slides showed a compilation of the X-ray photos taken from all over his body, with the broken and crushed areas of bone and damage to his spine circled in thick red lines.

After letting Max process the gruesome slideshow for a few seconds, Creedy pulled the tablet back and slid it into his inside pocket.

"This was the only option left to you, and having heard of your bravery and courage in pursuing this man in the face of great danger, I wanted to make sure we did everything we could to help you."

Shellshocked, exhausted and confused, Max responded, "Thank you... I suppose?"

Creedy nodded and smiled in response.

"I hope you understand, Max, the treatments that have been given to you are classified beyond top secret in terms of the public's knowledge of their existence. This is essentially a military facility and I'm afraid that until we can fully understand the effects that our variety of procedures have had on you... it's somewhere you are going to have to call home for a while."

Max looked down at the bed and nodded. He glanced once more to either side of the bed and his restrained arms and legs.

"Why am I... shackled like this? Is it really necessary?"

Creedy chuckled in an attempt to make light of it.

"That's just a precautionary measure. As a result of your treatments, injuries that should take several months to heal are now on track to heal in weeks. Or even less. It's pretty ground-breaking stuff and we don't yet fully know what the physical and mental side effects might be... you understand?"

Once again Max nodded. This wasn't a particularly pleasant place to wake up and his mind was extremely foggy, but from what he remembered and from the story being told to him, he was grateful to at least be alive. It was baffling and surreal that he could go from the condition shown in those pictures to his current state in one week.

Suddenly he remembered.

"My daughter... Can I get a phone in here? I want to call my ex... my wife. Does she know about what happened to me? Does she know where I am?"

Max was fidgeting around the bed anxiously as he reeled off the questions.

Creedy looked at the floor as he walked to the edge of the bed. This is where the performance he had been rehearsing for a week could now finally be put on display.

"Max ... there's no easy way for me to tell you this. From what we can piece together, it seems that following your altercation on the rooftop, this sick and twisted 'lone wolf' character was unaware that he had left you so severely injured.

"We can only assume that he felt as though there was some kind of score to settle between the pair of you. While you lay dying in hospital, he went looking for you with settling that score in mind. When he didn't find you, he apparently changed tack and went after the closest thing to you, Max. Your family.

"Your wife and your daughter... they were murdered. There are no words I can use that can express how sorry I am."

Max's first reaction was to laugh nervously at what Creedy had just said. This was all so surreal and ridiculous, surely? Was this some kind of elaborate nightmare? A top-secret facility, saved from the edge of death and now this? Who *was* this guy anyway and how could Max trust anything he was being told?

Like anyone who receives bad news that they just don't want to believe, his response was to go into a state of denial.

"What the fuck are you talking about? Just get me my fucking phone in here and let me call my wife and talk to my daughter. I'm tired of listening to this."

The frequency of the beeping coming from the ECG monitor in the background continued to increase.

Creedy turned around and switched on the small flat-screen television that was mounted on the wall, just to the left of the door. It was already primed to play a news clip that had aired five days ago — the breaking report after the bodies of three females had been found and identified as the immediate family of 'dead' policeman Max Carter.

As Max watched the aerial shots of his sister-in-law's house in Gloucester and read the scrolling text underneath, his whole world shattered in front of his eyes.

The screams of pain could be heard from all areas of the building. The walls and windows seemed to vibrate with the intensity of the sound.

Alexi and his assistant started running down the hall towards the room to make sure everything was OK.

As Max continued to scream, cry, hyperventilate and roar in anger, Creedy could see the white in his eyes beginning to turn blood red. The metal restraints that were holding his arms and legs in place were beginning to visibly bend as Max exerted all of his now superhuman strength trying to burst out of them.

Creedy stood perfectly still with a solemn look on his face as he continued to watch the TV screen with Max. He was finding it hard not to smile as all of this was going on, getting a sick enjoyment out of how well his perfectly laid plan was unfolding in front of him.

After a few more seconds, Alexi and his assistant burst in through the door and ran over to the control terminal on the right of Max, who barked at them with a ferocious and terrifying growl. The veins on his neck and face looked on the verge of exploding and his skin had turned a hot blood-red. Alexi immediately began administering a cocktail of strong sedatives through one of the IV lines connected to Max's body and within seconds, his outburst of rage became less intense.

In less than twenty seconds, Max was unconscious again. Alexi froze in fear as he saw the state of the metal restraints and how bent they had become. He looked over at Creedy, who smiled back in acknowledgement.

"Even stronger than we thought, Alexi. You're a fucking genius."

Alexi's terrified facial expression quickly turned into a cautiously proud smile. The pair were comfortable with completely turning a blind eye to the more worrying brain activity readings that had been displayed on one of the monitors and laughed as Creedy turned to leave the room once more. He shouted another order from down the hallway.

"Let me know as soon as the next round of treatment starts, Alexi."

CHAPTER TWENTY

Charles Creedy was not the type of character who liked business meetings of any sort. Firstly, he didn't really like the concept of sharing his ideas or the details of any of his projects with anyone else as a matter of principle. He only really trusted himself with that kind of information. He also was not a fan of working 'as a team'. If there was a shortcut to take; if there was a way he could put himself in a better position through an alternate route, he would take it. This was especially true as he had gotten older and his patience had all but disappeared.

Creedy's least favourite meeting was easily the virtual conference call that took place roughly twice a year with representatives from the various security agencies that contributed their funds and resources to his projects. They had these meetings with all of the 'initiatives' that they funded — both to track the progress of ongoing projects and ultimately decide whether or not to continue funding them. With Creedy's endeavours continually under scrutiny, it was always an awkward conversation. Today's meeting, he hoped, would be the last one he would have to attend.

The general format of the meeting involved Creedy joining an online teleconference from his agency-issued laptop, passing through a number of security protocols along the way. The screen would then divide into somewhere between six and ten small squares. Two or three of these would contain the faces of 'analysts' who would lead the call, with the remaining black squares representing the many silent participants who neither wanted to reveal their names nor their faces.

Today's call had been very similar to the ones that had preceded it. The few friends that Creedy had left in the agencies had bought him another two or three months of operation, maximum. He sat in the meeting receiving question after question but revealing very little, sticking to the line that he and his team were 'close to finding an agent that could significantly aid severely injured operatives' healing time'.

This, of course, did not accurately reflect the real purpose of the substance his team was developing.

No mention of the interest in the 'lone wolf' cases, the collection of the blood samples, the resulting breakthrough or of course, the small matter of his human patient whose family he had authorised to have murdered.

Creedy was in deep, and everything related to this project was going to be kept between him and his team for as long as possible. If those bastards thought they could pull his funding and that he would take it lying down, they had another thing coming.

Another week had passed since Creedy and the team had initially woken Max out of his slumber. Since then, the scientists had brought him in and out of consciousness several times as part of the final stage of the administration of Indigo2020.

The procedures had taken a toll on Max, physically and mentally. The additional week under heavy sedatives had given him plenty of time to mull over the things Creedy had told him. He'd been going around in cycles of intense rage, desperate pain and immense frustration, all while confined and restrained in this 'top-secret facility'.

Max opened his eyes and once again saw the blurry vision of Charles Creedy standing in front of him.

"Good morning, Max. How are you feeling?"

Creedy's voice seemed to echo in Max's mind, shifting in tone as his hearing and vision took a few seconds to stabilise. Having waited for some time to talk to Creedy again, it didn't take him long to find some words.

"I want blood."

Max's demeanour had changed somewhat since the last encounter. Where previously he was dazed, vulnerable and generally unstable, this time he appeared focused and alert.

Creedy pretended to look concerned by Max's comment, but secretly of course, this is exactly what he wanted to hear.

"I know, Max. That's completely understandable. That's why, against the wishes of my colleagues, I wanted to ask you if you would be willing to help me… us… locate and bring in this 'lone wolf'? So we can bring him to justice."

Max was once again quick to respond.

"If I'm the one who finds him… I will fucking kill him."

Creedy nodded with his lips pressed firmly together as if to say, 'I understand'.

"You're at the end of the procedures, Max. I'm sorry if some of your time here has been a bit uncomfortable. If there had been an easier way for us to do this, we would have taken it. Your vital signs are all looking good and the majority of your injuries are close to healing. Amazing, isn't it?"

Max looked off to the side and reluctantly nodded.

Creedy continued, "The next few days will be all about physical rehabilitation — getting a feel for moving around again you know? You might find that as you fully recover… your strength, speed and mental awareness may all be far better than ever. Be cautious with this at first, Max, we don't want you straining yourself. That being said, once you've had some time to adjust and you feel physically ready, you should feel free to experiment. It's good for all of us to know where we stand."

Max interrupted Creedy's flow as he winced.

"I get these headaches… these awful headaches behind my eyes."

Creedy looked over at Alexi, who was standing behind the terminal. The pair of them were still in a state of ignorance over some of the mental side effects that the treatment was appearing to have on Max. His brain activity waves had consistently shown some instabilities and, based on Alexi's initial calculations, the rate of muscle growth and regeneration throughout the body was unlikely to be sustainable. Neither of them wanted to even acknowledge any risk though; this was all going too well to consider taking any precautionary steps. Besides that, they also didn't have the luxury of time on their side. This was probably their best and last shot at getting this right.

Creedy was quick to offer Max some reassurance.

"Those are normal, nothing at all for you to worry about. Your body is going through some adjustments and it will take a little time for everything to level out. Be patient; I know this is a tough time but we both want the same things and I'm confident that we'll come out of this in a better place."

Max sat scowling with his eyes closed, in obvious discomfort from the severity of the headaches he was experiencing. Creedy signalled to Alexi, who then scuttled over to the side of the bed and administered a strong opioid-based painkiller through one of the IV lines.

Creedy added, "We'll give you some medication to help manage this out in the field, Max."

Max looked up at Creedy with a confused expression once more.

"What do you mean 'in the field'?"

Creedy sighed and took another deep breath.

"When you've gone through your rehabilitation and you've got a feel for things, there's a special assignment that we are going to have to ask you to undertake for us. Just one assignment. One hurdle to overcome and we can then focus all of our attention on finding and capturing our 'lone wolf' character."

The mere mention of Jay's moniker sent a tension running through Max's body. All of his muscles immediately tightened as he clenched his fists in anger.

Creedy continued, "This is going to be something that's a little outside the realm of the regular assignments you're used to as a police officer. From what I understand, though, it might be closer to the kind of thing DCI Fields may have asked of you in the past…"

Max immediately appeared less comfortable and looked off to one side as if to completely ignore the accusation.

"Relax, Max. There isn't going to be any judgement made here on the things you might have done in the past. In fact, quite the opposite."

Max looked back at Creedy with a surprised intrigue. Again, Creedy wasted no time in cutting to the chase.

"We can offer you the kind of lifestyle you have yearned for — and quite frankly, earned over the years Max. We can give you a brand-new life. The money, the house, the cars, the women… the power."

"None of it matters without my daughter."

Max butted in once more. A single tear ran down his cold, hard, pale face.

Creedy replied, "Even if it means you can avenge her at the same time? Personally ensure that the sick bastard who done this to you gets what he deserves? That's worth something, surely?"

A teary-eyed, tired and angry Max stared blankly ahead. A few seconds of silence passed.

"What do you want from me?" Max asked.

Creedy took another second to pause before he answered, this time putting on a 'regretful' expression as if he were going to ask for something he didn't really want to ask for.

"Your friend, DCI John Fields. He's a decorated and respected officer in the Met, there's no question of that. I'm sure his colleagues, former and current, would agree that for many years he did a fantastic job and made a real difference.

"Recently, however, his extracurricular activities and antics are causing problems and it's unlikely that his superiors will be able to protect him for much longer."

Max's intrigue quickly turned to a look of frustrated, confused concern. Creedy continued with his 'mission briefing'.

"We know that he has several friends and associates in certain positions and his fingers in all manner of pies. These 'Mason' characters are from a bygone era and their influence isn't what it once was. They are completely panicked at the information that those hackers have uncovered. The very fact that John asked you to do the things he did shows how desperate he was.

"To be clear though, as far as I'm concerned, you were just a soldier following orders. You were doing Fields' dirty work because he is far too much of a coward to even dream of doing it himself."

Creedy paused once more before cutting to the chase.

"John Fields and his interest in the hacker are going to get in our way and draw too much negative attention. He's made his last irresponsible decision. If we are to get some kind of closure on this whole thing, we are going to need to start by removing Fields from the picture entirely."

Max looked even more confused.

"Remove him?"

Creedy nodded with a stern, serious look on his face.

"Yes Max. I think you know exactly what I mean. What favours has he done you anyway? Threw a few thousand in your direction while he sat in that mansion out in Essex smoking cigars? He lets you take all the risk and look what you end up getting in return for your loyalty and hard work. Dragged into a godforsaken mess that's resulted in the people closest to you losing their lives."

Max stared blankly ahead once more, taking in the latest round of 'home truths.' It was a hell of a performance and a believable one that actually raised some valid points from Max's perspective. Of course, the intent and emotion behind it were completely false, but that was another matter.

Creedy had fully established himself as the 'reluctant hero' who had stepped in to save Max's life from the jaws of death. At the same time, he'd given Max another chance to pursue his attacker, the man who supposedly had gone on to kill his wife and daughter. Once he had digested all of the information, Max didn't have to think for very long before deciding upon what should happen next. He would recover, train, and dance to this man's tune if it would lead him to this 'lone wolf'. Killing Fields would only be a minor inconvenience and, as a matter of fact given the way things had unfolded, something that he might actually quite enjoy.

For Creedy, DCI John Fields was simply a loose end that he didn't want to leave untied. Given Max's apparent death in the line of duty, Fields was about to be under some intense cross-examination as to why the operation played out the way it did. Whose idea was it for Dave Shilling to be held in the new apartment complex and who else could have known about it? Why was a credit card in the witness' name used to do something as stupid as order food? It was only a matter of time before Creedy's name started being bandied about in the conversation.

Fields was a tough cookie, but under massive pressure and on the verge of retirement from the police force, it seemed likely that he was going to crack. Creedy couldn't afford to have the content of his conversations with Fields getting into the hands of the authorities. He wanted to be as low on the radar as possible, given the nature of his 'Free Spirit' operation. Aside from all of this, Creedy was excited to see what his new toy could be manipulated into doing and witness the extent of his abilities in the process.

Max's recovery continued to accelerate at a rapid pace. Within a few hours of struggling to walk for the first time in weeks, he could jog a couple of miles on the treadmill. The weights in his small, custom-made gym were being increased every day as the workout regime designed by Alexi was made tougher and tougher. His resting heart rate was continuing to rise and his metabolism was running faster. The team began administering more drugs by day three of the rehabilitation in an attempt to try to control these increases.

Max's reflexes went from 'good' to 'well above average' to 'off the charts' in a matter of days. Tests using virtual reality to simulate incoming projectiles showed that Max's ability to avoid them was higher than should even be possible. Within five days he could run 100m on the treadmill in just over eleven seconds, Olympian territory. His accuracy, strength, speed and power were all rapidly increasing as the bones and muscles in his body continued to heal at a seemingly implausible rate.

With every day of training, exercise and tests, Max would plead with the team to let him out of the facility. He was ready, he insisted, desperately wanting to get out into the world and take his revenge.

The splitting headaches and the muscle spasms were also getting worse, though, despite the increased amount of medication that the team were giving him. This, of course, continued to be ignored in favour of the more promising statistics.

Max looked ever the more monstrous with each session. His chest and abdominal muscles became more and more defined. His skin was looking paler, tighter and moister. His cheekbones became more pronounced and his face appeared thinner, even though his calorie intake was dramatically increasing.

Creedy had stayed at a bit of a distance in those following days, 'letting the scientists do their work'. He thought it best to keep Max focused on his training and give him less opportunity to ask questions. Questions that Creedy might not be able to fabricate a lie quickly enough to answer.

Max had also been informed of the fact that as far as the outside world knew, he was dead. The explanation being that it would be best if this 'lone wolf' and whatever organisation he may be working with were unaware of the fact that Max had survived. The very fact that Max had undergone this experimental treatment made him a walking 'top-secret' project that the world could not know about, until the time was right.

Max didn't care either way. The few things that he'd loved in his old life had been violently taken from him. The freedom of being a ghost with a 'clean slate' was actually welcome. Especially if it meant he was free to exact his revenge.

***

Meanwhile, deep in the Essex woodland, Tim Rolfe and his infamous co-habitant, the 'lone wolf killer', had now spent just shy of a month confined to the strangely homely bunker at Epping-255.

The daily routine continued to follow a fairly predictable pattern: Rolfe spent most of his days at his workstation digging around for more information with Fox either fiercely working out or meditating, patiently waiting for an outcome from the hacker's research.

At Fox's request, Tim had gathered and printed information on the Soviet 'project', as well as any documented information that existed about Jay's biological family. Sadly, there was very little concrete data on either the soldier from the Fox Unit or the woman from the small village who was apparently his wife. Given the nature of *his* job and the fact that *she* was from a very remote part of the world, there wasn't much written down about either of them.

Most of the information that Fox read through consisted of assumptions pieced together from declassified records. Reading it alone at night before he slept left him with a complex blend of emotions. The small part of him that still felt human was warmed by the fact that he could put together an idea of where his life might have begun. But that really was a small part. The overwhelming feeling was one of numbness and anger at the suffering that both of these people had faced. The parents that he would never know.

In parallel, Rolfe's research into the person who had killed his best friend and 'blackNet' co-founder had progressed significantly.

In the days following Harding's shooting, Rolfe had obtained Max's name from police files and carried out some preliminary research. He'd looked into several areas of Carter's life for some clues as to what else he could be involved in: his bank account information, his internet search history and his phone records, primarily. Nothing had really yielded anything fruitful. He had reached the point of considering the option that Officer Carter might have simply made a mistake or just been 'trigger-happy'. Of course, a lot more had happened since then that almost completely removed these scenarios as possibilities.

Using mobile phone location data from the areas that Max Carter was known to have been in, Tim had now succeeded in discovering a 'pay as you go' mobile number that likely belonged to the corrupt officer. One of the biggest giveaways was the fact that all activity related to the phone had ceased since the day the officer had been found mortally injured after falling from that East London rooftop.

Following this discovery, Tim spent hours looking at the various other numbers that were called and messaged from this phone in the hope of finding some clues. He soon hit the jackpot in tracing yet another 'unclaimed' number to its potential owner.

There was only one phone number that Max Carter called from his burner phone that wasn't registered in anyone's name. Looking at the location data of that phone, it seemed it spent a lot of its time either in Box Hill Police Station or a residential area in an Essex village. Running a search of the people who lived within that area and combining it with a search of the staff that worked at Box Hill produced only one overlapping result.

"John Fields… DCI John Fields of the Metropolitan Police."

Fox once again stopped mid-workout and walked over to Rolfe to hear more of what he had to say.

"He's definitely got something to do with all of this. Both the night before Michael's shooting and the day our dead copper was sent to that apartment complex to 'protect' Shilling, a number of calls were made between his and John Fields' burner phones. There's hardly any communication on the dates in between.

"I've looked through the Met's records and the whole idea of moving that witness to those apartments is documented as being on John's orders. It's likely he even picked the team that would be present there."

With a serious, confident and slightly proud tone in his voice, Tim continued to reel off the information he had compiled.

"He's also the only police officer that went to visit Carter in the hospital and looking through both of their social media accounts, I don't think they were exactly close friends.

"This Fields guy also seems to keep some interesting company. Some of the names that came up when I was looking at who he's been exchanging emails and instant messages with are familiar. Pretty sure I've come across them in some of the records Michael and I have uncovered in the past. I need to run through them again, but I think at least one was part of a major organised-crime family."

Fox had heard enough to warrant a visit.

"Perhaps I should go and have a word with him then?"

Rolfe turned round and looked at Fox, caught off guard at how eager he was to act on this information. Fox was quick to pick up on this.

"If our paths had not crossed, I would have died not knowing anything at all about my history, or how I became... like this. If they killed your friend and their aim is to kill you, then they are now *my* enemy."

Fox continued, "There is blood on the streets that they are falsely claiming I have spilt. I want to know why. I have a feeling that the answer will provide me with enough reason to kill every last one of them where they stand."

It never got any easier listening to Fox talk so casually about extreme violence and Rolfe knew from experience that when he said it, he meant it.

The faint sense of identity that Tim had provided Fox with was something that the latter had yearned for his whole life. It changed the context of everything. Only weeks ago, the idea that someone was trying to pin a murder on him wouldn't have even bothered him since his goals were so short-term, and in all likelihood, included his own death. Now, though, the idea made him feel sick with rage. He wasn't under any illusions of being sin-free — quite the opposite, but now he had an identity to uphold and a history to continue uncovering. He carried the symbol of the Fox, just like his father before him. The actions he had carried out were done so out of vengeance and he would not allow whoever these people were to use that in order to cover up their own murderous activities. Nor would he allow them to continue to hunt his unlikely accomplice and friend, Tim Rolfe.

CHAPTER TWENTY-ONE

Saturday, 2nd May.

After many sleepless nights, John Fields had reverted to his usual way of thinking and adopted a more selfish view of his situation as a whole. It was devastating that Max had died executing his orders, and Fields was certainly facing some serious questioning from inside the police force. As far as he was concerned, though, he would now keep his head down on the home stretch to his retirement. The pursuit of Timothy Rolfe was something he would have no choice but to leave to his 'Mason' friends and co-conspirators. After months of elevated anxiety, he was now purely focused on getting himself out of this mess, all the while reassuring himself that everything was going to be OK.

Today had been a fairly typical Saturday. John had spent the morning out on a dog walk through the Essex countryside with Sandra, his wife of ten years. They stopped for lunch at one of the overpriced 'well-to-do' pubs along the way. After walking home, John had video called his twenty-five-year-old son, Michael, who lived down in Brighton with his girlfriend, Georgina. She was carrying John's first grandchild and the family were all very excited, talking about the possible sex of the baby, what they would call him/her and how close to her expected date they all thought the baby might arrive. These kinds of conversations were more than welcome in John's life, a nice bit of positivity sprinkled among the violence and madness.

At five p.m., John walked a mile down the road to a small residential pub, The Builders Arms, to meet his friend Dave for their customary Saturday afternoon pint. The two of them would sit in their usual position at the far left of the bar on the high stools and spend a few hours putting the world to rights over some good, local ale. This was probably the only aspect in which John Fields had stayed grounded in his life. The one thing he never left behind in the pursuit of money and success in his career.

Dave was quite an unassuming man, really. A couple of years older than John at fifty-nine, he'd spent the majority of his working life on the railways. He'd worked a few different jobs in that domain but for the last five years he had been mainly on the platforms; making the announcements, giving people travel advice and manning the ticket barriers. He lived in a middle terrace two-bedroom house about a mile away from the stretch of lush £1.5m houses on John's street. The pair had known each other since they were teenagers, having become friends at a secondary school in Bethnal Green. Dave had a beer belly about two inches thicker than John's, enough to make a chunk of it visibly 'sag' over his belt and stick out from under his Slazenger polo shirt. Wearing the same pair of loose-fitting denim jeans and old Reebok Classics every week, he usually sat on the corner stool at the bar reading the newspaper for the hour or so before his mate John arrived to keep him company.

It was an unspoken acknowledgement that although the two men had come from very similar beginnings in life, John had done a lot better financially. He contrasted Dave's ill-fitting zippers and cheap jeans with his tweed blazers, tapered Levi's and freshly polished brown brogues. A lot of men in Dave's position would have felt jealous of their better dressed, wealthier friend with his younger and more attractive wife. But Dave just wasn't that way inclined. He was a man of far more simple tastes and was happy as long as his family was happy.

The reality of the situation was that over the past year or so, as things had begun to spiral out of control, John had looked at *Dave's* life and felt envious. Envious of the simplicity, of the security. Yes, he might not be able to buy the nicest car or holiday in the Bahamas every year, but at least when he turned the lights out at night, he could sleep. At least he could look at himself in the mirror and not feel the need to avoid eye contact.

Today's session in the pub had been a particularly pleasant one. The pub quiz going on in the background, that the pair never took part in, had brought up some amusing questions and answers that had got the whole place laughing and created a good atmosphere. The quiz had wrapped up by just after eleven p.m. and the pub had all but emptied shortly after that. Dave and John were the last two left, finishing their fifth 'one for the road' of the evening. Not wanting to let the night end and feeling like they were in their twenties again, they had decided they would go back to John's house for 'one more'. It had been a while since they'd had a game of pool in John's games room with a single malt whiskey and a cigar. John also knew his wife Sandra had gone to bed over an hour ago, so there would be no issue with his sneaky late-night drink on that front.

After a fifteen-minute walk on that mild May evening, the pair stumbled up to the gated entrance of John's five-bedroom house. On his third attempt, John entered the correct code to open the smaller black-and-gold entrance gate to the left of the larger gates for the cars. The pair chuckled as they walked the thirty or so steps along the brick-paved driveway. The warm lights illuminated the front of the house a soft orange before the brighter, harsher, white security light beamed down on them as they approached the front door. Both of them winced at the intensity of the light and screwed up their eyes.

The old friends walked through the grand double front doors as quietly as they could before John turned round to gently close and lock them behind him. When he turned back to face the hallway of the house, a cold shiver ran through his body.

Standing at the top of the staircase on the left-hand side of the hallway was a tall figure dressed in all black, wearing a balaclava over his face.

"Jesus Christ!"

Both men froze with their backs against the door, in shock at what they were seeing in front of them. Dave immediately began fumbling in both of his front pockets, scrambling to get his phone out to call 999.

John's thoughts immediately turned to his wife.

"What the fuck are you doin' in my house?! Sandra are you all right up there?!"

He angrily bellowed the question, instinctively walking towards the staircase as the figure casually began to take a couple of steps down towards them.

As John neared the bottom of the stairs, the figure reached and pulled a black police-issue 9mm Glock pistol from behind him. He pointed it down at the two men.

John stopped in his tracks with one hand on the thick, polished mahogany banister, looking up at the assailant. Dave was whimpering in a total state of shock and fear, still with his back pressed firmly against the front door, gripping his phone tightly in both hands. His arms were shaking far too much to even dial the numbers. He wanted to turn around and run back out through the door with every bone in his body, but the sight of the gun froze him in place.

"Tell your friend to put his phone down, John. We don't want there to be any accidents."

The first words spoken in the muffled, snake-like voice of the man standing on the stairs.

He took a few more steps down towards the two men as John reluctantly took a step back with an incensed, shocked expression on his face.

John was staring directly into the eyes of the man under the balaclava, eyes he began to think he recognised. He called out for his wife once more.

"Sandra? You better not have touched my fucking wife!"

John's voice was shaking and beginning to crack.

As the man approached the bottom of the stairs, Dave took a 'now or never' decision and swung round to his right to grab hold of the thick, gold handle of the front door.

Two gunshots rang out in the hallway. The sound was deafening and the smell of gunpowder instantly filled the room.

John instinctively jumped even further back from the stairs and hunched over with his hands over his ears. The ringing was so loud it felt like his brain was vibrating.

He turned round to see his lifelong friend Dave slide down the front door into a lifeless heap. Blood immediately began seeping out of two holes in his back.

"Dave… fucking hell!"

He scrambled over to his friend and leant down over him, putting his hand on his shoulder. He could immediately tell from the amount of blood that the odds of survival were not in Dave's favour, unless he received some medical attention immediately. John could just about hear him murmuring something with the little amount of energy he had left.

Weeping and with eyes full of tears, John turned round to face his friend's attacker, who was now standing in the hallway beside the staircase. Through a snotty, saliva-filled mouth, he shouted back at the gunman, *"You fucking bastard!"*

The man pointed the gun at John and gestured for him to stand up.

"He made a move, John. What could I do? Let's not make this any messier than it has to be, OK? Neither of us wants that."

John reluctantly stood up and sniffed a couple of times, trying to compose himself as he stared into his assailant's eyes with intense anger and sadness. The man began laughing and reached up to pull the balaclava off the top of his head with his left hand.

The paler, bonier face of Max Carter, sporting a maddening smile, was revealed.

John gasped and his eyes and mouth widened, his head jolting back in disbelief at what was in front of him.

"Max…? It can't be… you're dead… they told me you were… they told me you were dead!"

Max chuckled.

"Nope. Not dead, John. Although my wife, my kid, they *are* dead. Bullets through their fucking heads actually. I'm sure you've heard?"

John looked around the hallway in a total state of shock. None of this was making any sense.

"I… I'm sorry, Max. I know, I was at the funera… I don't understand what the fuck is happening?"

Max took a firmer grip of the gun and took a step forward as he gritted his teeth in anger.

"You don't need to understand shit. You fucking sent me out there into that mess for what? Fifty grand? A pat on the fucking back and pittance compared to the money you were getting! Now I'm like *this* and everything I loved in the world is fucking dead! I'm here to repay that favour."

Max took a deep breath before continuing.

"But first, I know you must have a big pile of money in here somewhere, John. All those backhanders you took, that amount of dodgy money takes a bit of time to launder. Go and get all of it and bring it to me now."

Still sniffling and trembling with a mixture of fear, shock and complete distress, John glanced at the staircase and then back at Max, who was now standing about two metres in front of him.

"Where's my wife, Max...? Have you... have you done something to her?"

Max showed no emotion and continued to stare directly into John's eyes.

"She's dead, John. I shot her in the head."

At that exact moment, a loud crashing sound came from the back of the house. It sounded like a small explosion. Max whipped his head around to face the far end of the hall, still keeping the gun in his right hand pointed straight in front of him.

John dived forward in a mad rage with both arms extended, making a grab for Max's gun. He managed to get hold of Max's arm and slam it against the wall in the second that he was distracted by the loud noise behind him. The gun flew into the air and landed on the staircase above.

Max's focus immediately kicked back in and he swung round and punched John's stomach hard with his left hand. Still fuelled off pure adrenaline, John managed to throw a punch that Max casually moved to the side to avoid, instantly swinging another left hook into John's stomach. As John hunched over, badly winded, Max kneed him hard in the head, sending him flying backwards before landing hard on the wooden floor. He was knocked unconscious.

Max immediately turned back to face the rear of the house to refocus his attention on the source of the loud bang.

As he did that, another figure, dressed in all black with a bike mask covering the bottom half of his face, stepped out of the open doorway to the lavish kitchen area. Jayden Amare Fox, 'the lone wolf', was now standing right in front of Max.

Both men were equally shocked to see each other there and froze, staring into each other's eyes as they decided what move to make next.

It wasn't long before the rage of coming face to face with the man who had supposedly killed his daughter took over and Max charged forward at Fox, screaming with anger.

Having less than a second to brace for the impact and caught off guard by Max's speed and strength, Fox leant over to absorb the blow of

Max's incoming 'rugby tackle' as he speared forward into Fox's waist with all of his strength.

The pair crashed through the door frame and rolled across the smoothly tiled white floor of the kitchen/dining room. As they violently wrestled on the floor, Max got the upper hand and locked Fox's body in between his legs below him. Letting out another scream of rage, he raised his right fist behind his head and drove it down at Fox with massive force.

Fox had just enough time to move his head to the side, narrowly avoiding the incoming fist. A loud, deep cracking sound bounced around the room as the punch left a hole in the thick, hard porcelain tile underneath him. Surprised, Fox turned to the side to look at the damage for a split second before turning back to get a grip on the fight.

As Max drove his left fist down with just as much power as the first punch, Fox reached up and caught it in mid-air. Both men jostled for a second or two, astonished at each other's strength.

Eventually, Fox turned his body to the side and threw Max off him with enough force to send him sliding across the polished kitchen floor and into the cupboards at the bottom of the breakfast bar. Both men quickly got to their feet to face each other, standing in a battle-ready pose.

"You're fighting the wrong person if you're attempting to avenge your family," said Fox.

Max only looked more enraged by Fox's attempt to clear the air.

"I am fighting a fucking *dead man!*"

Max reached over to the side and pulled out one of the large kitchen knives from the holder on the counter before slashing it wildly in Fox's direction.

Fox ducked the first swipe, with the blade getting close enough for him to feel it passing his face. As Max swung once more from left to right Fox stepped back, narrowly avoiding the blade again. The third slash seemed to come almost instantaneously after the second in an uppercut motion. Fox once again dived back, but not in time. The fast-moving blade ran up his cheek and forehead, instantly cutting him open, throwing blood spatter onto the ceiling above.

Max pulled back the knife and then drove it directly at Fox's torso.

With the blade less than an inch from Fox's stomach, he once again caught Max's incoming arm and held onto it with both hands. Again, the pair jostled to push and pull the knife, each of them still surprised that they were not getting the upper hand.

Fox broke the deadlock and turned to the side, throwing his left elbow up in to the side of Max's head while letting go and moving out of the way of the incoming knife.

Startled and hurt for a second, Max blindly swung the knife round to the right of him, where Fox was now standing. This far less threatening attempt was easily ducked before Fox leapt up and scissor-kicked Max in the abdomen with all of his strength. The force of the kick sent Max flying backwards through the air, crashing through a set of French doors that led into another seating area off the right-hand side of the kitchen.

Just as Max's body landed hard on the porcelain floor once more, Fox noticed someone appear in the kitchen doorway. It was the bloody nosed, rabid-looking John Fields. The white shirt under his blue waistcoat was now heavily bloodstained as he stood in the doorway, gripping his Mossberg 500 hunting shotgun firmly in both hands.

Both John's vision and his hearing had been badly affected by the hard knee to the head that had also broken his nose. His bitter rage and complete despair, however, remained intact.

He wasted no time in raising the shotgun, pointing it at the only person in his field of vision and pulling the trigger.

Fox turned to the left and dived over the kitchen counter as the whooping 'boom' of the shotgun rang out. Chunks of marble and woodchip flew in all directions as the pellets from the shot scattered all over the kitchen. Two of them skimmed Fox's leg as he flew through the air to the other side of the counter.

There was a brief silence followed by the distinctive metallic, chunking 'click' sounds of the shotgun being reloaded and the spent cartridge dropping out on to the floor below.

After taking a few steps, John saw something move in the small seating room off to the right of the kitchen. Without hesitation he turned, aimed and fired another shot through the already shattered and broken French doors.

Max dived underneath the long, solid stone table in the room as once again, dust and debris flew into the air.

"Arrrrgghhh!"

John let out a frustrated, enraged, tired and confused battle cry.

Still crouched behind the breakfast bar, Fox had decided that the moment immediately following the second shot would be the time to make his move and put John down. But he hesitated. Would putting John down now mean Max would kill him? Fox had come here to get answers out of the man, not *necessarily* to end his life.

Once again, the sound of the weapon being reloaded and the spent shell dropping to the floor could be heard. Neither Fox nor Max knew which way the gun was pointed.

Suddenly, loud shouting came from out in the hallway.

"Armed police! Armed police! Get down on the fucking ground now!"

John instinctively swung round to face the doorway back out to the hall with his shotgun still clutched firmly in both hands.

Confused, in a state of complete panicked rage and visually impaired, he took a step forward with the gun raised in front of him.

The first two officers who entered the hallway did what they were supposed to do in this situation. Before John could even concentrate long enough to focus on the sight of the armed officers approaching him, six shots had been discharged from their weapons.

Two bullets scraped John's lungs, one hit his heart and the other three were spread around his stomach. He dropped to the floor instantly.

It was ironic that of all the ways to go, DCI John Fields' life would end in a confrontation with the armed police. Standing in his own home, for that matter.

Although neither Fox nor Max had seen what had happened, the sounds were enough to piece together the situation.

With little option left, Fox dived up and smashed his way out of the locked door on the left-hand side of the dining area, leading to the garden. More armed officers were only metres away, approaching from the other side of the locked wooden gate.

Max looked regretfully into the kitchen area of the house before kicking out one of the windows in the neighbouring room to enable *his* escape. He let the sound of the footsteps of the approaching officers come right to the entrance of the room before committing to his decision and diving out of the window.

Everything inside him had wanted to stay and fight his 'lone wolf' nemesis and the thought that he might not get another chance at revenge genuinely terrified Max. The sheer number of approaching guns had made the choice for him though.

CHAPTER TWENTY-TWO

For the third time, Tim Rolfe was pleasantly surprised to see Fox return to the new 'family home'. Once again, he hurried to open the thick, metal hatch as soon as he saw Fox stumble into view on the network of surveillance cameras surrounding the property.

Fox slid down the ladder a little more clumsily than usual, crouching to the floor slightly as he reached the bottom. Rolfe, having walked over to the ladder, awkwardly put his hands forward to try to help him up. Before he could get close, Fox stood up and peeled back the bike mask from his face, revealing the fresh and bloody scar running up from his chin all the way to his forehead.

"Jesus Christ, man! What the hell happened up there?" Rolfe asked.

Fox turned to look at Rolfe, his face a messy collage of dried and wet red patches as blood continued to trickle from his scar. He was panting from the exhaustion of fleeing the scene and running the several miles back to the bunker. He walked past Rolfe towards the door that led into the corridor to the other rooms.

Having had no response from Fox the first time, Rolfe tried again, slowly following behind him.

"What... what happened with Fields? Did *he* do that to you?"

Fox stopped just short of the doorway and once again turned to face Rolfe.

"Fields is dead."

Tim stood still. He wasn't all that surprised to hear that information based on the way Fox had entered the bunker. It clearly meant there was some kind of struggle and he knew what Fox would have done in that situation. It was, however, a little disappointing since Fields was the last of the links back to Harding's death. Or so he thought.

"I see... I think you need some help, man. There's blood all over you!" Rolfe exclaimed.

Fox grunted back at him.

216

"I'll be fine. You'd better take a seat."

Rolfe looked back at Fox with a confused expression and then over at the seating area just behind the computers. Fox had his arm extended, pointing in that direction. After a second or two, Rolfe awkwardly walked over and took a seat facing the far wall and projector screen. Fox followed and slumped on to the adjacent sofa, sitting all the way back. This was unusual behaviour for him.

Fox took a few seconds to get his breath back and began explaining.

"I wasn't the only one looking for Fields today. Someone was already at the house when I got there... It was the policeman who killed your friend."

Rolfe leant forward, wide-eyed and clearly flabbergasted by this news.

"That's impossible! Isn't the guy dead?"

Fox turned his head to the side to look into Rolfe's eyes.

"Far from it."

"Jesus Christ! He's alive?"

Tim looked all around the room with his hands on his head. He had just got used to the idea that the man who had killed his friend had eventually met the same fate. Now all of that was reversed.

"But the news reports, the open murder case... it's all for someone who didn't really die? I've heard of faking your death but nothing like *this*. Why? And how?"

Fox didn't have all the answers yet, but he knew where they would need to come from.

"I think that's something you're going to have to find out."

Rolfe leant forward again and stared down at the floor in front of him, rocking with his hands clasped together as he started to ponder his options.

Fox wasn't finished.

"He looked different. Thinner, paler, cadaverous. His eyes looked like the eyes of a dead man. Like my own. He could move faster, punch harder. I think... I know he's been... tampered with."

Tim looked back up at Fox with eyes full of intrigue and fear.

"Tampered with? You mean like...? You mean tampered with like the man from The Fox Unit?"

Fox reluctantly made a single nodding motion.

"Wow. If that's actually true what does this even mean? This can't be some kind of freak coincidence. The man who tries to kill you gets killed and turns up a few weeks later looking 'altered', back from the dead?"

Fox added some more detail from the evening's events.

"He was there to kill Fields. I think I interrupted him before he could. There was a struggle; Fields had a gun. Eventually… it was the police that killed him."

"Jesus, the irony… Did you see if the other copper… Max Carter, got away?" Rolfe replied.

"I didn't see… but I didn't have to. He got away."

Fox took a couple of deep breaths as his heart rate finally began to level out.

"He thinks I killed his family. I can see it in his eyes; he's not going to rest until he kills me in retaliation. Maybe that will be doing us all a favour."

After a few seconds of silence, Tim jumped up from his seat and marched over to his computer, spinning the chair round and aggressively slumping down into it.

"If they really faked his death, they will have left a trace somewhere. I don't care how fucking smart these people think they are, there *will* be a trace somewhere. And I'll find it. That bastard killed my friend and now he's out there doing God knows what. We have to get to the bottom of this."

Fox said nothing in response. He stood up from the seating area and walked slowly back across the room and through to the living quarters to get cleaned up and rest. The experience of coming face to face with Max in his current state had, for the first time since his 'transformation', left him a little shaken. He could draw so many parallels with the suffering behind Max's cold, dead eyes. He had felt that exact same pain and for a moment, when he locked eyes with Max back in Fields' hallway, it felt like looking into a mirror.

Who had done this to Max? And who had pinned the murders of his family on Fox? It was the last thing he wanted, but Fox could feel a new rage building up inside him. This wasn't something he was going to be able to walk away from without someone answering for it.

***

With a black bag over his head and handcuffs on his wrists, Max Carter was helped out of the left rear door of an all-black Range Rover by two 'security guards'. He stepped out to the side and patiently waited for the guards to lead him through the several sets of doors and security checkpoints. The ambient noise from the outside world quietened down as they walked deeper and deeper into the building.

After about three minutes of turning left and right and stopping at various points, Max felt the cuffs being loosened as the bag was abruptly pulled off his head. He was back in the room that he had called home for the past few weeks at the North London 'Facility'.

With the sizeable hospital bed on the left, the vast space in the rest of the room had been kitted out with gym equipment, a television and a small seating area to make the place a little more 'homely' since Max had woken up.

The guard who had been walking him through the building had quickly left the room, with the door closing behind him shortly after the bag had been lifted off of Max's head. Standing just to the right of the bed, taking another look at some of the readings that were being periodically taken from Max's blood, was Charles Creedy. He looked even smarter than usual, wearing a dark-blue suit with a red handkerchief in the top pocket. It was the first time Max had seen him since his rehabilitation. He turned to Max and smiled as warmly as he could force himself to.

"Hello Max. I'm sorry about the… logistics of coming and going from this building. I hope it wasn't too uncomfortable for you."

Max grunted and walked over to the neatly made bed. There was a black ledger in the centre of it that immediately caught his eye.

Creedy continued, "It's not that we don't trust you of course, it's just procedure. If someone in your position were to be caught, for example… the team would be a little nervous that this person knew where we operated fro—"

219

"It's fine," Max interrupted.

Creedy nodded with an understanding look. He walked towards Max and cautiously reached out to put his arm on his shoulder.

"We've heard through our sources already Max. John Fields and his wife both shot dead in their home. And you're back in one piece."

He patted Max's shoulder before turning to face the other way.

"Well done; I'd say that was a damn fine result. He'd had it coming for a while and his wife... well I suppose she was collateral damage."

He turned back and smiled at Max as if to say, 'I know you killed her for the sake of it, and that's OK'.

The fact of the matter was that she was just making too much noise on the night and Max didn't want to have to deal with quietening her down any other way.

Max stared blankly ahead, clenching his fists and gritting his teeth as he replayed in his mind what had happened at the house.

"He was there."

Creedy immediately looked concerned, attempting to disguise it as just being inquisitive.

"I'm sorry, Max? *Who* was there?"

"The man who pushed me off that roof. The man who killed my family. He was there."

Creedy couldn't hide his reaction this time. He screwed his eyes up and his jaw dropped slightly in shock.

"How could he have known? How could he have possibly known that you were going to be th—"

Max interrupted Creedy once more.

"He didn't. He was as surprised to see me as I was to see him. I don't know what they wanted with Fields. But it nearly stopped me getting the job done. Fields got hold of a gun and it just so happened my old 'friends' burst in with *their* guns at the right time and put him down."

Creedy was both surprised and concerned by this news. In the heat of the moment, he wanted to criticise Max. *What do you mean you nearly didn't get the job done? Would you have accepted that?* He wanted to shout it in his face. That's how he would have normally talked to one of the men on his team. But this was no normal team member. In fact, nothing about this situation carried any of the characteristics of 'normal'.

He knew it was paramount to keep Max on side and for him to be mindful of who his enemies were.

Creedy took a deep breath.

"Well thank goodness you got out of there in one piece, Max. Did he though?"

Max looked down at the floor.

"I don't know. But unless there were any bodies found at that house other than the fat man, John and his wife, I would assume so."

Creedy nodded once more, again frustrated by Max's answer but putting on an 'understanding' facade. It was incredibly disappointing to hear that Max had found himself face to face with the 'lone wolf' and let him get away. The coincidence of him being there at the same time, aside from being alarming, felt like too much of an opportunity to have let slip.

"I think it's time for us to step this thing up a notch Max. That black journal over there contains a list of some of the projects that I hope we can work on together. I was going to talk you through a couple of them, but it seems removing this thorn in our side is going to have to take priority."

Max glanced over at the bed and then turned back round to face Creedy.

Creedy continued, "Hunting this man and his hacker accomplice would be a long and frustrating task no doubt. We have the resources but knowing that little weasel's history, I can imagine he will have their tracks well covered. Previous attempts to trace his activities were never successful."

Creedy stepped toward Max.

"Plenty of people want the hacker dead but *our* interest is, of course, in bringing that other sick bastard in. To do that, I think we have to make *him* come to us."

Max looked intrigued, anxiously waiting for Creedy to elaborate. He was visibly thirsty for the opportunity to be face to face with his enemy once more and to have another chance at revenge.

Creedy took another step closer to Max and lowered his voice, as if it mattered if anyone in that facility could hear him.

"The hacker has a five-year-old daughter."

Max instinctively jerked back at that sentence, instantly regurgitating the pain of losing his own daughter.

Creedy paused to let it sink in.

"She lives with her mother out in leafy Wiltshire. I'm sure if she were to end up... in someone else's possession, the hacker would be willing to sacrifice anything to get her back. That would include, presumably, his new friend."

Max looked troubled by the suggestion at first. Creedy's powers of persuasion and manipulation were far from being 'maxed out'.

"You know... this lone wolf wouldn't have been able to do what he did without that hacker's help. He's getting *all* of his intelligence from the hacker. *All* of the crimes he has committed have been carried out with the help of this little runt of a computer nerd."

This was, of course, an attempt to suggest that some blame lay with Rolfe for the killing of Max's wife, sister-in-law and daughter. With this lie tainting his perception, the more Max thought about Creedy's proposal, the more it started to seem like it made sense.

***

Being the mother of an international criminal's daughter, Tim's ex-girlfriend Joanne had been contacted by the police regularly since moving to Wiltshire a year ago. Each time they visited, she had told them the truth, that she hadn't seen or heard from Tim since she got there.

Following Tim's dramatic, headline-making escape from a cell in an East London police station, the family had been contacted once more and offered various forms of police supervision and protection. Joanne had almost laughed this off. *Protection? From Tim? He might be a big time criminal, but he's a geek!* she'd thought.

With the classification of Tim and his blackNet 'group' as that of a terrorist organisation, the threat was very real in the eyes of the law. Especially with the amount of media coverage the story was getting.

Regardless, Joanne had declined the offer to be moved or placed under any sort of police guard and once again reaffirmed that no contact had been made. She was only five foot two and skinny with long mousey brown hair and glasses, but she stuck up for herself and certainly knew how to stand her ground.

Although she considered herself to be 'over' Tim and actually quite bitter about the fact that he had dragged her and their daughter into this kind of situation — Joanne found herself both curious and very concerned by his breakout from police custody. It was hard enough trying to explain to Freya where her daddy was without having to shield her from all of the images of him being displayed on the news.

She couldn't shake the fear that one day soon she would be sitting Freya down to explain that her dad was never coming home. A fear she might have been better served keeping closer to home.

CHAPTER TWENTY-THREE

Tim Rolfe was walking himself through another morning routine in Epping-255. Waking up in the slightly unforgiving 1950s 'nuclear bunker' bed, dragging himself next door to the outdated but adequate bathroom for a lukewarm shower, and then out into the main room to switch on all of his equipment in his dressing gown. He'd also set the projector to come on automatically at six thirty every morning, displaying one of the less radical news channels for the morning headlines.

Starting the day with the morning television reminded him of a more normal life, a glimpse into the past before everything went crazy. Otherwise, it was easy to forget that there even *was* an outside world while living in a bunker thirty feet below the surface with no windows and limited fresh air.

As he walked out into the main room on this particular morning, what was displayed on the screen in front of him had absolutely no calming or nostalgic effect whatsoever. Three steps in, Tim froze with his mouth open and toothbrush still in hand. A large, foamy mix of toothpaste and saliva dropped out of his mouth and slapped on to the concrete floor below him.

"Police in Wiltshire have launched a nationwide manhunt today after a young woman was found shot dead in her home in Salisbury. Thirty-one-year-old Joanne Huntingdon was discovered late last night by local officers after they broke down the door to her property following a number of concerned calls from neighbours.

"Shockingly, Joanne's five-year-old daughter, Freya, is also missing from the property and police are said to be 'very concerned' about her safety. There have since been reports that a man was seen walking away from the scene carrying a large concealed object under his arm. This has led to a theory that the girl was taken from her

home after her mother's murder. Officer Michael Humphreys of the Wiltshire constabulary had this to say:

"We are obviously shocked and appalled at the horrific discovery that officers made last night at the property in Salisbury. Our focus now is one hundred percent on finding Joanne's five-year-old daughter, Freya, who is missing. We are circulating this image and asking people to take a close look at Freya's face and think hard about whether they might have seen a girl matching her description. We're also circulating a composite sketch of a man seen leaving the road at around the time of the murder holding a large, suspicious looking object under his right arm.

"The man's face was covered but he is described as being a well-built white male, six foot one, with medium-length wavy black hair and a pale skin tone. We are urging anyone with any information, no matter how trivial it may seem, to contact police immediately. If you think you have seen this man dial 999 and do not, under any circumstances, attempt to confront or approach him as he is considered highly dangerous."

The glass of water Tim was holding in his left hand slipped out of his grip and shattered into a thousand pieces on the floor around him. He didn't even notice it happening. He was lost in a trance as he watched his worst nightmare unfold right in front of his eyes.

Creedy had commandeered the use of an old warehouse on the outskirts of East London for the purpose of 'hostage accommodation' in this instance. It was owned by an old friend of his and sat among a mixture of industrial buildings and greenery. There was a long, declining dirt path with gates at the top leading down to the main site. At the bottom of the path was a vast derelict concrete square where a building had once stood. To the right of that was the large two-storey metal warehouse painted in a faded blue colour with patches of deep, orange rust. The warehouse sat right on the bank of a canal that ran parallel with the path down to the site and continued for miles in either direction. At the rear of the building was a steep hill, dense with bushes and trees that wrapped all the way around to the side, obscuring the whole site from view of anyone using the roads running around it.

Four armed men were stationed at the warehouse to guard the human 'package' that was being held in a small office at the rear of the first floor. None of them were particularly comfortable with what they had been called in to look after that day, but working for the kind of men Creedy employed meant they had done far worse things in the past.

This particular bunch were a group of Essex gangsters that Creedy's corrupt associate in the higher-ups of the police had done a deal with years ago. Like many informants who do these kinds of shady deals, they had avoided serious jail time in exchange for unequivocal co-operation. That co-operation had persisted until the present day and was being lent out to Creedy for a price.

The men stood guarding their various positions with 'high-vis' jackets on and dust masks covering their faces. They had jeans and yellow workman boots on and from a distance, they looked like a group of builders on a site, harmlessly working away. These guys weren't messing about; they had been told to come as heavily armed as they could and that they would be paid a high fee for this job. Their natural conclusion was that a group of really bad bastards must be coming after this little girl that they were 'guarding' for whatever reason.

Max Carter had insisted on handling the collection and transportation of the hostage. He'd stuck to his orders of returning to a rendezvous point where Creedy was to brief him on the next stage of the plan. This meeting would occur in the back seat of another black Range Rover, parked in a Docklands car park a couple of miles away from the warehouse.

Max got in via the back-right door and shut it behind him hard with an obvious attitude. The driver in the front, wearing a suit and sunglasses, immediately locked the door.

Creedy, sitting in the rear-left seat, wasted no time in getting down to business.

"You know you didn't have to kill the mother, Max. Some noise is good, but this kind of thing is only going to draw mo—"

"I got the fucking girl, didn't I?"

Max turned to look at Creedy with an expression that conveyed a mood Creedy did not want to make any worse. Creedy immediately changed *his* concerned expression to a contented smile.

"You did. You got the girl and she's where she's supposed to be."

"So what are we doing now then? I'm done with playing these fucking games. I want these guys dead," Max replied.

"Patience. Just a tiny little bit more patience and we can get exactly that."

Creedy extended his hand out and gestured as if to say 'calm down.'

He continued, "I've got people standing by to deliver our friends a message. The hacker will no doubt be immediately attempting to access all the files that the police have on what happened last night. He's probably even looking at local CCTV to try to find out who came after his daughter and where they went. Given that we changed vehicles twice along the way and took a deliberately stupid route, retracing ourselves several times, he's going to struggle to do that successfully."

"And if he does manage it?"

Creedy sighed before delivering another well-prepared answer.

"In the highly unlikely event that he does... we have men at the warehouse, heavily armed and ready for them. It will probably actually end up making this whole thing easier on all of us."

Max grunted.

"Not me."

Creedy paused, forgetting for a moment that he was supposed to pretend he cared about the terrible things that had happened to Max.

"Let's just hope he finds our little clue and gets in contact with us through the channel we've set up. If it all goes to plan then we will have one of them... maybe even both of them delivered to us. They will tell us everything we need to know and we can handle the rest from there."

"And the girl?" Max asked.

Creedy sighed once more.

"She might have seen too much. We'll cross that bridge when we come to it. The armed guards are there as a precaution for now. Maybe they will be asked to tie up the loose end."

Creedy could see that Max wasn't all that pleased with this plan, but for now at least, he needed him out of the way.

"Get some rest back at the facility Max, you've done enough for now. When we get these guys to come in, this 'lone wolf' will be all yours."

Two hours had passed since Tim had watched the headlines roll across the projected screen on the wall of Epping-255's basement. His six monitors were all busy, scrolling with information as various searches and algorithms continued to whirr away in the background.

Fox emerged from his quarters out into the main bunker space. Having gone to sleep after three a.m. and woken up at seven, he'd spent an hour meditating before coming through to immediately begin his training. As he walked past the seating area, he did a double take before stopping to read what was being projected on the far wall. The news clip detailing the shocking story of a murdered mother and missing girl.

Fox turned to look at Tim, who was staring at his screens with wide, thickly glazed eyes. His face was red raw, especially around the eyes, and he had clearly been crying heavily. By now he looked exhausted and almost drained of emotion. Fox didn't even need to know or recognise the names on that news report. From the look on Tim's face alone, he knew who they must be.

Without even turning round to acknowledge Fox's presence, Tim began to speak in a muted, exhausted monotone.

"They left me a clue. An email address to contact. I don't know… I don't know what they want but they've got my daughter… Joanne is dead."

Fox turned to look at the monitor at the top left of Tim's six-screen setup. Of the many crime scene photos being displayed, an image of a bloodstained handwritten note stood out from the others, photographed on the floor of Tim's daughter Freya's bedroom.

Written in black pen, the short note read:

'The Policeman.
Back from the dead, could it be true?
Search for his name next to yours for a clue.'

"It's a note for me. A riddle."

Tim had quickly worked out the simple meaning of the note and began running searches for appearances of his name next to Max Carter's throughout the internet. It wasn't long before he found a match in the form of a short, cryptic post on a dark web forum with an email address contained within it.

'AllveButF0rH0wL0ng@Gmail.com — Let us know if you want to let the timer keep ticking?'

"I… I sent them a message."

Rolfe looked down at the floor and began sobbing once more, overcome with the pain and stress of the fact that these men had taken his daughter and what he was being reduced to in order to try to get her back. He'd been telling himself over and over for the past two hours that he couldn't lose it, he had to stay focused and do everything he could to get Freya to safety as fast as possible.

Fox began to step forward as if to offer some kind of comforting gesture, but he hesitated.

After a few seconds Tim pulled himself together again, lifting his head with another snuffle, followed by a deep breath through his nose.

"I sent them a message asking what they wanted. They can't trace it. I assume that's what they'd try. They want to set up a meeting with me… with us. They haven't given me a location yet, but they want both of us to come in within twenty-four hours… or they say they are going to kill her."

Tim still hadn't turned to look at Fox. He was staring dead ahead at his screens, trembling with the unbearable amount of fear and anxiety that was coursing through his veins.

Rolfe continued, "I don't expect you to hand yourself in. I will go on my own and just hope that I can offer them something or convince them to give me my daughter back in one piece. I'll… I'll do anything to get that. At least if I go, I'll know that I tried."

Fox's attention turned to another monitor that displayed a static pink dot laid over a Google Maps image. The location looked like a field by the side of a motorway. He could see that Tim's eyes had darted over to this screen a few times as if he were continuously checking it for something.

Fox nodded at the screen.

"What is that?"

Tim saw his hand out of the corner of his eye and for the first time that morning, turned to face Fox. His eyes were as black as a panda's and the skin all around them appeared scarred. He even looked slightly thinner and the colour had completely left his face. His lips quivered as if he was freezing cold, even though the bunker had been kept at a steady 20 °C since the day they entered it.

As he saw where Fox was staring, he turned back round to face the screen and sighed. He took another deep breath through his nose before beginning to explain what they were both looking at on the monitor.

"It's the last known location of a bracelet that I sent my ex to give to my daughter when she was three years old… it's got a GPS tracker and a transmitter inside it. One of the only things that's kept me somewhere close to sane over the past couple of years is being able to know where she is at any one time. The last time it transmitted was quarter past eleven last night from the M4 motorway — looks like heading East. They must have found it and disabled it somehow… at least I hope that's what has happened, and it hasn't stopped transmitting because something terrib—"

"She's alive," Fox interrupted.

Tim turned back to look at Fox once more with those helpless, drained eyes.

"She is the only leverage that they have over you. They won't jeopardise that. Yet."

A very slight look of relief washed over Tim's face for a second. It did very little to detract from the massive pain and anguish.

Fox hadn't finished quite yet.

"She *is* alive. But if you do as they say and meet with them, they will kill you and then kill your daughter anyway."

Tim looked confused and even more distressed, screwing up his face as he looked left and right between the news story being projected on the far wall and Fox standing right in front of him.

"They've got my daughter, man! I can't just fucking sit here and do nothing! They say I've got twenty-four hours and I've got no moves left to play! I can't take even the slightest chance… they've killed her mother already; why would they hesitate to do the same to her?"

Fox looked down to the floor and exhaled.

"If you go looking for her, both of your lives will end today. Her only chance of survival is if I go… and I must go alone."

Rolfe's face wore a look of shock and apprehension as his eyes darted around in his head, searching for the right thing to do. He was surprised that Fox would even offer such a thing.

"What? No! I can't let you do that! She needs me. I need to go—"

Fox took a step closer to Tim, who shuddered with the cocktail of emotions running through his body.

"These people cannot be reasoned with. It's the only option."

Rolfe hadn't really given any thought as to what his game plan would be, if and when he turned up to such a meeting. The blind panic and emotion involved in the fact that this was his little girl being held — and in God knows what kind of condition — was severely compromising his ability to reason.

In the two hours since this had all become apparent, Rolfe had immediately begun trying to pull CCTV from the area around his late ex's home and access the traffic camera information for the stretch of the M4 motorway that his daughter's bracelet had last transmitted from. The CCTV was taking some time to collate from the various sources — there isn't always an easy way to find 'all of the cameras in one area'. Some are operated by the council, some by local businesses and some even by homeowners themselves. Not all of these were accessible through the internet and the subset that were took some time to gain access to.

The results from the traffic cameras were similarly disappointing. There were several 'candidate cars' that Tim could see on the three-lane motorway at that time, but the image was so dark and grainy that the number plates were not visible, even after extensive image enhancement. This was unfortunately on a stretch of the road that was utilising those ridiculously bad low-frame-rate black-and-white cameras that should have been a thing of the past by now.

He *could* follow the trail along each of the suspect cars' various potential routes, but this was a 'needle in a haystack' scenario. Tim didn't feel like he had anywhere near the kind of time he needed to gather information using his normal methods.

The kidnappers had set out the twenty-four-hour window and told Rolfe they would follow up soon with a location for the meet. He wasn't going to give up searching, but until then it seemed, he wouldn't have any way of knowing where his daughter was.

CHAPTER TWENTY-FOUR

Max Carter nestled into his position, around two hundred metres inside the steep, elevated woodland behind the canal-side warehouse. From where he was perched, he had a perfect view of the near side of the warehouse, including the barren open space at the side and the 500m long dirt track leading down to the site. The view was even clearer through the long scope of the Heckler & Koch M110A1 sniper rifle he had mounted on a stand in front of him.

Max had received his instructions and understood them loud and clear. Underneath all of the pain, rage and bloodthirstiness, he did genuinely feel grateful to Creedy and his team for what they had done for him. At least what they had *claimed* to have done for him. That did not, however, change the fact that the idea of sitting and waiting for a meeting to be set-up between his enemy and 'someone else' from Creedy's band of mercenaries was something that he was far too impatient to comprehend.

After giving Creedy the impression that he would go along with the plan and meet one of the other team members for transport back to his new home at the North London facility, Max had gone to visit an old lock-up that he and a few of his equally corrupt colleagues had been using before his untimely demise. This particular lock-up contained a mixture of weapons, money and other nefarious items that they had uncovered during raids and kept for themselves, rather than handing them over to their undeserving employers. A collection of 'just in case' items that, given the kind of lifestyle they were living and the friends they were keeping, they thought it best to have at their disposal.

As well as the long-range rifle and Glock pistol that he had on his person, Max had taken a variety of seized explosives from the garage lock-up. This essentially consisted of a handful of grenades smuggled in from Eastern Europe and a box of ten home-made pipe bombs that were wired up to be detonated remotely by mobile phone.

Before scaling the hill, Max had entered the warehouse below and talked to the heavily armed men stationed inside. He had told them that if anyone hostile turned up, they were to contact him directly and immediately. He also gave them strict instruction, in the form of a threat, not to tell anyone that they had seen him at the site. Especially not Creedy. These men were hard East London gangsters but from the moment they had seen Max's face a few days earlier, side by side with Creedy, they knew that he was not someone they wanted to mess with.

As the days had gone by, Max's appearance had become less and less natural-looking. His skin had become even more pasty and pale and his eyes even more bloodshot. His veins were thicker and protruded out from his skin like there were plastic tubes inserted into his arms and neck. It looked like he was swelling and in constant discomfort.

Max's visit to the warehouse was not simply to 'check in' with the men guarding it. He had also been carefully placing six of the pipe bombs down there, tucking them behind various tall piles of disused wooden pallets while no one was looking.

Among many other things, the owner of the warehouse used the property for the storage of butane gas canisters. These were mainly sold in bulk to the various canal-orientated businesses in the area that would then sell gas by the individual canister to barge and boat owners, for instance. Several small clusters of these canisters were spread around the ground floor of the warehouse. Max made a point of placing some of the pipe bombs in their vicinity.

From his perch up on the higher ground, with one eye over the scope and his hand on the small metal wheel on the side, Max adjusted the focus once more to make sure everything was perfectly visible. He looked down at the old Nokia 3310 that was now his remote detonator, neatly placed on the ground beside the left foot of his rifle's stand.

On the other side of that rifle stand was the pink plastic wristband that Tim Rolfe had given his daughter Freya on her third birthday. As his ex, Joanne, had reluctantly promised Tim, she had made sure Freya had worn it every single day after that.

The circular bulge in the middle of the wristband had been cut open and the tiny microchip and transmitter removed from it entirely. The two thin wires that connected those to a thin, black solar power strip that ran round the circumference of the band were simply fraying out to either side, not connected to any power source.

As instructed by Creedy, once Max had abducted Freya and delivered her to the getaway vehicle, one of the henchmen had scanned the car for any radio or cellular signals with a high-tech handheld detection device. Sure enough, they had found a signal and narrowed it down to the wristband on Freya's arm. Creedy thought he might have been giving Rolfe too much credit in asking his men to check for this, but his paranoia proved to be completely justified. He would not be at all impressed to learn that the device was not destroyed as he had been led to believe it had been.

Max was not going to let this opportunity pass him by. He was not going to let anyone else be in control of an encounter between him and the man who had supposedly taken everything from him.

He looked down at the exposed transmitter and took a deep breath.

From his kneeling position behind the large, mounted rifle set back in the small woodland behind the warehouse, Max carefully reached forward with both hands and began twisting the exposed transmitter wires back into those running into the solar strip around the strap of the watch.

After a few seconds, the cellular detection device that he had switched on and placed on the floor at his right-hand side began pulsing and crackling ever so faintly. The transmitter was beginning to send out a signal once more. Now, all he had to do was wait.

Back at the North London facility, Creedy was blissfully unaware that Max was engaging in all of this 'extracurricular' activity. In the same way that Max had deviated somewhat from the agreed plan of action, Creedy, too, had been keeping his real intentions under wraps.

Carter was going to be an invaluable asset and the first dividend of that would be the capturing of 'the lone wolf', this was true. It was also true, however, that Creedy had little intention of letting Max have his revenge. He knew it would be difficult for Max to contain himself in a one-on-one situation and it felt likely that one of them would end up dead, a less than ideal scenario, regardless of which one of them that was. Max was possibly one of the most valuable military weapons in the county at this time and the lone wolf was a treasure chest of information on altered human DNA that had already given Creedy's 'Free Spirit' project a steroid injection of a boost. Even if Fox had to be killed to be brought in, and Creedy had acknowledged that this was a distinct possibility, he wanted that done on his own terms. Not ripped apart or dismembered or blown up in whatever godforsaken eventuality that the two meeting each other again would result in.

For these reasons, Creedy had decided that the proposed meet should be arranged without Max's knowledge of the time or place. He would eventually contact Carter in a panic, stating that their target had 'shown up' somewhere and that some of Creedy's other men had captured him before Max could arrive. How to keep Max preoccupied after that while they kept Fox in the lab was a bridge they would have to cross when they came to it. Money, cocaine and prostitutes were some things he had enjoyed in the past and these penchants were unlikely to be too affected by his 'treatment'.

For now, though, Creedy stood behind a seated Alexi in one of the small offices in the North London facility. His right-hand man had handled the creation of the email address for Tim Rolfe to contact, as well as responding to his queries.

So far both sides had confirmed that they would meet at eleven p.m. that evening. Alexi had sent over a location and sent a follow-up message asking Rolfe to confirm that both he *and* the 'lone wolf' would be present at the meet. He added that the safety of Rolfe's daughter 'could not be guaranteed' otherwise, just to add a little extra incentive to stick to the letter. They had simply received the response: 'OK'.

The location that Alexi and Creedy had decided upon was a disused parking lot on an industrial estate on the outskirts of North-East London. Creedy was familiar with the surroundings, since the building a hundred metres away housed the Bentley service centre he used to take his Continental GT to every year. It was a fairly private estate and had only one way in and out from the main road.

Creedy had called in a few more favours to get the additional armed men he needed to guard this proposed meet. As per their orders, they would be doing so without Tim's daughter in their possession, who was of course being held at the canal-side warehouse. Once the identities of the two targets had been confirmed, they were to be tranquillised and transported to another location for interrogation and subsequent testing. Creedy had decided he would go as far as letting Tim see his daughter over a video call to confirm she was safe, in an effort to make the men more compliant. After all, it was only fair to let him talk to Freya and see her face one last time before they were both killed.

***

Monday 4th May, 5:00 p.m. Twenty-four days since Dave Shilling's death, two days since Fields was shot by the police, eighteen hours since Rolfe's daughter was taken and six hours before the proposed meet.

After spending hours compulsively checking his monitors, Tim had to blink and rub his eyes several times to confirm what he was seeing in front of him was real. The static pink dot on the Google Maps image displaying his daughter's location had now jumped over to a new point on the map, pulsing to confirm the signal was actively being received. The audible 'beep, beep, beep, beep' repeating every two seconds or so, filled the underground bunker with suspense and anticipation.

"I jeesh... it's..."

Tim gasped and stared wide-eyed at the screen. He tried to form some words to say something, but he couldn't get anything out that made sense.

Fox had already made his way over to the computer to look over Rolfe's shoulder at what the source of the pulsating beeping was. It was clear what they were both looking at.

After about five seconds of staring in complete disbelief, Tim frantically pulled his chair in closer to the computer and began zooming in on the location of the beacon. How did this happen? Could it be that Freya had been put in some kind of metal box that had prevented the signal from transmitting? Maybe she was out of it now?

Having established where exactly it was, Rolfe immediately began running a search against the history of the site address, looking for council documents, online copies of the deeds, planning permissions, listings for sale or rental — anything that could give him more information about what he was looking at. The centre-top screen remained frozen on the zoomed-in overhead satellite image showing the warehouse site.

Fox had seen enough. With Tim still manically typing away at the keyboard, he turned and began walking towards the far end of the bunker. It took Tim a few seconds to notice and swing round in his chair.

"What are you... Where are you going?" Rolfe asked.

"We've discussed this."

The gravelly, 'straight to the point' tone of Fox's grunted response brooked no argument.

"But I..."

Tim took a deep breath and looked down at the floor. If his daughter really was at this location, Fox would have a far better chance of bringing her back alive. It was probably the only option where at least one of them survived. Rolfe had resigned himself to the fact that he was going to hand himself over to them that evening, knowing that there was a chance that it would be the end of him. This little pink bracelet had offered an alternative... but would it be enough to save her?

He looked back up at Fox with tears in his eyes, his lips quivering.

"Are you... sure about this?"

His desperate expression begged for Fox to bring his daughter back alive without the need for any words. With one hand on the red metal ladder that led out of the bunker, Fox turned to face Tim once more.

"I came to you looking for people, looking for vengeance. What you have given me has far exceeded that in a way I could have never hoped for. I now know who 'Jayden' was. I know the origin of his name and who his family might have been. Blanks that have existed since the beginning have now been filled. That comes with a certain peace before the end. For that, I have to thank you. No harm will come to your daughter."

With that, Fox ascended the ladder for what seemed like the final time. As the thick, metal hatch at the top hammered shut behind him, Rolfe immediately lost his composure and began sobbing wildly, crouched over with his head in his hands.

CHAPTER TWENTY-FIVE

An hour had passed since Max had sent out his 'message' through the reconnected tracking device. The red evening sun was now reflecting off the canal next to the warehouse just down the hill from him. It was a warm, breezy evening and the roads surrounding the site were beginning to quieten down after the post-work rush hour. Dressed in their 'construction' attire, the four armed men inside the warehouse remained vigilant, given the reminder that Max had come in to deliver them a little while back.

The 'builder' patrolling the area around the warehouse had a 9mm semi-automatic pistol stuffed down the back of his jeans with an extra clip of ammunition in his pocket. Not far behind him, chain-smoking in a seat right in the middle of the barren warehouse floor, was his friend who was holding a meatier Smith & Wesson M&P 15-22 semi-automatic rifle. The same gun, in fact, that the third man had, who was positioned on one of the walkways that traversed above the open floor, keeping guard from above. Finally, the man who was lucky enough to be stationed in the office with the five-year-old girl that they were guarding, had chosen a Glock 17 handgun along with a bag of military grenades.

The men cracked the odd joke between themselves and agreed that one of them would take a smoke break out the back of the warehouse every so often, leaving the other three on duty. Aside from that, though, the mood in the warehouse was fairly serious. None of them had any idea why they were holding this little girl here and who exactly it was that might come looking for her. Having seen the news stories from the West Country and the pictures of the little kidnapped girl whose mother had been murdered, they had made the connection, only adding to their concern about what the hell they were into. Still, this was business, and they were being paid handsomely to carry it out.

The evening sun beaming in through the small windows around the top of the warehouse meant the lighting was reasonable, but there were still pockets of darkness that were getting harder and harder to see in as the night approached.

As well as a door on the near side of the warehouse leading out to the gravelled wasteland, there was a corresponding door on the far side that led out to a small 'jetty' on the canal. The bottom half of the door had been damaged at some point and covered over with a bodged job of hammered down planks of wood. The glass from the small window at the top was also gone and that too had been partially covered with smaller chunks of the same old, partially rotten wood.

The patrolling guard leant his head out of a small opening between the panels to check left and right of that side of the warehouse before turning to walk back over to the near side of the building.

As he reached about halfway across the ground floor of the warehouse, he heard a loud, sharp cracking sound come from behind him that immediately stopped him in his tracks. By the time he had turned around, with one hand reaching back to grab hold of the pistol tucked in his jeans, the full force of a flying kick connected flush with his jaw.

The sound of the guard's jaw breaking reverberated through the vast open space inside the warehouse. His head jolted back so violently it very nearly broke his neck as well. The cracking of bones was quickly followed by the sound of his body slumping onto the floor. Unconscious, his limp body slid a metre or so across the ground before coming to a stop. The gun that he had just had time to grab hold of slid further still as it loosened from the grip of his hand. That was just enough for it to slide into the view of the second guard, sitting in the open area of the warehouse. His view of the first guard's patrol was obscured by highly stacked wooden container crates, but he could see around four metres to the left and right of them, including both doors into the building.

He froze for a second, staring at the gun on the warehouse floor. Given that he was around twenty metres away from it, he had to squint slightly to make sure that it was in fact a gun that he was looking at. He stood up from his seat, took the safety catch off his rifle and turned to face the third guard sitting behind and above him on the walkway of the first floor.

"Heads up, boys!"

239

He pulled down the black balaclava that had been rolled up on top of his head, to cover his face. The guard on the walkway above did the same as he too stood up and began readying his rifle. The fourth and final skinny, bald guard who was sitting in the small office at the rear of the first floor heard the muffled shout. He turned to look at the terrified little girl sitting with her arms and legs tied in front of her on a small mattress at the back of the room. She had tape covering her mouth, and she was sobbing and murmuring as she rocked back and forth to comfort herself.

The thug instinctively got out of his chair, picking the Glock up from the table in front of him as he walked over to the front window of the office that looked out into the warehouse. He stared out at his two 'comrades' below as he pulled back the slide on his weapon to hop a bullet up into the barrel, ready to fire.

Holding the pistol in his right hand, he reached into his pocket with his left and sent a pre-written message to the number that Max had given him.

Potential trouble.

The guard down on the ground floor carefully approached the opening on the other side of the stacked crates. By now, he could clearly see the sprawled-out body of his friend lying next to the gun. He wanted to call out to him to see if he was OK, but he knew that it was tactically better to remain silent.

As he approached the edge of the crates, gripping his long, powerful black rifle out in front of him, he took a deep breath and stepped out to face the area where his friend had been struck down.

Nothing in sight except the downed guard, the gun, a few barrels at either side of the room, and the door out to the jetty at the rear with the wooden panelling kicked in.

Just as he began to lower his weapon, he heard a whipping, whistling noise come from the middle section of the warehouse. This was quickly followed by a dull thud and a shocking, intense shriek of pain. The sound of it sent chills through the two other men. It was so bad that they wanted to cover their ears.

The guard on the ground floor quickly but cautiously peered around the crates to look up at his comrade standing on the steel walkway above. He could see that something was embedded just below his left shoulder, with blood pouring from an open wound under his black T-shirt. A small, sharp throwing knife was handle-deep in his body.

Almost immediately after the cries of pain came the deafening, metallic booms of the semi-automatic rifle he was holding firing off in all directions. Bullets hit the roof, the wooden crates, the windows around the top of the building and the warehouse floor as concrete, glass and wood fragments flew into the air.

The guard on the ground floor dived back into the front area of the warehouse, taking cover behind the wooden crates.

The skinny guard who was up in the office with Freya ducked down behind the door as soon as the firing started. He shuffled back into the room closer to the frightened little girl, already positioning himself to hold a gun to her head if the situation called for it.

Max had received the message and heard the gunfire come from the warehouse below almost simultaneously. He knew this was it. Showtime.

Max immediately grabbed hold of his rifle and leant in to look down the long scope once more. He turned to face the window of the upstairs office at the rear of the warehouse, the side closest to him, where the girl was being held. Both occupants of the room were too low for him to see. He could, however, see the red flashes from the muzzle of the gun being manically fired inside the building, reflecting off the metallic walls and glass windows.

Max wanted to run down the hill to that warehouse and kill this bastard with his bare hands, but he would stick to the next move in his plan. Having scanned the scenery like a hawk for the last hour, he didn't know how his target had managed to enter the building unseen. He would not be allowing him to leave.

Max looked down at the phone he was holding in his left hand with his thumb hovering over the 'call' button.

The sound immediately after the tenth shot was the far quieter, distinctive 'clink' of a trigger being pulled with no rounds left in the magazine. Two more followed in quick succession.

"Arrggghhh. Fuck's sake!"

The tired, frustrated guard on the walkway, still in agony from his shoulder wound, let out a defiant roar as he frantically continued looking around the room, scanning for who had done this to him.

Suddenly, three metres along the walkway from him, a figure leapt up from out of sight, vaulting over the metal rails on the side. A man dressed in all black with a mask low enough to reveal the top half of his pale, scarred face.

Standing right in front of the stabbed guard, this terrifying man with blood-red eyes and shoulder-length jet-black hair stared into his eyes for what seemed like a minute, but in reality was only a couple of seconds.

The guard threw the empty rifle over the rails and began to reach down to his side to pull the small Walther PPK pistol from his holster. Just as his hand grasped the gun, he felt the wind being forced out of his body as a powerful kick crashed into his stomach. Jolting backwards, he leant over in agony, his hands thrown out in front of him from the force of the blow.

Fox grabbed hold of the guard by both shoulders and threw him off the right side of the walkway, taking the pistol from his right hand as he flew over the edge.

The guard on the ground floor, having heard that the firing had stopped, emerged gingerly once more from behind the crates. This was just in time to see his friend's body clatter against the cold, hard concrete floor. He immediately looked up and began raising his rifle up to the walkway above.

Fox fired three shots down into the guard's chest before he could even pull the trigger, killing him instantly.

In the moment of silence that followed, Fox could hear the muffled sound of crying coming from the small office at the rear of the warehouse.

Max Carter pressed down on the 'call' button of the mobile phone he was holding.

The initial explosions echoed around the metal warehouse structure, making the gunshots seem like pin-drops in comparison. Blinding flashes of hot-white flooded the building as the six pipe bombs detonated at almost exactly the same time. Dense, pungent smoke filled the vast warehouse area.

Secondary explosions from the nearby clusters of gas canisters began popping off almost immediately. One after another, the whizzing, hissing sound of the gas escaping from a breached container was followed by the cracking *'boom'* of the canister exploding, often firing up into the air. The various piles of dry, wooden pallets and crates were quick to catch alight and within seconds, over half of the warehouse was on fire.

The door into the office at the back of the first floor had been bolted shut. With the raging fires and explosions going off underneath and behind him, Fox had little intention of stopping to try and open it the conventional way anyway. Having sprinted along the steel walkway and leapt into the air, he came crashing in through the window of the small office, followed by plumes of smoke and hot air. He rolled over a desk and on to the floor, coming to rest in a crouched position on one knee.

Cowered in the corner of the room, the last remaining guard grabbed hold of Freya by the hair and held his gun out in front of him, pointed at Fox. The guard was shaking with fear and shock from the sensory overload of what was happening around him. He let out a couple of deep, whooping coughs and shouted over the sound of the roaring, crackling flames licking against the walls of the warehouse.

"Get fucking back! I'll shoot her in the fucking head; I swear to God, I'll do it!"

Fox stood up and glanced over to his left. The sight of flames touching the edge of a pile of twenty or so gas canisters on the ground floor had caught his eye.

He quickly turned his attention back to the situation unfolding in front of him. The wide-eyed quivering nutcase waving a gun at a little girl's head. The guard had taken his balaclava off in the moments preceding Fox's entry, allowing him to see what the hell was going on unimpeded.

Both men tried to remain undistracted by the intense muffled screams coming from little Freya.

Fox kept his focus one hundred percent on the position of the man's head next to the girl's. The guard had a firm grip of Freya's hair, alternating between aiming his gun at Fox and holding it against her temple.

Fox raised his right hand out in front of him and pushed the air back with an open palm, as if to say 'wait', leaning into a readied stance with his right knee bent.

With his left hand, he reached behind him, pulled another small, sharp throwing knife from his belt and with a lightning-fast flicking motion, hurled it through the air.

The knife travelled fast and true in an unwavering trajectory. It cut through several strands of Freya's hair before lodging deep into the bottom of the thug's neck. His head flew back as he began to choke, struggling to breathe. The blood immediately started to pour from his neck at an alarming rate.

At that moment, the flash of another gas container exploding on the ground floor came beaming in through the window on the left. They had a couple of seconds at most to get out of the building.

Fox leapt forward, cut the ties around Freya's arms and legs and scooped up the terrified girl, holding her under one arm. He ran towards the thick first-floor window facing the warehouse yard, turned to the side to shield Freya and dived through the glass as it shattered into fragments.

A huge *boom* followed as the entire stack of twenty gas canisters on the ground floor simultaneously ignited. A tall, hot ball of fire thundered through the building as flames shot out of several of the windows at the top of the warehouse, closely behind Fox and Freya. Thousands more shards of glass were blasted out in all directions.

Up on the hill, Max pulled back from his scope and looked down at the inferno, slightly caught off guard by the size and sound of the explosion. He could feel the heat on his face from all the way up there.

Carter saw the two bodies fly out of the office window and immediately leant back down to look through the scope of his weapon once more.

Fox turned in the air, falling for about three seconds before landing hard on his back on top of a dark blue metal freight container that stood next to the building. The deep, metallic thud made it sound like he was made of solid metal.

The force of the landing dazed Fox and hammered the wind out of him. Anyone else would either be dead or very badly injured from such a fall.

Having completely shielded Freya from injury, Fox's grip on her loosened and she slumped out of his arms and off the side of the container. She landed on the dusty, sandy wasteland below, luckily only hard enough to leave bumps, cuts and bruises.

Freya quickly got up to her feet and pulled the duct tape away from her mouth before turning to look back at the warehouse. Instinctively, she began running away from the site up the long dirt track road entrance.

Max watched the whole thing through one eye behind the scope lens. He took a deep breath and moved his finger down to rest on the trigger.

"You've come all this way to watch her get shot in the fucking head my friend. Here's a fraction of the pain you've caused me."

From his supine position on top of the container, Fox looked back to see a brief but bright orange light flash from inside the woods. The low evening sun reflecting off Max's rifle scope. He looked down at little Freya as she ran for her life towards the site exit.

Realising what he was watching unfold, Fox rolled to his left and took a two-step running jump, launching himself into the air towards Freya.

Having tracked Freya as she ran, Max aimed the sights a couple of centimetres higher than her current position and pulled the trigger.

The gun jolted back violently as the loud, whipping crack of the shot echoed off the side of the warehouse and washed over the wasteland next to the building. It sounded like thunder had struck the area.

The 7.62×51mm round from the M110A1 ripped into Fox's body, entering through the right side of his stomach, ricocheting off his hip and exiting through his lower back.

The force of the bullet's impact sent his body into a slow spin in the air as a puff of bloody mist sprayed from the exit wound.

Hearing the massive bang from behind her, Freya ran off to her right to a small path through the woodland.

Having seen his lens fill up with a black object for a second, Max pulled back from the scope of the rifle to get a look at what had happened. He stared in shock as he saw Fox's spiralling body crash to the ground, sending up a cloud of sandy dust. This distracted him for just long enough to allow Freya to disappear into the woodland on the right.

Max quickly leant back into the rifle and fired three wayward shots into the trees before letting out a frustrated growl through gritted teeth.

He stood up from his sniper's nest and began running down the hill towards the site below.

Still alive but bleeding heavily and badly injured from the high-calibre gunshot and fall, Fox was now dragging himself across the ground towards the far end of the warehouse. He left a trail of blood in his wake as he painfully hauled himself across the gravelly floor.

Max watched with pleasure; in no rush at all, he now boastfully strode towards his dying enemy. He chuckled to himself with every step he took.

Fox managed to drag himself all the way to the water's edge at the front of the burning warehouse, resting up against a short brick wall. He panted in complete exhaustion as he looked up at the blurry, wobbly image of Max walking towards him wearing his old all-black police marksman uniform. Fox was covered in dirt and the rips in his clothes exposed bloody cuts and bruises all over his body.

Max walked over until he stood directly in front of Fox, looking down at him with his arms crossed. With the extent of his injuries and the amount of blood Fox was now losing, he could feel his pulse slow and the energy start to completely fade from his body.

CHAPTER TWENTY-SIX

"Well, well, well."

Max straightened the police-issue baseball cap he had put on since scaling down the hill, shielding his eyes from the low evening sun.

"You know I should just fucking finish you right now… but I want to leave you alive to suffer just that little bit longer. Leave you to suffer like I have suffered."

Fox took deep breath after deep breath, desperately trying to conserve his energy as the blood continued to stream from his open wounds. The overwhelming heat, smoke and smell from the burning warehouse in front of him was making that all the more difficult.

Max knelt down, now face to face with Fox. He reached forward and grabbed hold of his cheeks, squeezing hard like a clamp closing in from either side of his face. The two men stared into each other's eyes. Fox could once again see the same red tinge in Max's eyes that he saw when he looked in the mirror.

"Why the fuck did you do it? Throwing me off the roof and leaving me to die is one thing. But the kid? Why did you have to do that?"

Max shoved Fox's head over to one side as he let go and suddenly stood up. He turned and walked a couple of steps back to compose himself.

Max continued, "They should have let me die. I wish more than anything that they left me to die in that alleyway, but they didn't. Now I am in constant pain. I can feel my muscles bursting out from under my skin and I look like a *fucking monster*."

Max threw back his head and screamed the last words with a primal rage. Fox managed to muster enough energy to talk.

"I… I didn't touch your daughter… I didn't throw you off that roof. They are lying to you. Manipulating you into doing their dirty work."

Max looked down at Fox with an even more furious expression on his face. His muscles were tensed, rock solid and his teeth gritted firmly.

His heart was pounding and the veins in his arms and neck swelled even more as he took deep, panting breaths.

Just then Max noticed some movement in the bushes on the other side of the warehouse yard. He could see a strand of blonde hair and a little red shoe poking out from behind a tree. Freya. Having run into the woodland, she did the first thing that came naturally to her and hid from all the madness.

Fox flopped his head over to the left and squinted to focus his eyes for a few seconds before he saw the same thing.

Max looked back down at Fox with a smirk on his face and began walking in her direction.

"It's OK. You can come out now; I'm a policeman. The bad men have all gone."

Fox watched Max walk across the dusty yard from his slumped position with a feeling of helplessness. He had promised Tim that no harm would come to his daughter and yet, he feared, he was about to watch that very eventuality unfold right in front of him. That was not an option.

He could see Julia's face in his mind as he feared he was nearing the end. For a moment, he remembered those times. Memories of a past life. After all the losses, all the blood that had been shed, it could not end like this.

Fox took a deep breath and reached down, ripping a long, thick patch of black fabric from his top. He looped it around the wound on his stomach and tied it up as he winced in pain.

As Max reached halfway across the warehouse yard, without even turning round, he reached behind him and caught the incoming throwing knife by the blade in mid-air.

He stopped and turned to inspect the knife as blood slowly trickled out from his palm, running down onto the blade.

Fox looked up at Max, hunched over in a knelt position with his arm extended from throwing the knife.

Flinging the blade off to one side, Max began walking back towards Fox once more.

"That wasn't very nice now, was it?"

Max stopped about a metre in front of Fox, who was steadying himself to get to his feet. Without warning, Max drove a hard right hook into Fox's ribcage, just above his gaping, bleeding gunshot wound.

Fox winced and fell backwards a couple of steps, dropping down onto one knee.

He looked up to see Max laughing hysterically, those wild, red, demonic eyes staring down at him menacingly. To the side of him in the distance, Fox could still see the outline of Freya hiding behind the tree.

By now, the sound of faint sirens had begun ringing out in the background. Drivers on the surrounding roads had reported the plumes of smoke rising out from the site and the fire brigade was on its way.

If he could keep the girl alive for just a few more minutes, that might be enough.

Fox slowly stood up, reached down and tightened the knot he had tied around his wound with the ripped clothing. As he pulled tightly on the fabric, thick droplets of blood were rung out, oozing onto the ground below. He summoned every ounce of strength left in his body and readied himself to fight, leaning down into a combat-ready stance.

Max watched what was unfolding in front of him in disbelief, continuing to laugh at him.

"Hahaha. You can't be serious? Do yourself a favour and get back down on the floor. I'll be back over to finish this in a s—"

Max was cut short by a well-executed jab to the nose that sent his head jolting backwards. It caught him completely off guard as he steadied himself with a shocked expression on his face. He put his hand up to his nose and looked down at it to see a droplet of blood.

Max looked up at Fox with an even wilder smile. Fox stared back, desperately holding back from displaying the massive amount of pain that he was in.

"Last chance Max. Let the girl go. I never touched your wife or your daughter."

"Arrrgggghhh!"

Max let out another battle cry as he began swinging punch after punch in Fox's direction. Fox shuffled a step back with each incoming blow.

He managed to dodge the first couple. Blocking high, blocking to the side.

Then *boom*, a rib-shattering right connected, followed by another on the left.

As Fox hunched over to protect his body from the onslaught, Max leant all of his weight into a hard punch that clattered into his face.

Fox's head jerked backwards as he stumbled a few steps back from the impact of the blow. On his third step he very nearly tripped on something, but just managed to keep himself upright. It was Max's black duffel bag containing the remaining pipe bombs.

Max moved forward to continue the assault. Fox steadied himself once more and threw a surprise right hook that Max reacted to, just in time to block. He raised his right leg up and snap-kicked into Fox's stomach in response.

Fox fell backwards over the bag and rolled on to the dusty yard floor. He coughed and spluttered as he once again tried to steady himself, spitting a mouthful of blood out on to the ground.

With a face full of dirt and blood, he looked up at the wild-eyed Max walking towards him. Everything seemed to slow right down and move at a reduced pace. He could feel his senses heighten even further, smell the smoke more, hear the crackling of the flames louder, taste the blood and sweat in his mouth. He had the overwhelming feeling that this could really be the end.

As Fox got up into a knelt position again, Max stepped over the bag and lunged forward, swinging his leg up to knee Fox in the head.

Fox stopped the knee with both hands clasped together and jumped up to his feet in the same move.

Shocked and angered by this, Max immediately threw a straight punch with his right arm.

Fox parried it off to the right and forced his knee up into Max's stomach.

Max leant forward and winced, stunned by the force of the unexpected impact.

Fox leant over and pulled the black Glock pistol out from under Max's belt buckle at his back.

As he attempted to draw it back over Max's head, Max reached up and grabbed hold of Fox's wrists, turning and throwing him over his shoulder to land hard on the ground once again.

Max was at the end of his tether, panting with frustration as *he* now held the gun out in front of him, pointing it at Fox.

"I'm done playing these fucking games with you now. See you in hell."

As Max's finger compressed the trigger of the Glock and the firing hammer drew back ready to strike the bullet in the chamber, Fox reached out with his right arm, grabbed hold of the black duffel bag of pipe bombs and pulled it up in front of him.

The hammer hit the back of the round, causing the explosion inside the barrel that propelled the spinning bullet out of the end.

After travelling only a metre, it tore through the fabric of the bag before directly striking one of the home-made pipe bombs.

The bomb immediately exploded, along with the three other bombs that were packed tightly around it in the bag.

The massive, hot fireball from the explosion violently ripped and burned through both men's bodies.

At that distance, it wasn't survivable for either of them.

The wailing sirens of the two fire engines reached the gates at the top of the site just in time for the occupants to see the burning aftermath of this latest explosion.

The large blue warehouse was now an inferno, with red-hot flames licking out of the windows. Thick, black smoke was billowing from all holes in the building, forming a large, dense, ominous trail in the sky above.

The fire crews cautiously drove down the sloping entrance road and rolled to a stop a few hundred yards from the ferociously burning warehouse. It wasn't long before one of the firemen spotted the little girl hiding in the woods and went in to get her to safety. The police would arrive soon after, not managing to identify the girl until hours later.

***

Tim Rolfe had anxiously waited hours for an update back at Epping-255. He'd had to read about the fires on social media and follow the progress of the emergency services at the scene via his hacked radio feed. The feeling of relief when he'd heard that a little blonde girl had been found and taken into protective care was overwhelming. He burst into tears, collapsing with exhaustion onto the concrete bunker floor.

Rolfe wasn't sure what would happen now, with Freya's mother being dead and her dad an international criminal on the run. His potential involvement or influence in where she would end up would be a bridge that he would have to cross at some point in the future. He wanted more than anything to just run out to wherever she was, pick her up and hold on to her for dear life. For now, though, it was good enough that she was safe. Her grieving grandmother Margaret had already been in close contact with the police since her daughter's murder, and it was likely they would send Freya home with her.

The following morning's news report laid out the facts as they had been unravelled.

"Several hours after emergency services arrived at a blazing warehouse in East London, the shocking discovery of human remains was made amongst the charred rubble. The fire service had initially thought the blaze to be accidental since they knew that gas canisters, among other flammable objects, were being stored inside the ageing building.

"As well as the four badly burned bodies found inside the warehouse, the police say they have found evidence appearing to point to the use of firearms and have locked the entire site down for a thorough forensic investigation to take place.

"Perhaps equally as shocking and bizarre is the fact that a five-year-old girl was found wandering alone, very close to the site, with no sign of any parent or guardian. The authorities are now looking into the possibility that she is the missing child, Freya Huntingdon, who was of course kidnapped from her home in Wiltshire a week ago.

"More on this shocking turn of events as the news comes in."

Four bodies found inside the warehouse. Tim read over the various articles as they came out, time and time again. He had no way of knowing who exactly had been discovered and it would take some time before that information became available, if they could ever be identified. One thing he could be sure of, though, was that no one had returned to the bunker that evening.

That first morning waking up in Epping-255 alone was altogether strange and surreal. It had been one hell of a journey up until this point and it would take Tim a while to figure out how to feel. He'd come to the realisation that given all he had seen, there was no authority he could hand himself in to, no prison he could be sent to that he would be likely to survive. Living on the run was his only option for a life at all.

Of course, Rolfe felt grateful to have met Fox in the way that he had. On top of the fact that he was real-life proof of some of the most infamous conspiracy theories out there; he had saved Rolfe's life.

It was immensely painful that the mother of his child had lost her life and that his only daughter would now likely have to go into care. Between that and losing his new co-inhabitant, Tim Rolfe really felt that he had little left to lose.

Rolfe had no desire to do anything other than pursue the people behind Joanne's death and the kidnapping of his daughter. Furthermore, he wanted to uncover the mysteries behind the 'Free Spirit' project and burn it all to the ground.

Miles away in the bushes by the side of an East London canal, the blood-red eyes on a badly charred body opened as he took a deep, gasping breath.